WET DREAM

WET DREAM

Hotties of Haven

Jenna Jacob

Wet Dream
Hotties Of Haven
Jenna Jacob

Published by Jenna Jacob

Copyright 2017 Jenna Jacob
Print Edition
Editing by: Blue Otter Editing, LLC
ISBN 978-0-9982284-1-9

This is a work of fiction. Names, places, characters and incidents are the product of the author's imagination and are fictitious. Any resemblance to actual persons, living or dead, events or establishments is solely coincidental.

WET DREAM
HOTTIES OF HAVEN

Brea Gates has spent a lifetime surrendering her paycheck, her body, and her ever-lovin' soul to one worthless man after another. She's determined to steel her spine and give up romance for good. No one possessing a Y chromosome for her. No way. No how.

No men!

When she visits friends in tiny Haven, Texas, she finds blessed peace—for five minutes. One glimpse of rough-hewn cowboy Sawyer Grayson blows Brea's man-ban to hell, making her ache to get her hands on what he's packing in those tight blue jeans.

After a failed marriage, Sawyer swapped "Mrs. Right" for "Ms. Right Now." Though he refuses to risk forever with a gold digging she-devil again, he's all about a cold beer and a willing woman…or three. But he knows instantly that Brea is different. She's the kind of wet dream who tempts him all night. And she just might be the only one who could lure him back to the altar…

USA Today Bestselling author Jenna Jacob presents the second book in her new romantic comedy series, Hotties Of Haven.

For Brea

CHAPTER ONE

After a double shift at the Mocha Hut, Brea Gates wanted to go home, peel off her nylon uniform, and sink into a hot bubble bath to soak her throbbing feet. It was days like this she wished she'd gone to college. If only she could go back in time, she'd bitch-slap some sense into her naïve, younger self. But oh, no…Amos was going to marry her and they'd live happily ever after. But that didn't happen. When things went south with Amos' cheating ass, she'd hooked up with Brady, love-struck-confident that he was the man of her dreams. Of course, he wasn't. Neither was Beau, Charlie, Drew, Elliot, Garrett, Malcolm, Stan, Tommy, Travis, or Randall.

Though Brea suspected that her faulty hunk finder should have been recalled at birth, she refused to give up searching for her soul mate. One day, she would fill the obligatory quotient of kissing frogs and find her Prince Charming…or at least a doable facsimile of one.

While her current lover, Weed, had his fair share of character flaws, life with him was a zillion times better than it had been with Randall—a raging alcoholic who'd pissed the bed nearly every night. Once Weed found work, they'd bounce over this temporary bump in the road, and she'd be happy again…or at least she hoped so. If only he'd put forth a little effort and get off his lazy ass, actually look for a job—instead of lounging in his boxers, listening to heavy metal, playing video games all day—and start having sex with her again, they might be able to patch up their relationship.

As she pulled into her normally quiet neighborhood, she was

shocked to see the street clogged with police cars and television crews. To her horror, she discovered the chaos of activity was focused on their house…or rather, Weed's. She had no claim on the property, simply paid the damn rent.

With her heart in her throat, she pulled to the curb. After shoving Weed's car into park, she cut the engine and stared in disbelief as two uniformed officers led Weed off the front porch…in handcuffs?

Shit! She hoped they weren't the same pair from their bedside toy drawer.

What the hell…?

Her pulse thundered a speedy staccato. Suddenly, an officer appeared beside her car door. Bending, he peered at her through the open window. "You can't park here, lady. You need to move along."

"I'm not going anywhere. I live here!"

Taken aback, the cop arched his brows. "In that case. Step out of the car and put your hands above your head."

"Do what?" Terror wrapped its icy hands around her throat while dread coiled like a rattlesnake in her stomach. "But…but…why?"

"You live here, right?"

"Well…yes, but—"

"Out of the car," the officer barked.

She opened the door and stood on trembling legs as she lifted her hands in the air. Weed snapped his head in Brea's direction, as if sensing her arrival. Apology was written all over his face. She had no clue why he was being arrested, but the shame in his eyes told her he was guilty as hell.

Disregarding the cop's instructions, she slapped her hands on her hips. "What did you do?"

"I'm sorry, baby," Weed whined.

Confusion sliced through her fear. Snapping her head back at the cop beside her, she scowled. "What is he being arrested for?"

"He's been selling meth to some kids over at the high school."

"Meth?" she screeched. Fury charred her veins. "Where the hell did he get meth? That stupid son of a... I'm going to kill him. Give me your gun. I'm going to put a bullet through his idiotic brain."

The cop chortled. "It's probably not wise to make death threats in the presence of an officer, ma'am."

"I don't care!" Brea fumed. "How could he do such a thing? He doesn't even take aspirin, let alone drugs."

Seething with anger, she turned toward Weed again. Narrowing her eyes, she shot him a look meant to vaporize his sorry ass. Unfortunately, it didn't, so she bared her teeth at him instead. "Really? Selling drugs? Have you lost your damn mind?'

"Don't be mad, baby," he begged.

"You know something, Weed? On a scale from one to asshole...you're a dick!"

Collective laughter rippled through the throng gathered on the lawn. Weed shot her a sneer that had her wanting to march her way to him and kick him square in the balls. Instead, she watched in shock as her miserable excuse for a boyfriend crawled into the back of a police cruiser before it drove away.

Pissed beyond reason, Brea scanned the crowd of neighbors assembled across the street. Embarrassment began filling her system as the group stood wide-eyed and whispering, watching the action unfold.

"Oh, I am so through with that asshat. I'm going inside and pack my things, then I'm getting the hell out of town." As she lunged toward the house, the cop stopped her with a hand at her arm.

"I'm afraid I can't let you do that."

"Why not?"

"Because you're under arrest."

"Arrest?" A new wave of terror erupted like a volcano inside her. "But *I* wasn't the one selling drugs. I had no clue the idiot was doing such a thing."

"You'll have to sort it out with the judge."

"Judge?" Brea squawked.

"Afraid so." The cop nodded somberly. "Please turn around, miss, and put your hands behind your back."

Doing as she'd been told, she felt the cold cuffs snap around her wrists.

"You have the right to remain silent..."

A reporter rushed past the other cops and shoved a microphone in Brea's face. The woman's questions didn't even register. But the cameraman's lens certainly did. Dropping her chin to her chest, Brea hid her face. The last thing she wanted was her friends to see her on the six o'clock news.

What friends? she reminded with an inward groan.

Brea didn't know if she wanted throw up or cry...or both. Of their own accord, fat tears rolled down her cheeks. Her brand-new Nikes were saved from death by barf-fest.

More terrified than she'd ever been in her life, she sobbed all the way to the police station. The entire time they processed her, like a common criminal, Brea's stomach pitched and swirled. Her head pounded in time with her racing heart. All she wanted to do was wake up from this demented nightmare. Though she tried to convince every officer she encountered, her pleas of innocence fell on deaf ears. Finally, a kind-hearted female officer must have taken pity on Brea, because the woman offered to call someone for her. Of course, she jumped at the chance but drew a blank when it came time to rattle off a number to the cop. Not only wasn't there any phone number, but Brea couldn't think of a single soul she could reach out to for help. She couldn't call her parents...even if she were sitting on death row. They'd wiped their hands of their only daughter the minute she'd announced she was moving in with Weed. Her mother had cried, asking God how she'd failed her only daughter. But her father had blown a gasket. He'd pounded his fist on the table and shouted. She could still hear the fury in his voice: *We're through picking up the pieces every time some asshole breaks your heart. Until you start making better choices, you're on your own. We're not going to bail your ass out of any more stupid romantic mistakes.*

No, they wouldn't bail her ass out of jail either.

She didn't blame her folks for giving up on her... Well, she did, but...it was Brea's long and distinguished track record for picking the douchebaggiest boyfriends on the planet that forced them to give up on her. She'd endured years of her parents' constant lectures to "find a nice boy worthy of your love and settle down". When Brea met Weed she thought she'd finally found a nice boy. He'd had a job, back then, working as a mechanic. But Weed turned out to be one more clown in her circus of bad decisions.

Brea thought about calling her boss, Charlie, but quickly nixed the notion. Asking him to bail her out of jail because her dipshitiot boyfriend got popped for selling meth was a termination letter in the making.

When she'd made the rash decision to move to Denton with Weed, Brea severed all ties with the friends she had back in Austin. Well, all but one...Colton Maddox. She called the hunky man-whore, who'd been a member of her old high school clique, from time to time. While the two had never *wrinkled the sheets* together, they still kept in touch. Ironically, Colton now lived a short distance from Denton in the tiny town of Haven. But she didn't know his number off the top of her head. And since she'd had to hand over her belongings, she didn't have her cell phone either.

After she explained her plight, the helpful cop not only found Colton's number but dialed him up for Brea as well. Pressing the phone to her ear, she sent up a prayer that the man was home and not at a bar picking up women to take home and warm his bed.

"Maddox residence," a woman answered in a low, sultry voice.

Brea cringed, hoping she hadn't interrupted him playing slam-the-banana with his woman of the hour.

"Um...is Colton there?"

"He's out in the barn right now. Can he call you back?"

There was something hauntingly familiar about the woman's voice, but at the moment, Brea's mind was so warped with angst and fear she couldn't focus on trying to place it.

"No. Um…it's kind of an emergency. Can you get him for me, please?"

"Sure. Just a minute." The woman sounded suspicious but thankfully didn't ask any questions.

After what seemed an eternity, Colton's deep voice on the other end wrapped her in a blanket of relief.

"Colton, it's me, Brea. I'm in a bit of trouble here and wondered if—"

"What's wrong? You sound like you're about to fall apart on me."

"I am." Her voice cracked and tears tumbled down her cheeks once more.

"Are you hurt?" Colton demanded.

"No," she said with a sniff.

"Okay. Take a deep breath and tell me what's wrong."

"I'm in jail," she wailed pathetically.

"Jail? Where? Why?"

"W-weed. H-he was selling meth. They arrested him and hauled me in, too. I swear I didn't know he was doing something so s-stupid. I keep t-telling the cops I'm…I'm innocent, but they don't believe me."

"Don't cry," Colton moaned sympathetically. "Tell me where you are. I'll come pick you up or bail you out or whatever you need me to do. You can come stay with me or I can get you a hotel room, but listen to me…don't you go back to him. Got it?"

"Yes. I don't want to see that worthless prick's face ever again," she huffed.

"Good. You leave Weed to me. I'll take care of that *late, great* sack of shit when he gets out of jail, sweetheart."

Brea choked on a watery laugh and thanked him.

She gave Colton the address to the police station before the female cop escorted Brea back to a holding cell. In an attempt to keep from super-gluing her ass to the pity pot, she watched the comings and goings beyond the scuffed plexiglass barrier. As an officer led Weed past her cell, she launched to her feet and pounded on the faux glass wall.

"You fucking bastard! I'm in jail because of you!"

Weed paused and shot her a hateful glare. "If you hadn't been harping on me to get a job and support you, neither of us would be here."

"What?" She gaped in shock. He actually had the balls to blame *her* for his stupid stunt. "You were supposed to get a *real* job to help support us both, you dipshit! I hope they lock you away for life!"

"They might. But you'll be going down with me, baby!" he sneered.

"Bullshit! You did the crime, so *you'll* do the time."

As the guard urged Weed forward, Brea flipped her rat-bastard ex the finger. Shaking with rage, she forced herself to sit back down on the unforgiving metal bench. She hung her head and moaned.

No way in hell would she sit by and not defend herself if Weed tried to implicate her for his crime. She had to find a way to prove her innocence. But how could she do that when it would most likely boil down to his word against hers? She didn't have money for a lawyer. The thought of spending five minutes, let alone years, in a federal prison had her all but climbing the walls. Fears and what ifs rolled through her brain like storm clouds. Numbed in despair, she shrank inside herself and stared blankly at the floor. But her mind continued to spin out of control. As she sat plotting several unique and horrifically painful ways to end Weed's life, the door of her cell swung open. A tall, middle-aged man wearing glasses and a wrinkled suit stepped inside.

"Miss Gates, I'm Detective Estes." He extended his hand. She shook it warily. "I'm sorry for the inconvenience caused by bringing you to the station. You're free to go now."

"I am?"

Like a dolt, she questioned her freedom instead of leaping from the bench and screaming *See ya later* as she made a beeline out of the station.

"Yes. We've had your boyfriend—"

"Ex-boyfriend," Brea clarified.

Estes bit back a smile. "We've had your ex under surveillance for over a month. We know that you were never present during any of the drug transactions, but I needed to make sure you were unaware of his…hobby. I need to tell you that Mr. Sherman…Weed, tried to throw you under the bus. But when I reminded him during our little meeting that you were never present at any of the drug transactions and asked your role in his…hobbies, Weed couldn't give me an answer. His lawyer advised that Mr. Sherman tell the truth, and finally he assured us that you had no part in any of his illegal drug activities."

"That's what I've been trying to tell everyone!" She threw her hands up in frustration.

"So I've heard." Estes grinned. "The friends that you called are waiting out front."

"Thank god! Can I go to by Weed's house and get my things?"

"I think that's a good idea." Estes nodded. "The team is still there gathering evidence, but I'll call Detective Nickel, who's there now, and ask him to assist while you gather your personal belongings."

"Thank you." She didn't care if the Dallas Cowboys or the Mormon Tabernacle Choir wanted to watch her pack. All she wanted was to get her shit and get out so she'd never have to lay eyes on Weed again.

"I assume you're leaving your ex?"

"You bet your badge I am," she stated emphatically.

Estes smirked and nodded, then handed her his business card. "Leave a number with the desk sergeant where I can reach you before you go. You may need to testify against Mr. Sherman when his case gets closer to trial."

"Any chance he'll get the electric chair? I'd pay money to see that."

Detective Estes laughed and shook his head. "Nope, sorry."

She sent him a disgruntled frown.

"Miss Gates," he began tentatively. "I know it's none of my business, but you're a bright, funny, and seemingly smart woman. How did you get mixed up with someone like him?"

Her throat constricted. *Because I wanted him to love me.* Shoving down her pathetic reasoning, she shrugged absently. "I'm not sure…especially now, but you can bet money I won't make that mistake again."

Oh, but she had. Shitloads more than once, and it depressed the hell out of her. It was past time for her to learn some lessons from mistake after mistake and change her ways.

With a nod, Estes led her out of the holding cell. As she signed for her belongings from a stoic-faced officer, Brea couldn't simply brush aside her foray with the penal system or Weed's disregard for her freedom. Scared straight, she was going to live her life totally different from here on out…starting with her unreasonable infatuation with the male species. Suddenly, a light bulb went off in her head.

"I'm going to give up men."

"Excuse me?" The cop arched a brow in surprise before handing Brea her purse.

"Oh, nothing. I was thinking out loud."

And it was a wonderful idea. So what if she turned into the crazy, celibate cat lady from Denton. She'd be fine without a penis messing up her life. She had toys! Those vibrating puppies had been taking care of her needs more thoroughly than Weed's hard-on ever had.

Life without a man would be great. Eating microwave meals, reading books, watching something other than sports, and listening to her own choice of music. Sure, it might be boring, but it was safe.

Pushing past the security doors, Brea found Colton and her

long-lost bestie from high school, Jade Hollis, sitting beside him. It instantly dawned on her that the woman who'd answered the phone was Jade.

"Jade? Oh, my god!" Brea screamed as she ran, then hugged her friend tightly. "Where the hell have you been?"

After Jade's mother died, the girl had dropped off the planet. Colton had spent years trying to find her to no avail. Obviously he'd finally succeeded.

"Are you two…together now?" Brea asked, still hugging her bestie from high school.

"Yes." Colton beamed with a smile so bright it rivaled the sun. "In fact, we're getting married in September."

"Seriously? That's fantastic! It's about damn time."

"Yes, it is." Colton beamed with pride, then glanced around the police station and sobered. "What do we need to do to get you out of here? Post bail or…"

"No. Oh, hell, I'm sorry. I was so caught up in seeing Jade I didn't even say thank you for coming to save me." Brea felt like a ditz for ignoring the man. "There's no charges, no bail for me. I'm free to go. I'll fill you in on all the gory details later. Right now, I just want to get out of here. That and hear how you two finally found each other."

"She found me." Colton grinned. As he relayed how he'd found Jade on the sidewalk in Haven, his happiness never wavered.

She pinned her wayward friend a scowl. "Do you have any idea how worried we were about you?"

Her chastising tone, scathingly reminiscent of her mother's, made Brea cringe. Guilt for jumping Jade's shit thrummed through Brea. Making it worse was the look of remorse that wrinkled her friend's face.

"I didn't mean to worry you guys. I was going through a bad time and needed to be alone while I got my head straight."

"No. I'm sorry. I was so preoccupied with the first Mr. Wrong, I wasn't there when you needed me."

"It's all right. Life is perfect now." Jade tipped her chin and gazed up at Colton with a love that was blinding. "I don't miss Denton a bit."

"Denton?"

"Yeah, I used to live not too far from here."

"Shut up!" Brea gaped. "I've lived here with Weed for almost two years."

"You shut up!" Jade blinked in disbelief.

"Both of you shut up, and let's get out of here," Colton teased. "We can catch up on the way home."

As they headed toward the parking lot, Brea remembered she wanted to pack her things. "Would it be too much trouble to run by the house? I want to pack."

"Can I torch the prick's place when you're done? Of course, I'd prefer to do it with the little twit beaten unconscious inside…" Colton grinned evilly.

"That's tempting, but the cops are still there."

"Damn." He scowled.

Wanting to keep from focusing on her own troubles, Brea listened as Jade explained her mass exodus from Austin. After burying her mother, the bank repossessed her friend's home. Bereft at losing everything, Jade pulled inside herself instead of leaning on her friends.

Brea knew pride was an evil bitch. It's what kept her from reaching out to her parents after all.

"Good thing is, Colton and I are together now."

"By the looks on your faces, it's better than good."

"It is," Colton piped in. "It's incredible."

"I don't need any of the X-rated details." Brea held up her hand. "I've decided to give up men."

She didn't know why she'd blurted out her strategy. Was she subconsciously hoping, by saying the words aloud, it would stop her from tumbling into bed and taking up playing house with the next man who showed her the slightest hint of attention?

"Yeah, right," Colton scoffed in disbelief. "There'll be a star in the east and another virgin birth before that's going to happen."

"Laugh all you want, but I'm serious. Until I find a guy who worships me for more than doing his laundry and scrubbing the toilet bowl, they can all pound sand."

Colton sent her a frown. "Not all us men are pricks, sweetheart."

"I know that, but I'm not a man magnet, I'm a jerk-wad aficionado. I've played the fool so often I should have a collection of Tony Awards in my thong drawer."

"Oh, honey," Jade sympathized. "One day you'll find—"

"Someone who deserves me. Yeah…yeah, my folks tried drilling that into my head since my first menstrual period. I'm convinced that all the good men have either climbed out of the dating pool or they drowned."

"Don't give up on the whole male species yet," Colton insisted. "There are lots of good men out there waiting for the right woman. You'll find your guy. You're too special not to enjoy a solid, loving relationship."

She was special all right…a special mess.

Brea sent him a smile of appreciation, biting back a retort that she thought him full of shit. "I do know one thing. I'm done handing out my heart like a Hallmark card to every guy who thinks giving me the best fifteen seconds of my life is enough."

Jade gasped.

Colton frowned and shook his head. "Fifteen seconds? Oh, honey!"

When he pulled the truck to the curb in front of Weed's house, cops milled about, as Estes had promised. While her friends waited in the truck, Brea approached the crime tape that stretched around the porch.

"Miss Gates?" a blond-haired man in a dark suit asked.

"Yes."

"I'm Detective Nickel. Estes said to expect you." Raising the yellow tape, he nodded for her to duck under. "I'll escort you through the house."

"Thank you."

Stepping inside her soon-to-be-former home, she saw the place had been practically turned upside down. A little smile curled her lips knowing Weed, the lazy prick, would have to clean the mess up all alone. Brea was going to be long gone.

She knew she wouldn't get far on the seven hundred dollars—originally allotted for the house payment—in her purse. But Colton had offered her a place to stay, and with any luck, she'd find work in Haven and soon be in a position to fully support herself. Ready to be rid of any memory of Weed, Brea stormed into the bedroom. Shockingly, she realized that nothing had been touched.

"We're working our way through each room. We haven't made it back here yet," Nickel explained.

Like a robot, she nodded, but her focus was on the bed she'd shared with Weed. That she'd gotten mixed up with the asshat sent revulsion pulsing through her veins. After grabbing two duffle bags from the back of the closet, she tossed them on the bed.

"I'll need to look inside those," the detective stated.

"They're not Weed's, they're mine. And they're empty…see?"

Pulling the zipper apart, she shook out each bag over the bed. With a curt nod, the man stood watching—a silent sentinel—while, like a Tasmanian devil, Brea filled the totes.

"I'd like some privacy to change out of my work uniform if you don't mind?"

Nickel sent her a blank expression. "I'm sorry. There aren't any female officers on site. If you'd like to wait, I'll be happy to call the station and have—"

"Never mind." Brea shook her head. "If you haven't seen a woman in bra and panties by now, then today's your lucky day."

Nickel chuckled. "If it's any consolation, I have a wife and three daughters."

"Good. I didn't want to make you blush."

Turning her back on him, Brea whipped off her uniform shirt. Weed's actions had stolen not only her freedom but her home and privacy as well. She yanked on an oversized T-shirt before tugging off her skirt, then quickly pulled on a pair of black yoga pants and slipped into her sandals. Unabashedly, Brea opened the drawer of the nightstand and retrieved her vibrators.

One corner of the detective's mouth twitched as she shoved them into her bag.

"At least B.O.B. and his friends won't send me to jail or break my heart like every other man in my life," she quipped.

"Indeed they won't." The detective had the good grace not to laugh.

Back in the truck, the three headed toward Haven. Brea struggled to put thoughts of Weed, jail, and drugs behind her. But Estes' question remained, haunting her: *Why did you choose someone like Weed Sherman?*

Not only was she a hopeless romantic with too many imperfections, but also, it was safer choosing men riddled with more flaws than she, in hopes they'd be content. Content with her mousy brown hair, unremarkable matching eyes, and the unattractive curves of her five-foot-one and slightly chunky body. She'd hoped that if her lovers could ignore her imperfections—as she did theirs—one day, she'd find the storybook ending she'd always dreamed of. Unfortunately her love stories turned into epic yelling matches brimmed with hurt or platonic, sexually frustrating sagas of boredom. In reality, all were nothing but horrific horror novels.

Stripping the layers of fantasy and staring at her reality head on, Brea realized she'd been living a fool's paradise. That sobering enlightenment only served to bolster her boycott of men…or at least a long dry spell until she came to terms with her own inadequacies. Of course, the more likely scenario was that hell would freeze over first, but she was willing to at least try.

"Jade and I haven't had dinner yet. Are you hungry?" Colton asked, interrupting Brea's internal musings.

The thought of food made her stomach cramp. Instead of answering, she simply shrugged.

Jade shot her a sympathetic smile. "Don't crawl inside yourself. Take it from one who's been there…it's a cold and empty place. Lean on us. We're here for you."

"That's right." Colton nodded. "I'll be more than happy to vet the next guy you want to date."

Brea shot him a crooked grin. "Thanks, *Dad*."

"Aw, what a sweet offer," Jade cooed with a starry-eyed gaze. "You are such a love."

He darted her with an equally mooning and sickening expression. "No, sweetheart. You are."

"Lord, I can tell already that I'm going to need insulin injections around you two," Brea moaned.

"I can stop by the pharmacy after dinner if you'd like." Colton teased.

"That's okay, I'll just skip dessert," Brea countered with a cheesy grin.

The couple kept her engaged in conversation, staving off her Dr. Phil internalization. Before long, Colton had turned onto the main street of Haven and pulled in front of a café called Toot's.

Brea couldn't hold back a giggle. "You've got to be shitting me. Toot's? Is the food so toxic it gives everyone gas?"

Jade cracked up laughing. "Oh, my god. I thought the very same thing."

"Ha ha." Colton turned off the motor. "Toot is a great cook. You'll see."

"She really is. The food is to die for." Jade nodded.

When Brea entered the café, her senses were assaulted with such luscious aromas her stomach growled loudly.

"Heavens, Brea. I think you just woke the old folks at the nursing home across town. When did you eat last?"

"Dinner yesterday, I think." Brea couldn't honestly remember.

She'd skipped breakfast this morning, fighting with Weed—

for the umpteenth time—over his refusal to find work. Unbeknownst to her, the dumb ass *had* a job…an illegal one. Lunchtime had come and gone. The coffee shop had been inundated with customers ordering a one-time special, twenty-five-cent mango-passion iced tea. Though she'd thought she'd never eat again while at the police station, Brea was suddenly famished.

After passing several booths with tables draped in red-and-white-checked gingham, Brea sat down next to Jade on a red spinning stool, at the long, gray-speckled Formica-topped counter. The place had a fifties vibe.

A teenaged waitress handed them menus and ice water before darting away once more. When she returned, Brea ordered the chicken-fried steak, then excused herself and trekked to the ladies' room. After sitting in a dirty holding cell and bawling her eyes out, she'd have given her well-worn virginity for a steaming shower or that silky bubble bath she'd been dreaming about driving home from work. With neither luxury available at the moment, she washed the scuzzy residue of jail from her hands. After splashing cold water on her face, she peered up at the mirror. Blotchy skin, swollen eyes, and her hair a fright, Brea dragged a brush from her purse and tried to tame her wild hair. She looked and felt as if she'd been shit through a rusty sieve. There was nothing she could do about that now, so she tossed her brush back in her purse and strolled out of the bathroom.

Stopping dead in her tracks, she nearly swallowed her tongue as she drank in the hunky cowboy who'd hijacked her seat next to Jade. Brea couldn't peel her eyes off his über-broad shoulders, cinnamon-colored hair, and sun-kissed skin. When he smiled at something Colton said, a tingle rippled over her flesh. Jade retorted something, and the man threw back his head and laughed. The vibration of his rich, deep tenor stroked her spine and roused primal feminine desires she didn't know were inside her.

Down, girl. You've given up men…remember? Besides, he's a

ginger.

She wasn't usually attracted to redheads, but for this copper-haired Adonis, Brea would happily make an exception...*if* she were still shopping the man market.

As if feeling her stare, the man turned his head. Her pulse leapt. His emerald-green eyes rimmed with flecks of gold locked onto her with such intensity she felt as if he were dismantling her defenses and delving into her very soul. He flashed her a seductive lopsided smile, and Brea's knees turned to rubber. Reaching out, she clung to the countertop and dropped her gaze for fear he'd see hunger reflecting in her eyes.

Man ban? Hello? her conscience mocked.

She felt like a newly converted vegan who'd just been offered a fat, juicy steak, and her hormones screamed in outrage. The cosmos had once again aligned to say...*fuck you, bitch!*

"There she is." Colton smiled.

Forcing her feet to move, she swallowed tightly.

"Brea, I'd like you to meet Sawyer," Colton continued. "Sawyer, this is our good friend Brea. She's staying with Jade and me for a while."

"My, my, you sure are a pretty little thing." Sawyer's gaze locked with hers as he tipped his white Stetson before flashing her a confident wink.

His silky, deep voice slid over her flesh like gooey syrup, sending a hard quiver to rack her system. Sawyer rose from her seat. He was tall, at least six-foot-billion, and towered over her miniature five-foot-nothing frame like a mountain. He made her feel like a damn Oompa Loompa.

The man was too tall.

Too pussy-clenching handsome.

Too damn intense.

Everything about him was quickly abolishing her non-penis pledge. She wanted to look away...hide from his dissecting stare, and try to quell the heat surging between her legs, but couldn't. Instead, she stood like a deaf-mute, drinking in every sinful inch of the man as her imagination took over her brain. She could almost feel the cinnamon-colored scruff on his face. And his lips…good Lord above. They were full, firm, and enticing. It took every ounce of willpower she possessed not to lift to her toes and latch her mouth to his.

Somehow she managed to tear from his gaze. Brea wished she hadn't as she skimmed her eyes over the sinewy muscles of his partially exposed arms. His narrow hips made her want to wrap her legs around him, and his long, sturdy thighs looked as if they could easily keep pace while he thrust into her all night long. She nearly sighed out loud as she drank in his expansive chest stretched beneath a blue chambray shirt.

Her palms itched to feel every thick-corded muscle packed beneath his clothes.

"It's nice to meet you, Brea. I hope you don't mind that I kept your seat warm."

Still unable to form a single syllable, Brea prayed she wasn't drooling like a Saint Bernard as she ogled the chiseled features of his face.

No mortal man had the right to look so damn gorgeous. He was a living, breathing work of art.

Cursing her ill-timed vow of chastity, she studied his every nuance. The knowledge that she'd never have the chance to live out the fantasies crowding her mind was mournful as hell. But alone in bed, Sawyer could roam free inside her head…and his imaginary tongue, up and down her body. Of course, she'd likely burn through a package of batteries a night, and quite possibly kill a B.O.B. or two—but a girl's gotta do, what a girl's gotta do.

As Sawyer moved in behind her, his scent, a masculine mixture of leather, sweet grass, and man, stroked her senses. When he placed his palm on the small of her back, she jolted with surprise while tiny pinpricks of heat fanned her skin beneath her shirt. As he chivalrously helped her to her seat, the energy from his touch sent a seismic wave rippling through her.

Either the air in the room shot up a hundred and twelve

degrees or Brea was in the throes of a hormone-induced lust-flash. With his hand lingering at the small of her back, the nipple-tightening hottie was turning her inside out. Never before had she ever met a man who evoked such potent and instant sexual attraction.

She needed to say something before he began to wonder if she ate soup with a fork.

Brea somehow found her voice, though it came out low and breathless like a 1-900 sex phone operator. "No, not at all. It's nice to meet you, too."

An approving hum sounded in the back of his throat as he sent her a knee-knocking smile.

She had no clue why she was flipping her shit over this ginger-haired cowboy. Maybe it was because everything about him screamed self-assurance. Brea had no doubt the man possessed all the right skills and the stamina to blow her horny little mind. She lifted her chin and forced a smile to keep from eyeing his crotch and doing something stupid, like fall to her knees and peel his snug blue jeans off with her teeth.

As if able to read her thoughts, Sawyer cursed under his breath and then cleared his throat. "What brings you to Haven?"

His innocuous question stilled the air in her lungs. She felt as if her fragile emotions were being tossed to the wind, like dandelion seeds in a summer breeze. Her cheeks caught fire. Sawyer's copper brows slashed in concern before he darted a curious glance Colton's way.

Answer him, you fidiot. Lie if you have to, but say something!

"Oh, I-I'm just catching up with old friends," she stammered.

Sawyer gave her a dubious nod before his expression smoothed and he pinned her with a wide smile. "Well, it's nice to have such a beautiful woman here to pretty up our town."

Hands down, the man was a charmer. No doubt he'd charmed the panties off every willing woman in Haven. Even assuming he shared his bedroom skills with half the town didn't keep her hormones from singing in hopefulness like a Southern

Baptist choir.

But Sawyer would never get the chance to plow her lady garden. Not until she found a way to sever the link that connected her pussy to her heart. Most likely a chainsaw couldn't cut the sucker, and that was a shame of biblical proportions.

Disappointment wrinkled her brow as she settled onto her seat.

Sawyer bent in close to her ear. "I know you're here for other reasons besides catching up with your friends. I see you carrying the weight of the world on your shoulders, darlin'. If you ever want to talk, I can help share that load."

His über-keen observation made the hairs on the back of her neck stand on end. The last thing she needed was the Long Island Medium's second cousin twice removed to dissect all the piss-poor choices she'd made in her life.

"Are you a psychic, or do you have some weird fetish to help out damsels in distress?"

A sensual smile kicked up one corner of his mouth, and Brea wanted to slide her tongue over the tempting bow.

Sawyer inched in even closer. "Trust me, darlin'. My fetishes might scare a pretty little thing like you."

The lure of his silky seduction was a torture all its own. Before she could think up a witty comeback, the waitress set a plate of food down in front of her.

"I'll let y'all enjoy your dinner." Sawyer lifted his hand from her back. Still devouring her with his gaze, he tipped his white hat. Strands of inviting copper fell over his forehead, and Brea clenched her hands to keep from brushing her fingers through it.

"I hope we get to see each other again before you leave town, Brea. Have a good night, everyone."

After flashing her one last panty-melting smile, he turned and strolled away. Gazing at his retreating form, Brea bit back a whimper. It seemed a sin to watch that sexy ass, dipped in denim, walk right out the door.

"I think Sawyer likes you," Jade murmured for only Brea to

hear.

"He'll have to un-like me. No more men. Remember?"

Her protest sounded reasonable, but Brea ached to wrap herself around that hunk like a three-piece-suit from a thrift store.

Sawyer was as dangerous to her man-free diet as a caramel sundae with whipped cream and a cherry on top. She couldn't cave and sate her sexually needy sweet tooth. One taste of his sugar cone would only leave her wanting more. If Brea had any hope of getting her life in order, she'd have to stay far, far away from that clit-throbbing hottie.

CHAPTER TWO

WITH HIS BLOOD pumping lava, his body humming in need, and his heart beating like a sledgehammer—like it had since laying eyes on Brea—Sawyer jogged across the street to the only bar in Haven, the Hangover. He needed a cold beer to put out the fire she'd ignited inside him. His palms itched to slide over every lush inch of her naked curves. Hell, even his cock ached and yearned to squeeze into her hot little body, then soar them both beyond the heavens.

He was baffled by the instant attraction he felt toward the woman. Sawyer had his pick of the women in Haven, but since he'd drunk in the sight of Brea, he didn't want anyone but her. But why...he didn't know. She hadn't been overly friendly or flirtatious. In fact, she seemed almost shy—which was definitely not his style. He liked his women experienced and uninhibited...women who wanted exactly what he did—multiple spine-tingling orgasms without any messy emotions like love.

Yet there was something unique about Brea he couldn't quite put his finger on or ignore. She'd instantly intrigued him. Though she wasn't the kind of brave and brazen kitten he was used to playing with, he wanted to discover all the luridly carnal ways he could to make her purr and roar out his name.

As he stepped into the dimly lit bar, a country-western song blared from the jukebox and assaulted his ears. He'd rather hear the eighties rock and roll his mom had listened to as he was growing up. She often claimed that Def Leppard, Aerosmith, and other great bands from that era kept her sane raising six rambunctious boys. It was probably true. The woman had managed to keep her cool in a daily avalanche of fistfights, foul language, and chaos he and his brothers had regularly instigated. As an adult, he admired her even more for not killing one or two of her sons.

Jerking a nod to his younger siblings—twenty-five-year-old twins, Noble and Nate—playing pool toward the back of the room, Sawyer strolled to the bar. Another younger brother, Nash, sat nursing a beer. Clapping him on the back, Sawyer sat down beside him.

"What's up?"

"Nothing." Nash shrugged with a sullen expression. "Just hanging out."

"Where's Megan?"

It was a rare sight to find Nate alone. Usually he and his grade-school sweetheart were joined at the hip, or the lips.

"Washing her hair." He scoffed and rolled his eyes.

Uh-oh. There was trouble in paradise. "What are you two fighting about?"

"Same shit…different day." Nash let out a heavy sigh. "She wants to pin down a wedding date."

"Then do it."

"I'm not ready yet."

"What are you waiting for? A better offer?"

"Maybe."

"Pull your head out of your ass, man. Do you honestly think another woman is going to put up with you the way Megan does?"

"No," Nash mumbled.

"Then why are you dragging your feet?"

"I want to marry her…it's just…marriage is a huge step. We're still young. A lot can happen between twenty-three and eighty-three."

"Yeah, it's called life."

"That's not what I mean. What if we wake up one morning and decide we want to be with someone else? Sara did."

Knives of regret stabbed Sawyer. He'd strived to set a good example and be a decent role model for his younger brothers but failed miserably. Swallowing the bitterness tainting his tongue, he shrugged. "I'm living proof there's no guarantee of happily ever after. Sometimes all you can do is roll the dice."

"I hate gambling."

"Do you really love her?"

Nash growled and sent him a glare. "How can you even ask that? You know I do."

"Then stop sitting here like a whiny little bitch, sulking in your beer, and call her."

His brother's shoulders slumped. "I already tried. She won't answer."

"So you're just going to give up? Sit here with your dick in your hands? Get off your ass, go to her house, and apologize to her."

The man sent him an indignant stare. "For what? I didn't do anything!"

Gina—the late thirties owner and bartender with pale blue eyes, strawberry-blonde hair, and the mouth of a seasoned sailor—handed Sawyer a mug of beer. He nodded a silent thanks, took a gulp, then said to his hardheaded brother, "You're right. Don't set a date. You're not ready to make a commitment yet."

"What do you mean I'm not ready? I am, too!" Nash lifted his chin and squared his shoulders, ready to fight.

"No you're not. If you can't swallow your pride and apologize just because *she* needs to hear it, you're definitely not ready. Marriage isn't about who's right and who's wrong. It's about making compromises."

Sawyer's words of wisdom weren't born from watching Dr. Phil or listening to shrinks dishing out advice on talk radio; they came from six long years struggling to make his own marriage work. Unfortunately, that was a losing battle. Sara, his ex, didn't have an apologetic bone in her centerfold-model body. The woman was self-centered, uncompromising, and right...even when she was wrong. Sawyer had spent six long years making concessions without the woman giving an ounce of reciprocation.

After flying to Dallas for her third plastic surgery—a breast augmentation after a rhinoplasty and tummy tuck—Sara confessed that she'd been having an affair with her plastic surgeon. Sawyer had been almost relieved at the news. Though Sara had grown up in Haven, she hated small-town life. She coveted diamonds, jewels, and designer underwear—thongs studded with diamonds if he could have afforded them—not barn dances, chili cook-offs, and shit-kicking piddly parades. And most definitely not the plain gold wedding band he'd placed on her finger.

After that debacle ended, Sawyer had vowed the words *I do* would never roll off his tongue. Of course, he had no qualms saying *I'll do you all night long* to the single women of Haven.

Out of the blue, Brea's face surfaced in his brain. Glancing toward the door, Sawyer longed to sprint across the street. He wanted to take the dark-haired vixen home with him and *do* her every which way but Sunday.

"I can too apologize," Nash challenged.

Sawyer blinked and focused once more on his brother.

"I apologize to Mom all the time for her having given birth to you!"

"Aren't you a fucking comedian?" Sawyer smacked his brother on the back of the head. "Stop busting my balls, and go make things right with your woman."

Grumbling, Nash stood and tossed a five on the bar. "If she kicks my ass, I'm coming back to beat the fuck out of you. Got it?"

Sawyer grinned and nodded as his brother walked toward the door. Neither he nor any other man in his family would ever think of raising a hand to a woman. If Megan decided to take a frying pan to Nash's head, Sawyer would accept the payback.

Grabbing his beer, he traced his brother's steps. He paused and peered out the window as Nash drove away. Turning his attention toward Toot's and, most importantly, Colton's truck, Sawyer clenched his jaw. What the hell had crawled up his ass? He never chased after women like a slobbering Saint Bernard. He didn't have to. They willingly came to him. What the fuck possessed him to think about pursuing her? Well, besides the need to drown in her luscious body? Still, he lingered at the window hoping to catch one more glimpse of the sultry sprite.

Noble pressed in against Sawyer's back, startling him. His brother peered over his shoulder. "Whatcha lookin' at out there?"

"Nothing. Just watched Nash head out to Megan's with his tail between his legs."

"How'd he fuck up this time?"

"He ran."

"Ran from what?"

"Commitment."

Noble, the older twin—by a whopping minute and a half—clinked his mug with Sawyer's and winked. "I'll drink to that."

The man was a confirmed bachelor. Not so much a man-whore, but bold, cocksure, and full of himself. Sawyer doubted there was a woman on the planet who could entice Noble to make a hint of commitment. On the other hand, Nate was the polar opposite—quiet, shy, and resolved to remain a virgin until his wedding night.

"I knew you would." Glancing toward the back of the bar, Sawyer arched a brow. "How many times have you whupped Nate's ass?"

"Six," Noble preened. "How about you? Want to try and redeem your miserable luck?"

"Not playing pool with you. I like keeping my money. You're a fucking shark."

"Pussy." Noble grinned.

Movement across the street caught Sawyer's attention. He watched as the trio walked toward Colton's truck. At the sight of Brea, Sawyer's heart rate picked up a couple notches. She was smiling at Jade. Brea damn near looked like a goddess. And

Sawyer realized he was already obsessed with the girl. The only way to purge her from his system was to forget her or fuck her. Sawyer hoped it would be the latter of the two.

"What are you gawking at now?" Shoving in alongside Sawyer, Noble nearly pressed his nose to the glass. "Oh, you're either a brave son of a bitch or the stupidest fuck-face to walk the planet. If Colton catches you eyeing his woman, you'll end up in a body bag."

"I'm not lusting after Jade, you fuck-nut."

"Oh, momma. "Who's that juicy cut of prime beef with them? She's pretty." Noble let out a long, low wolf-whistle. "Oh, yeah. Come to Daddy, sweet thing!" His brother's voice held a predatory edge. Sawyer wanted to beat the man bloody. "Hey, do you think she, Jade, and Colton are doing some kind of kinky threesome shit?"

"No! She's a friend of theirs, you pervert."

"Yeah, but are you sure she's not *with* them? 'Cause that shit would be hot as fuck to watch."

"Do your Internet porn sites know you're cheating on them?" Sawyer smirked.

"Fuck you. Those sites are the bomb."

"I can't believe we came from the same mother. But then, you spent every second of your formative years jacking off to Dad's *Playboys*. I shouldn't be surprised."

Using a wall of smoke and mirrors, Sawyer tried to hide his own kinky penchants by focusing on his brother's instead.

Noble simply laughed. "Don't pull that innocent choir boy crap with me. You're as twisted as the rest of us, and you damn well know it. You made me repeat every detail of the action I used to get with the Lauderbach sisters." A wistful expression crawled across his brother's face. "Damn, I wish they hadn't moved away."

"Are we playing pool, or are you two gonna stand up there comparing dicks all night?" Nate yelled from the back of the bar.

Noble leaned in and, with a conspiratorial whisper, said, "He gets testy when he loses." He started walking toward his ill-tempered twin. "If yours wasn't so fucking small that you needed a pair of tweezers and a magnifying glass to take a piss, you could join us, too. But since you don't measure up with the big boys—"

"Go fuck yourself," Nate groused. "My dick's bigger than both of yours combined."

"And you give it one hell of a workout…alone in the shower, don't you, bro?"

Noble's jab at Nate's vow of celibacy turned his chaste brother's face a deep shade of red.

"Kiss my ass," Nate snarled.

Sawyer rolled his eyes at their banter, then glanced out the window. Hope evaporated and disappointment sluiced through his veins as the taillights of Colton's truck faded into the night. Sawyer scowled. He didn't know how, after barely meeting the girl, Brea had maneuvered herself under his skin. He felt the need to race home and scrub the prickly sensation from his flesh, *after* he hauled ass to Colton's and dragged Brea beneath him for the night. Unfortunately, the lurid images clawing in his head would be put to rest, later, with his own fist. Unless…a willing playmate or two popped into the bar before the night was through. Tipping back his beer, Sawyer drained the mug. The thought of taking anyone home but Brea soured his stomach. He didn't want another woman…he wanted her.

The revelation shook him to his toes and nearly cracked the foundation beneath him. A burst of panic slammed his system. Sucking in several slow, ragged breaths, he wiped the sweat that had formed from his brow. He was a billion and one ways twisted over the girl, but this wasn't the time or the place to lose his shit. He didn't want his brothers getting the slightest whiff that he was interested in Brea or there'd be no stopping the ball busting they'd give him.

With a bitter sigh, he started toward the bar. Watching the twins battle it out on the pool table would give him something to focus on besides Brea.

"You boys keep your big, bad dicks in your pants, or I'll toss you out for indecent exposure," Gina warned from behind the bar.

"That's not what you told me last night, darlin'," Noble teased with a crooked grin.

"You're right. Last night I told you to go out with Amanda."

"Amanda? Who the hell is Amanda?" he asked clearly confused.

"A-man-da-hand relationship, dumb ass!" Gina countered with a grin.

Sawyer and Nate laughed at her raunchy comeback. There wasn't another woman in Haven who could cut a man down, or lift his spirits, using just her words; Noble grinned and blew her a kiss just as the front door burst open.

Victor LaCroix, the surliest bastard in town, stomped to the bar. Sawyer stood a couple seats away watching the smile on Gina's face turn arctic.

"What can I—"

"Whiskey," Victor interrupted. "Hold the small talk, bitch. I've had a shitty day."

Instantly, Noble and Nate sidled up beside Sawyer as he bristled. Anger hummed through his veins, and irritation rolled off his siblings. They'd been raised to respect women, unlike LaCroix.

Sawyer sent Gina a quizzical stare. Did she want him and the boys to step in on her behalf? She subtly shook her head and turned a brittle smile on Victor. After plucking a bottle off the shelf behind her, Gina held it to her chest. "Your day's about to get a whole lot shittier if you don't apologize to me, LaCroix."

Her sickening-sweet tone didn't faze the surly old man. He simply sent her an evil sneer. "You're testing my patience, girl. Give me that bottle and go find yourself a man who will keep you in your place."

Tension spiked. The air grew thick. A flash of fury rolled across Gina's face. She cocked her head as if appraising the loathsome prick. Sawyer had seen Gina deal with ugly drunks—twice Victor's size—and unleash the ruthless tigress inside her. But LaCroix was stone-cold sober. That made him a much bigger threat than a shit-faced drunk.

Warning bells clanged in Sawyer's head.

He stood poised, ready to intervene if needed, ready to spill the rude bastard's blood. Sawyer wasn't going to undermine the woman's authority in her own place of business…at least not yet. Without out a word, Gina slammed the bottle on the bar. Victor jerked in surprise and then glared. Bending over ever so slightly, she pulled Martha—her coveted Louisville Slugger—from beneath the bar and gripped it with both hands. Lifting the bat over her right shoulder, she swung the brown-stained wood against the bottle with all her might. Glass and booze exploded with a deafening crash. Ignoring Victor's thunderous cry of shock, Gina leaned in close to the man and flashed him a predatory smile.

"The only thing I need from a *man*, I can buy from the store and put batteries in. You may think I'm a weak little woman who needs to be coddled and taken care of, but I don't. You don't get to come into my bar, call me names, or order me around. You have two choices. Apologize and enjoy your drink, or leave. But if you insult me one more time, your head is going to be as fucked up as that bottle of whiskey. Got it?"

Gina pounded the end of the bat on the bar to emphasize her words. Twisting the wooden tip, she ground the fragments of splintered glass into dust.

Victor gaped in shock. Then a look of retribution grew over his face, red and fiery.

"All right. If that's how it's gonna be…" Gina lifted the bat and pointed it toward the door. "You lift your wrinkled old ass off my barstool and get the fuck out. The next time you come here, I'd better hear an apology roll off your tongue, or Martha here's gonna teach you some manners."

Sawyer admired her bravery, but the threat LaCroix posed

was far from over.

"You can go to hell, you crazy bitch! While you're there, buy yourself some batteries for your mechanical dick, you fucking dyke."

Gina raised the bat, taking aim at Victor's head. Sawyer and his brothers advanced, determined to physically remove the man so Gina didn't spend the rest of her life in prison for murder. But before they could reach him, Victor leapt off his barstool, sending it crashing to the floor. Backing away, he jerked a glare at the brothers.

"You all better get the fuck outta here. That bitch is crazier than a wet panther."

Gina jerked a tactical knife from beside a lime off the cutting board and sailed it past her ear with a seamless flick of the wrist. The gleaming blade sang through the air and landed with a thud in the wooden post behind Victor's head.

"I'm not a bitch," Gina spat. "I'm *the* bitch. Now get the fuck out of my bar!"

Victor's face turned a pasty gray. Muttering curses under his breath, he sprinted out the door.

"Jesus," Noble hissed. "What the fuck crawled up his ass?"

"Not a clue, but I think we can stand down now, boys." Sawyer flashed Gina a look of pride. "This is one damsel who's obviously not in distress."

"And I never will be," she snarled. Shoving back an errant curl from her forehead, she clenched her teeth. "That dusty old bastard scares me."

"Hopefully, he won't come back." Sawyer wanted to not only sooth his own anger but erase the visible fear in Gina's eyes. "Are you all right, darlin'?"

"I will be. I'm just pissed at myself."

"Why?" Sawyer blinked.

"Because the son of a bitch made me lose my temper. I hate it when that happens."

Wearing a starry-eyed expression, Nate rushed behind the bar to Gina's side.

Sawyer cocked a brow as his brother started wiping up glass and whiskey off the bar while swooning over the woman…the much older woman. Gina had to be at least fifteen years Nate's senior. By the look on his brother's face, Sawyer wasn't going to put a wager on Nate keeping his virginity for his wedding night. No, that goal was definitely in jeopardy. This whole situation had heartbreak written all over it…Nate's heart.

"Where did you learn to throw knives like that?" Nate's question dripped in awe.

"I learned to take care of myself a long time ago, honey."

Oblivious of Sawyer's brother's infatuated gaze, Gina cleaned up along side Nate.

"Here, let me do that for you," Nate offered like a lovesick puppy.

Sawyer rolled his eyes and slapped Noble on the back. "Come on, let's go play some pool. Loser buys a round."

Noble's eyes lit up. "You can save yourself a metric ton of embarrassment, and just buy me a beer now."

"I never give up on a bet or a challenge, fucker," Sawyer chuckled.

AFTER TOSSING AND turning, Brea rolled out of bed. Colton's guest room was cozy, the mattress soft and inviting, but her brain refused to shut down long enough for her to fall asleep. She'd lain awake all night while her thoughts seesawed between Weed, drugs, the cold and unforgiving holding cell, and the feverish arousal of Sawyer's blood-pumping stare.

At any other time in her life, Brea would have fucked the man's brains out…and moved in with him the next day. She scoffed at the thought of Sawyer inviting her into his bed, let alone his life. He didn't swim the loser pond of scum-suckers she usually skinny-dipped in when seeking out her next heartbreak.

No, Sawyer was the type found doing the front stroke in a bottomless blue ocean. Yeah, maybe she shouldn't be thinking about him bottomless and front stroking, but Brea couldn't help herself. The man was…

Way out of reach!

Unfortunately her inner reality checker was right. She had as much chance of living out her naughty fantasies with Sawyer as she did with Matthew McConaughey—the former lead role holder of her masturbation fantasies. Sawyer had seized the title last night.

If Brea hadn't been so pigheaded, determined to prove she was smarter than her parents when it came to love, she'd have set her man standard higher. Thinking she had all the answers, she'd paraded down the same perilous path and wound up with Weed, yet one more douchebag jerk.

She had to stop pining for a future with every man who stuck his cock inside her or she'd never find happiness. It was time to turn over a new leaf, but as a new day began to dawn, maybe putting her sex life on hold was too extreme. Giving up warm kisses, tender caresses, and sweaty, thrusting orgasms left her feeling bereft. Like starting a new diet, it made Brea want to binge before D-day, but instead of pigging out on food, she wanted to gorge on Sawyer. Get her fill of him until—like an insertable turkey timer—she popped.

"Get a grip. He'd probably turn you down. Then you'd be nothing but a walking, breathing embarrassment," she grumbled out loud.

She knew the only way she'd ever give up men totally would be to join a convent. But she heard somewhere that nuns had to wear underwear—white cotton, granny panties to be exact. She'd be banned from wearing her coveted skimpy lace thongs. Oh, and masturbation was probably a no-no along with sex.

"Looks like the nunnery is out of the question for this orgasm-craving butt-floss queen."

As dawn began breaking on the horizon, she stood and drank

in the beauty unfolding before her. Fingers of gold touched the grassy pasture, catching sparkles of dew to glisten like diamonds. In the distance she heard cows bawling for breakfast and a rooster crowing, announcing the start of another brand-new day.

Her first day without men.

The idea made her feel as if she were taking a slow walk to the gallows.

"Ugh!"

As she watched Colton stride toward the barn, guilt joined the rejection and depression pumping through her veins. Grateful that he and Jade had come to her rescue, Brea didn't want to mooch off their kindness indefinitely. Since they'd been apart for nearly a decade, she needed to give them privacy so they could fuck like bunnies and make up for the years of sex they'd missed. Nothing killed romance quicker than having a third wheel hanging around.

She needed to start making plans for her future and figure out where she wanted to start planting her roots. Sailing away to her own private island, complete with scantily clad cabana boys and a couple of margarita machines, sounded heavenly. But that was as unlikely as living out her *other* fantasy with Sawyer.

The scent of coffee tickled her nose. After showering and dressing, she wandered down to the kitchen and found Jade cooking breakfast at the stove.

"Good morning." Her friend's tone was far too chipper for Brea's tumultuous state of mind.

"The jury is still out on whether or not it's a good one."

"Coffee will help. Mugs are in the cabinet to the right of the sink. Make yourself at home…you're family." Jade turned to get a good look at her, then sent her a frown. "You didn't sleep a wink last night, did you? Is the bed—"

"No." Brea shook her head. "The bed's perfect. My mind is what's lumpy and uncomfortable."

"Of course it is. You had a hell of a shock yesterday."

"You can say that again."

"Pop a squat at the table. I'll be done here in a few minutes."

"Is there anything I can help you with?"

"Nope. Sit back, enjoy your coffee, and chat with me. I usually don't have anyone to keep me company while Colton's out playing with his cows." Jade giggled. "Don't tell him I called them cows. He's ubër-sensitive about his *cattle*."

Brea smirked. "Your secret's safe with me."

"They always were."

The warm smile Jade sent her lightened Brea's heavy mood. While a part of her still wanted to bop her old friend on the head for disappearing like she had, Brea knew there were times you simply had to hide away and lick your wounds…like she was doing now.

"I'm glad you and Colton are together. I can feel the depth of happiness pouring off both of you."

A melancholy expression slid over Jade's face as she paused and slid the pan of bacon off the flame. After wiping her hands, she picked up her mug of coffee and sat down across from Brea.

"I am, too. I didn't plan for things to turn out like they have. But the moment we saw one another, it was like I'd finally found home." She issued a scoff and shook her head. "That sounds stupid and corny, but it's true."

"It's not stupid or corny…it's romantic. That's how it's supposed to be when you find your true love. So what made you decide to look him up again?"

"Well, after I walked in on my ex jacking off while real-timing the chick he'd been screwing behind my back on his phone, I decided to find a new life."

"Ewww." Brea wrinkled her nose. "I bet you were crushed."

"Pfft, I was surprised but definitely not broken-hearted. I just packed my bags, told him good-bye, and left."

"You didn't love him?"

"No. I didn't love any of them." She shrugged. "I always picked emotionally unavailable men I knew would never fall in love with me. I'd lost my heart to Colton back in high school. I'd just let my stupid pride get in the way."

"God, we're a pair. You protected yourself while I let any sweet-talking scumbag sweep me off my feet. I've made such a mess of my life."

"Stop being so hard on yourself. You'll get your shit straightened out...it just takes time and a lot of soul-searching."

"I'll have plenty of time for that after I find a place of my own where I'm not sidetracked by fuck-nuts."

"Explain something to me. Why do you think you have to give up men totally?"

"Because I'm a hopeless, brain-dead princess, I guess. I spend the night with a guy and presto! I want to believe he's my knight in shining armor...saving me from having to be alone with myself. It's ridiculous, I know."

"First of all, being by yourself isn't a bad thing. Everyone needs time to learn who they are and what they want. But there's nothing wrong with a couple of one-night stands to blow the cobwebs out of your system. Find a fuck buddy. Hell, Haven is crawling with available men, and I know for a fact that cowboys are damn good in the saddle. Well, at least Colton is." Jade grinned like a cat who'd eaten the canary.

If Brea ever solicited a fuck buddy, Sawyer would be that man.

The back door opened, and Colton stepped in as Jade hopped up from her seat and hurried back to the stove. "I see how it is. Your best friend comes to town and you go off gabbing instead of fixing my breakfast, huh?"

Jade narrowed her eyes. Fury lined her face. "Excuse me?"

Colton burst out laughing as he took two strides toward his girl. Wrapping her in his arms, he hugged her tight. Jade smacked his shoulder and squirmed to break free.

"Settle down, bobcat. I was only teasing."

"I don't like your sense of humor," she spat.

"So I see." Colton lifted her off the ground, kissed her hard before setting her back on her feet. "Go sit down and visit with

Brea. I'll finish making breakfast, baby."

"Oh, I see how *you* are! Being a bossy butthead isn't going to get you fed, so now you're ready to step in so you don't starve to death. Is that it?" Jade scolded but, being unable to hold back her grin, lost her irritated cred.

"Something like that," Colton laughed.

Jade handed him the spatula, dramatically tossed her nose in the air, and sat down again. With a grin, she called out over her shoulder, "I like my eggs over easy."

"Ungrateful wench," Colton grumbled in mock annoyance.

Brea smiled while the couple bantered back and forth, but inside she was choking on envy. She'd searched high and low to find that exact kind of love, or a man like Colton. One who taunted and teased playfully and openly showed his unconditional love. The ringing of her cell phone ripped her from her delusional longings. Pulling the device from her pocket, she stared at the screen.

"It's Weed," she announced. Her skin crawled and indecision warred within.

"Hand it over. *I'll* talk to him." Colton stalked toward her, palm extended.

She found his protective mien endearing but shook her head. "I've got it."

Rising from the table, Brea wandered into the adjoining family room and answered. "What do you want, Weed?"

"Brea…baby. Look, I'm sorry," the bastard began in a contrite tone. "I didn't mean to hurt anyone. I was simply looking for a way to make some fast cash."

"And you thought selling drugs was the answer?"

"Stop being so judgmental. I didn't kill anyone."

"That you know of. If those kids accidently overdose on that shit you sold them, you'll be going to prison for murder."

"I know. Dammit, I know," Weed barked. "My lawyer already told me that. But they haven't and I'm not, so settle your ass down. Listen, I need you to find a bail bondsman and come get me the fuck outta here. The judge set my court day for two months from now but won't let me out on my own recog..cognatants"

"Recognizance," Brea corrected. What had ever attracted her to the Darwin Award-winning man?

"Whatever…I need you to post bail so I can come home."

"You've got balls asking me to do *anything* for you after you tried to throw me under the bus, you prick! You made this mess. You figure out how to find your own bondsman. I packed my stuff and left your sorry ass last night. You're on your own."

"You what?" Weed barked. "Don't say shit like that. You know I love you. Come on. Get in the car and come down here to pick me up."

"You don't love me. You never did. Even if I had a car, which I don't—it's in your name, remember?—I wouldn't drive around the block to help you. Go fuck yourself, Weed. And oh, don't ever call me again."

"You fucking bitch," Weed screamed. "You can't leave me. You need me."

Brea hung up and stared at her phone. "Not anymore, I don't."

Shaking with rage and regret, she closed her eyes and sucked in a ragged breath. The clouds of denial parted, and she finally grasped that Weed was nothing but a low-down disgusting pig. So why had she given her body and heart to the prick? A sick feeling sank to the pit of her stomach. Because he'd done what all the others had before him—flashed her a hungry smile and said a few flirtatious words. Sawyer had done the same thing last night, and Brea was ready and willing to fall into his bed and fuck his brains out.

You're never going to learn, are you?

Clenching her teeth, Brea let out a low growl. She'd spent the night coming up with excuses to circumvent her man ban, so she could have her cake—her Sawyer cake—and eat him…err, rather, it, too. Unable to hide the truth from herself any longer, Brea knew she had to begin her man diet here and now.

Filled with a sense of determination greater than any she'd known, she turned to find Jade and Colton standing in the doorway, wearing matching pensive expressions. Determined to navigate this new road of self-enlightenment and emotional and financial independence, Brea vowed to never relinquish the reins of her happiness to a man again.

"Is it time to eat?" She flashed her friends a confident smile.

Dissecting her with a hard stare, Jade slowly nodded. "Yes. Are you all right?"

"I'm actually better than I've been in a long time." Flashing Colton a mischievous grin, she arched her brows. "Are the eggs over easy?"

A crooked smile kicked up a corner of his mouth, and he nodded.

"Then let's do it," she stated before marching into the kitchen.

The meal started off enveloped in an awkward silence, but after a few minutes, the three were eating, laughing, and reminiscing about their teen years.

"I never did tell Chelsea Walters it was me who threw the rock that broke her window. How did I know she slept like the dead? But one thing I'll never forget was the sound of her daddy pumping those shells into his twelve gauge or the buckshot that sailed over my head as I ran elbows to asshole out of there."

Brea and Jade were laughing so hard at Colton's story, tears spilled down their cheeks.

"You're lucky you didn't end up stuffed and mounted over his fireplace," Brea snorted.

"I know, right? Her dad was a taxidermist's fantasy. He had six or seven deer, three wild boars, and two cougar heads, all stuffed and mounted in his shed," Colton said with a visible shudder. "The crazy son of a bitch even had a family of squirrels hanging on the wall by the shower in the bathroom. I don't even want to think what he mounted over his own damn bed. That man was scary as fuck! It wasn't any wonder Chelsea didn't have many dates."

"What's she doing now? Do either of you know?" Jade asked, wiping her happy tears.

"Last I heard, she was still in Austin, working for a big oil company," Colton replied before draining his mug and pushing back from the table. Standing, he bent and planted a soulful kiss on Jade's lips, then gave her a wink. "I need to get back to work. Breakfast was wonderful, sweetheart. And those eggs? Best I've ever tasted."

Jade rolled her eyes and flipped him off. He just laughed, all the way out the door.

"After I get these dishes done, I need to run to town and get some groceries. Wanna come with?"

"Only if you let me clean up the kitchen."

"You're on. Thanks. I'm going to grab a quick shower, then we can be on our way."

With her life plan in place, Brea's soul felt lighter than it had in…forever. Belting out her favorite Blake Shelton song, she started loading the dishwasher.

CHAPTER THREE

SITTING IN JADE'S rusted pickup, Brea couldn't wipe the grin from her face. Memories of them cruising their favorite haunts back in Austin inundated her. For several long minutes, she savored a time long past, when life had been easy and carefree. She brushed a hand over the faded cloth seats while wistful melancholy fluttered through her.

"Boy, if this old truck could talk…" she chuckled.

"We'd be in jail," Jade snorted. She quickly slapped a hand over her mouth and darted Brea a look of sympathy. "I'm sorry. That was the wrong thing to—"

"It's the truth," Brea cut her off with a laugh. "I can't believe you still have this beast…and that she actually still runs."

"This old girl's been the only constant in my life." Jade patted the cracked vinyl of the sun-bleached dashboard. "At least so far. Hopefully, Colton and I will last as long, if not longer. I hope this old truck will still be with me and not in a junkyard, if I have to start over again."

As if in warning not to mention a scrapheap, the engine coughed and sputtered before once more purring down the road.

"You're not going anywhere. Colton won't let you. He's in this for the long haul," Brea assured.

"Me, too." Contentment smoothed Jade's face as she pulled in and parked in front of the post office. "I'll be right back. I need to pick up a package, then we'll run across the street and get groceries."

Brea leaned forward and spied the supermarket. "Why don't you meet me over there, while I get the shopping started?"

"Sounds great. See you in a few."

Jade darted into the post office while Brea stood at the corner waiting for a couple of cars to pass. All of a sudden, a shiny black pickup truck pulled to a stop beside her. When the tinted window slid down and she saw Sawyer behind the wheel, her heart tripped in her chest.

His emerald eyes danced over her like a gentle caress. And the wide smile on his lips made Brea's whole body tingle. Like a bolt of lightning, heat awakened between her legs with a familiar throb.

"Good morning, gorgeous. What brings you to town so bright and early?" he asked, shoving his truck into park.

She swallowed the lump in her throat. With shaky fingers, she raised the grocery list. Dropping the paper quickly, she darted a glance behind her. "Oh, I'm just helping Jade with some errands. What about you?"

"I'm heading to work a little early." Sawyer leaned over the cab and opened the passenger door. "Hop on in for a minute, let's talk."

Talk? She had plenty to say to the man but it wasn't with words. Brea wanted an in-depth discussion that involved lips, tongues, and every inch of his naked body.

What about your man ban? You know…that orgasm-prohibited diet plan you started today? You'll never heal your heart deep-throating his long john and sucking the cream out of it!

"I can't!" Brea barked and slammed the door. Sawyer blinked in surprise. "I-I mean…I'm meeting Jade at the store in a minute. I need to go."

His intense gaze set her body on fire, yet goose bumps peppered her flesh. Her nipples drew up hard and tight, sending tempting tingles to spark her blood.

"Then join me for a drink tonight at the Hangover, say around eight o'clock?"

No way. Brea and booze didn't play nice. Alcohol went straight to her pussy and turned her into a hooker hosting a yard sale. Her attraction to men was hard enough to contain. Tequila was an accelerant that ignited a ravenous bonfire of lust inside her. A willing appendage that made her combust was the only way to put out the flames.

"I-I don't drink," she stammered.

"Then let me buy you a soda," Sawyer countered.

The irresistible twinkle in his dazzling green eyes was short-circuiting her brain.

"Hey, Sawyer." Jade nodded to the man as she moved in alongside Brea. "Are you hitting on my bestie?"

"I'm trying, but unfortunately, I think I'm striking out." His lips turned down in a mock frown before he wiggled his brows and grinned. "Wanna put in a good word or two for me?"

"Oh, god," Brea mumbled under her breath.

"Normally I would, especially for you, but my girl isn't interested in men. Sorry." Jade looped her arm with Brea's.

Wrong, Jade, I'm hella more than interested.

Though Brea knew she should at least try and deny the fact, she couldn't.

Sawyer's gaze stalled on the women's linked limbs before shock made his eyes grow wide. "Oh, hell. I didn't realize that you…you two were lovers. Wow. Okay, it makes perfect sense now. Fuck! Colton's one lucky son of a bitch."

Brea's mouth fell open. "What? We're not… You thought that we…that Colton watched while Jade and I… Oh, hell no!"

While Jade tossed back her head and howled, a vibrant red blush crawled up Sawyer's face. Brea was too stunned to laugh and simply stared at him, slack-jawed.

"I'm sure Colton would *love* that, but the three of us are just friends…*platonic* friends," Jade explained through giggles.

Sawyer's blush grew deeper crimson as he held up his hands in surrender. "Hey, I'm not one to judge or pry…it's just…" He narrowed his eyes at Brea. "Why won't you let me take you out for a drink?"

Because I'll be on you doing the lust thrust before we make it to the bar.

"Wait! Do *not* give her alcohol," Jade barked out in warning.

"Okay. I won't." He looked startled by her sudden outburst, but focused back on Brea. "Let me take you to dinner, then."

"No. I'm sorry. It's not you. I-I don't date. I'm on a man ban." Brea lifted her chin defiantly.

While she didn't want the whole world to know her plan, Haven was small, and she'd likely run into the man over and over again. She needed to shut him down, nip his stirring flirtations in the bud, and she had to make it quick, painless, and final. What he'd do to her in bed, when she was alone with B.O.B., would have to satisfy her…somehow.

Sawyer's golden brows slashed with a frown. "A man ban…what the fuck is… Oh, I get it. Damn. That's a cryin' shame. A pretty little thing like you shouldn't do without the pleasures a good man can give."

His low, silky voice set a fifty-pound can of sexually curious TNT off inside her. Knowing she couldn't possibly do anything about it had her girl parts weeping in regret.

Then, like a colossal masochist, she opened her mouth. "And I take it you're that good man?"

"I've never had a complaint yet."

He flashed her a bad-boy grin. Promise flickered in his eyes. Brea wanted to howl in frustration.

"I don't doubt that for a second, but my man ban remains."

It might remain, but it was crumbling and cracking like an oatmeal mask in the Mojave.

The corners of his mouth kicked up in a mischievous grin. "Good. I like a challenge. See you soon, darlin'."

With a wink, Sawyer pulled away. She watched him drive out of town as she trembled like a leaf. Slowly his words registered. He planned to decimate her defenses.

What defenses? The ones he just destroyed with that sexy, lazy smile?

His smile…his lips…one kiss and he'd melt her like lip gloss in August. Her plan was in serious jeopardy. She had to build a sturdy wall around her before encountering that sinful man again. Locking herself in Colton's guest room was an inviting alternative, but hiding from Sawyer until she grew strong and secure wasn't a viable option. She'd have to work fast with all the determination she could muster.

Good luck with that, her subconscious scoffed. *That big, bad wolf will blow all your houses down, and you damn well know it.*

Though she didn't want to admit it, Brea knew deep inside she was in serious trouble.

As if sensing her dilemma, Jade squeezed her arm, then dragged her across the street.

"You stood your ground firmly. I'm proud of you."

Brea wanted to be proud as well, but she was too busy processing the shock of turning down the first date of her life. She thought of calling her parents, or *Ripley's Believe It or Not*, to share her miraculous feat, but instead, she grunted and followed Jade into the store.

The overhead vents blasted cold air over her body, freeze-drying the flames of estrogen still licking up her spine. Unfortunately, doing a handstand to take care of the heated wetness between her legs might be frowned upon and cause grave embarrassment as well. Sucking in a ragged breath, Brea forced thoughts of Sawyer aside. She focused on pushing the cart behind Jade as they walked up and down the narrow aisles.

Pausing in front of the milk cooler, Jade placed her hand over Brea's. "You haven't said a word since he drove off. If you're that attracted to Sawyer, go out with him. One date isn't going to hurt."

Brea adamantly shook her head. "No, it only takes one date. I'll end up doing something stupid, like let him fuck me into a coma."

Jade laughed softly. "You say that like it's a bad thing."

"It is, because I won't stop there. I'll keep going until I maneuver myself into his life, until we're both miserable and can't stand each other."

"I'm not suggesting you move in with him. I'm just saying have some fun, but hold on to your heart."

"If only it were that simple." Brea rolled her eyes.

"It is. You don't need a man twenty-four seven."

"I'm not ready to use him like a vibe and then send him out the door, as if stowing my toys back in a drawer."

"I'm sorry. I'm not trying to push you into doing something you're not ready for. It's just that…Sawyer's a good man. You need to stop plucking partners out of the gutter, or you're going to keep getting junk. You should be start plucking your men from the sky… like stars." Jade sent her a sad smile. "You of all people deserve big, bright, beautiful stars."

"Is Sawyer a star?"

"He definitely ain't no broken beer bottle, sugar," Jade chuckled.

"No, he isn't."

"At least think about it. Okay?"

Since laying eyes on the man, she'd done nothing but think about it. That was the problem! Biting her tongue, she sent her friend a nod before they proceeded to the front of the store.

Brea stopped the cart behind a thin, older blonde. The woman turned and skimmed a cursory glance over the two. Looking back at the cashier—a heavyset woman wearing a tag stamped LUCY, was eyeing the friends as well—the blonde issued a heavy sigh.

"I don't know what to do," she moaned. "Kristen will be in the hospital for at least a week after they do the surgery on her broken leg. Like an idiot, she was the only one I had lined up to take care of things for me. My flight takes off at eight in the morning, and there is no one left to call. I can't cancel this trip! The girls will have to forfeit if I'm not there."

"Lordy, Barbara, I'd help you out if I could," the cashier commiserated as she shoved her wire-framed glasses on top of her bottle-black hair. "We're so short-handed here that Ray's got me putting in sixty, sometimes seventy hours a week. I can help you out by going by the house before and after work, but Ozzie'll be alone for ten, maybe twelve hours a day."

"No. That little monster of mine will have eaten the entire house the first day. Of course, Troy's closing the vet clinic next week to take his family to Disney. I tried every other vet and kennel from here to Dallas." Barbara tossed her hands in the air. "I am so screwed."

The angst in the woman's voice pained Brea. She'd been between a rock and hard place more times than she could count.

"I know that woman doesn't know me from Adam, but I would love to help her out," Brea whispered to Jade.

"I don't know her either," Jade murmured. "But I bet she knows Colton."

Before Brea could stop her, Jade tapped Barbara on the shoulder, flashing a sincere smile. "Hi. I'm Jade, and this is my friend Brea. We weren't trying to eavesdrop, but you sound like you're in a fix. We might be able to help you out."

"I'm sorry. I don't know you two. Do you live in Haven?" Barbara was clearly suspicious of Jade's offer.

"This gal here"—Lucy pointed at Jade—"she's the one who moved in with Colton Maddox."

"Oh, I heard he finally found someone special." Barbara smiled. "I'm sorry. I haven't had the pleasure of meeting you yet. I'm Barbara Rhymes."

The woman extended her hand and Jade shook it. "It's nice to meet you. This is my friend Brea Gates. She and I… well, and Colton, we've all been friends since high school. Brea is staying with us for a little while."

"Hello, Brea." Barbara studied her appraisingly.

"Nice to meet you," Brea replied politely.

"Where you from?" Lucy asked curiously.

"I was living in Denton."

"Was? You running from the law or something?" Lucy narrowed her eyes.

"No. No, nothing like that. I just got out of a long-term relationship."

"Men," Lucy tsked. "They're all swine."

"Are you planning to stay in Haven?" Barbara asked.

"I can, as long as you need me to." Brea didn't want to confess that at age twenty-eight she didn't have a life plan. Or that she'd wasted her dreams of having children, a home, and the love of a good man on losers whose lofty ambitions were achieved by keggers and video games.

"Can you stay a month?"

"A month?" Brea had expected to fill the woman's needs for a week…two at the most.

"That's going to be a problem, isn't it?" Barbara frowned.

"No. I can stay as long as you need me." She didn't have anything else to do.

"Oh, thank god. All you need to do is take care of my dog, Ozzie. He's a love. And then water my gardens. I've raised everything from seed and would be heartbroken if they died."

"Is your ex dangerous? Is that why you left him?" Lucy blurted out, obviously warier than Barbara.

"No. He's a lazy ex-mechanic who has more skill romancing a transmission than a woman," Brea drawled. "He got fired a while back and stopped looking for work. I got fed up supporting him and left."

She'd keep Weed's extracurricular drug activities to herself. Why cast doubt on her shredded moral fiber? Still, the cashier sent Barbara a scowl and a subtle shake of her head.

"I…I don't know." Barbara indecisively bit her bottom lip.

"I'm not a murderer or anything," Brea began, hoping to ease the other women's fears. "I'd never harm an animal. I love dogs. I won't think of destroying your house or pilfering the silver flatware. I'm trustworthy and honest. You can ask Colton. He's known me forever. He'll vouch for me."

"I will too." Jade nodded emphatically.

Their words seemed to melt Lucy's distrust, as her expression softened. And soon after, Barbara and Lucy were regaling her and Jade with stories of their own heartbreaking experiences with men.

"I like you, Brea…" Barbara paused. "No offense, but I'd like to talk to Colton."

Jade whipped out her cell phone, scrolled to find his number, and handed it to the woman. "Here, you can call him now."

Barbara thanked her, pushed the button, and walked toward the produce section.

"If you all don't mind…while she's making that call, I'm going to hit the ladies' room. My bladder is fixin' to bust!"

Without waiting for a reply, Lucy turned and ran toward the back of the store.

"I really hope this works out. I feel horrible invading your and Colton's privacy."

"Don't be silly." Jade waved dismissively. "You haven't invaded anything."

"Still, I don't want to hinder your sex life. And with what I've got to do, lying in bed listening to you two go at it like a couple of monkeys on Animal Planet…I'll need new toys in a week."

"We don't want that now, do we?" Jade giggled.

"No. I need to go easy on B.O.B. since he's the only thing that'll be getting near my flower patch for a long time." Brea sobered. "I've never lived alone before. It's time I give it a try and figure out what I want to do with my life."

Jade blinked. "You've never lived alone?" Brea shook her head. "Wow. I didn't know that. You should stay here in Haven. Find a job and settle down, close to Colton and me. It's not a bad thing to have friends around in case you need them. And you know we'll both be there anytime you need us."

"I know, and I love you both for it. Thank you."

Barbara came rushing back excitedly and wearing a huge grin as she handed Jade back her phone.

"Brea, you're hired," Barbara announced with a laugh. "Oh, my god, Colton couldn't stop praising you. Thank you so much for doing this for me. You've saved my butt. I'll pay you a thousand dollars for the month…is that fair?"

"A thousand dollars?" Brea gasped. "Yes. More than fair. Oh, my god. Thank you."

"I don't mean to be nosy," Jade began. "But where are you going for a whole month?"

"I belong to a women's cycling group." Barbara looked around, then leaned in close and whispered, "We call ourselves the Menstrual Cycles."

"Oh, my god," Brea chortled. "That's priceless."

"I know," Barbara giggled. "In the morning, we're flying to Italy to compete in the Giro d'Italia Femminile. It's the women's equivalent to the Tour de France. The men won't allow us to ride the Tour. I think they're afraid we'll beat them and they'll have to all turn in their man cards."

"Oh, wow. That sounds exciting," Jade cooed.

"What? What did I miss?" Lucy asked as she hustled behind the cash register.

"I was just telling the girls about the race. Brea is going to take care of Ozzie and the house."

"Wonderful!" Lucy cheered.

"Here, let me give you my address." Barbara quickly scribbled the info on a small grocery sack and handed it to Brea. "Come by anytime this afternoon. I'll introduce you to Ozzie and show you around the house."

The three women watched as Barbara sailed out of the store. Once out of sight, Lucy pinned Brea with a fierce stare.

"Barbara is a good friend. She's been through a lot and is finally getting her life back on track. You mess with her and I'll hunt you down. You got it?"

Taken aback by the woman's threat, Brea couldn't help but admire the fierce protection Lucy extended her friend.

"Trust me. I have no hidden agenda. I don't want to hurt her in any way. I'm simply helping a fellow woman in need. That's all. I promise."

"Good. That's what I wanted to hear." Lucy glanced behind her and cringed when an old man entered the store. "Good afternoon, Emmett."

"No. It's not a good nuthin'," the seventy-something man snapped curtly. "That damn Bigfoot is back. He was prowling outside my house last night. By the time I'd loaded up my shotgun, the big, ugly sucker ran away."

Brea sucked in a gasp of fear. Lucy rolled her eyes and gave a barely perceptible shake of her head. "That's nice, Emmett. Just make sure you don't mistake Maynard Pierce for Sasquatch and blow his head off."

"I know what my neighbor looks like, you darn fool woman," Emmett huffed. "You'll see. One day I'm gonna be on the evening news."

As the man stormed away, Lucy shook her head. "Oh, I'm sure you will...for blowing your gall-darned neighbor's brains out, you crazy ol' coot."

Brea flashed a worried glance first at Jade, then Lucy. "There isn't a real Bigfoot around here is there?"

"Only Emmett. The man's got the biggest feet I've ever seen." Lucy grinned with a wink.

SAWYER'S PULSE FINALLY slowed to a normal rhythm as he turned down the gravel road toward his parents' ranch. Unfortunately his straining cock wasn't ready to give up its fight for a good time with Brea. His hungry appendage had stood up the second Sawyer spotted the woman standing on the corner. The way the sunlight had streamed around her, casting the sexy vixen in an ethereal glow, made her look like a beautiful angel. She'd stolen his fucking breath.

Everything had been going smooth as silk...until she'd turned him down.

"Spurned by a ridiculous man ban," Sawyer spat in disgust.

"What the fuck is that all about anyway?"

He would have liked it better if she'd turned him down because she batted for the other team, like Sawyer had first thought. But finding out she'd kicked all men to the curb rankled. Some prick-assed fuck-nut must have hurt her something fierce. He wanted to find out who, hunt the weasel down, and rearrange his face. While the notion would satisfy Sawyer immensely, it wouldn't heal Brea's wounds, no matter how badly battered they might be.

Questions about her past…no, worries of what she'd endured rolled through his brain. The need to know everything about her rode him harder than a sumo wrestler on a Shetland pony. But he'd never discover a damn thing as long as Brea continued to shut him down. With a curse, Sawyer slammed his palm against the steering wheel.

Frustration ate at him until he saw the two-story log home in the distance. He'd grown up here, and a much-needed sense of peace began to settle through him.

Parking beside the barn, he watched, Norris, his youngest brother, who, at eighteen, was stronger than most men twice his age, lead one of the horses toward the pasture. The oldest of the brothers, Ned—who was married and lived a half mile up the road with his wife, April—was busy saddling the horses with Noble in preparation for the guests arriving soon.

"About time you dragged your ass out of bed," Noble playfully taunted.

"Kiss my ass! You haven't been outside more than ten seconds," Sawyer scoffed in return. "Mom and Dad still up at the house?"

"Of course. Dad's in the bathroom, taking his morning constitutional, and Mom's cleaning up the kitchen. She's fixed enough food to feed an army."

"We eat like an army."

"That's no lie." Noble grinned.

As Sawyer headed toward the back patio door, the last of his brothers, Nate and Nash, stepped onto the massive wooden deck. Both were wearing serious expressions.

"Is something wrong?" he asked.

Angrily jerking his head up, Nash sent him a wicked glare. "Everything! If you'd kept your nose out of my business and given me time to let Megan cool down, none of this shit would be happening."

The venomous tone and fury rolling off Nash's tongue caught Sawyer by surprise. "Whoa. What the hell happened with Megan?"

"There is no more Megan," Nash spat. Inching into Sawyer's personal space, he raised a finger and poked him in the chest. "I should have never listened to any of your piss-poor advice."

"I sent you over to apologize."

"Oh, I tried. She tore into me like a panther with a toothache. Verbally kicked my nuts down my throat, then gave me an ultimatum."

Sawyer cringed inwardly. The word *ultimatum* told him shit had gone south in a bad way. The six brothers shared the same genetic flaw—an overactive bullhead chromosome. When pushed into a corner, they either came out fighting or turned into frosty obstinate, pricks.

"Which was?" Sawyer arched his brows.

"She told me to shit or get off the pot. Either set a date and marry her or she'd find someone who would. Then she pulled off her engagement ring, threw it at me, and slammed the door in my face. Happy now?" Nash barked.

Guilt, slick and hot, sluiced through Sawyer's veins. "No. I'm not! If I'd known things were going to end up like this, I never would have told you to—"

"Forget it. What's done is done."

Nash turned and stormed away, leaving Sawyer feeling as if he had both feet crammed in his mouth and was nothing but two inches tall. "Son of a bitch!"

"This isn't your fault, and you know it," Nate assured. "All

Nash had to do was set a goddamn date. Instead, he got his hackles up and…dumb shit needs to learn to kiss ass a whole lot better."

"If he wants to stay married longer than five minutes, he does."

Nate chuckled. "I'll take your word for it. Mom tried to tell him a little bit of space might do them some good. God knows they've been breathing each other's air since grade school. She told him that every couple spats now and then."

"I suppose he's not listening to Mom either, right?"

"You know the answer to that. He's like the rest of us…single-minded, stubborn, and too damn tenacious for our own good."

Sawyer scrubbed a hand over his bristly chin. "Of course he is! Fuck!"

"And just like the rest of us, he'll get over it once he's had time to cool off." Nash slapped him on the back, then walked away.

Inside the house, Sawyer found his mother, Nola, in the kitchen, washing dishes. He came up behind her and kissed her on the cheek. She smiled and nodded toward the plate covered in foil on the table.

"Good morning, sweetheart. I thought you planned to come in early today."

"I was, but got held up in town."

"Ah." She nodded. "Sit down and eat before your food gets cold. Did you talk to Nash?"

Sawyer couldn't miss the worry clouding his mom's moss-colored eyes. He popped a piece of bacon in his mouth and nodded. "It wasn't a talk really. More like he chewed my ass, and I listened."

"If my cast-iron skillet hadn't been full of eggs, I'd have smacked him in the head with it." Nola sighed heavily. "What on earth was that boy of mine thinking? Megan is his soul mate. Everyone on the planet knows it…sees it. Why can't he?"

Washing his food down with a gulp of coffee, Sawyer shook his head. "Because you and Dad blessed us, or rather cursed us, whichever the case may be; our heads are far harder than your skillet. It's a wonder we're all not brain-dead from butting our heads together for one reason or another."

"Well, *you* finally stopped beating yours and wised up. Hopefully Nash will too…soon."

"I didn't wise up, Mom. I gave up. Big difference," Sawyer replied grimly.

Nola wiped her hands and sat down at the table. "Oh, honey. Sara left you no choice. You did the only thing you could and divorced *Her Majesty*."

Sawyer grunted in reply. It might have been his only option, but he'd never been able to shake the guilt for failing. Failing to keep his vow to God, his family, and himself.

"Don't worry, Mom. Nash will pull his head out of his ass one day. If he and Megan are meant to be, they'll work it all out."

"I know. I still want to knock some sense into him." She issued a heavy sigh. "Let me get you the register."

"Thanks."

Nola retrieved a thick binder and set it on the table beside Sawyer before returning to her dishes. He sucked in a deep breath and steeled himself, then opened to the first page. He silently read the bios and studied the photos of the handicapped children en route to the family ranch.

Their spread of land was known as Camp Melody, a respite from hospitals and clinics for mostly terminally ill children. The ranch was a vision realized by his father, Newton. It was an escape for children to try and forget about their illnesses while they spent a week experiencing new adventures in the great outdoors.

His dad's youngest sister, Melody—the only aunt Sawyer never had the chance to meet—had been born with a rare blood and bone disorder. From an early age, Melody had been confined to a wheelchair. His father had spent every minute of free time making sure Melody didn't waste away in her room, reading books, glued to the television, or watching the rest of the family work and play outside.

Newton would secure his sister on his horse, and they'd ride out to the river. They'd enjoy a picnic in the shade or fish in the sunshine. He taught her to shoot several types of guns, and even built a slide-board that fit between the garden rows. She was able to weed and harvest the vegetables with the rest of the family.

When she passed away at age seventeen from a lung infection, his father had taken it hard. He vowed to his family, and his sister's spirit, that he would find a way to keep her memory alive. He'd instilled that same moral conviction in all six of his sons. They grew up providing memories and experiences for sick children all over the country.

Sawyer continued studying the pages as sadness gripped his heart. This was always the hardest part for him…reading about the unfair, shortened life expectancy of each innocent child.

Raising his head as his father entered the room, Sawyer sent him a grim nod. Meeting his gaze, Newton gripped his son's shoulder firmly, acknowledging the torment in Sawyer's eyes.

"You're the one with the softest heart. You always have had, probably always will, son." Newton smiled sympathetically.

"You calling me a wimp?"

Newton chuckled. "No. Never. You're kind, compassionate, and caring. A father couldn't ask for more honorable qualities in a child. Don't let yourself get strangled by the injustice of it all. Find peace in knowing we're giving these kids something special to take back as they wage war on the diseases that are ravaging their tiny bodies."

"I do, Dad. I just wish they could all live long, happy lives."

"Hopefully, some of them will."

His father's gentle words smoothed some of the raw and jagged edges on Sawyer's soul. But the children's struggles weren't the only issues weighing heavily on his mind. Brea's rejection, and Nash's angry words, had left a hallow void inside him. As his appetite waned, he closed the notebook, pushed away from the table, and took his dishes to the sink.

Tucking the binder beneath his arm, Newton slapped Sawyer on the back. "Let's do this. Momma, are you ready?"

Nola smiled and nodded as she dried her hands. When the three stepped out on the deck, she reached up and rang the weathered copper bell hanging from the rustic fascia. The alert usually meant it was mealtime, but this call was for his brothers and Melody employees to gather on the deck for their weekly staff meeting.

Sawyer watched as the doors to both the girls' and boys' barracks opened wide. Like ants, jean-clad, Stetson-wearing paraprofessionals, nurses, and a multitude of counselors and volunteers hurried across the yard before gathering in a half circle on the deck. Their faces glowed with excitement. Sawyer's spirits lifted, well, until he glanced Nash's way. The man still wore an angry scowl on his face.

While his mother handed out activity agendas, his father addressed specific needs of their scheduled guests. Sawyer darted another glance Nash's way. His brother's brooding, angry sadness had Sawyer releasing a guilt-ridden sigh. When the meeting was over, he hung back and gripped Nash's shoulder before the man could walk away.

"I'm sorry I butted in last night. I honestly wasn't trying to stir up trouble between—"

"No. I'm the one who should apologize," Nash interrupted. "I ripped into you because I'm unable to inflict the anger I feel onto myself. I'm the dumb fuck who dug my feet in and refused to budge. I'm not pissed at you or the world, just myself."

The remorse in Nash's voice sliced Sawyer like razor blades. Their family bond was strong. When any one of them was hurting, the pain rippled out and affected them all. Nash's heartbreak was no exception.

"I'm here if you need me. We all are." Sawyer slapped him on the back with a grim nod.

"Thanks."

The sound of crunching gravel and the hum of diesel engines came from the driveway, announcing the arrival of the guests. The staff gathered on the poured concrete walkway that connected the barracks, mess hall, showers, and shelter houses, waving and cheering excitedly. Each new group of campers was welcomed with an overabundance of enthusiasm. Sawyer, and even Nash, couldn't help but grin and holler from the deck.

"Come on, let's give these angels something wonderful to remember," Sawyer urged.

As he made his way to the first bus, images of another angel filled his head. But he shoved his memories of Brea aside and scanned the little faces for a blond, blue-eyed pixie. Sawyer had a special surprise planned for the little girl. He smiled as they lifted six-year-old Tina Ellis off the bus. The timid expression on her face gave way to a look of awe, and a dreamlike sparkle danced in her eyes when she spied the horses. Sawyer moved in close as a counselor handed the girl her metal-cuffed crutches, and with lumbering steps, Tina headed straight toward the fence of the pasture.

"Horses," she whispered on a breathless sigh.

Goose bumps peppered Sawyer's arms, and tears stung the backs of his eyes, while his heart nearly burst with joy. Though he'd never met aunt Melody, he knew by the tone of Tina's voice that his father's sister was looking down on this family with nothing but pride.

After making his way over to Tina, Sawyer dropped to one knee and smiled. "You're Tina, and you love horses, right?"

The little girl blinked up at him as if he'd read her mind, and nodded ever so slowly.

"I'm Sawyer. Would you like to ride one of them?"

Her mouth dropped open in unadulterated shock. "Can I?"

"You bet. I'm afraid our first trip will have to be a short one. We still need to get you settled into your barracks, but after that long bus ride, I thought you might like to breathe in some good ol' fresh Texas air."

"I would. I really, really would."

Sawyer smiled, then turned to Jason, one of the counselors. "Miss Tina and I are going for a little ride on Thunderbolt. We'll be back shortly in case anyone is looking for us."

"Got it, boss. You two have fun." Jason nodded as he helped another child in a wheelchair clear the lift gate.

"Thunderbolt?" Tina asked with an audible gulp. "Does he go fast?"

"As fast as you want him to."

Tina reached up and lightly brushed her thin fingers along the horse's shoulder. "Not too fast, okay, Thunderbolt?"

The horse jerked his head as if answering. Tina's face filled with wonder all over again. The horse stood motionless—as he'd been trained—while Sawyer hoisted himself onto the custom-fabricated saddle. Gripping the metal horn, he leaned over and plucked Tina off the ground. She let out a tiny squeal of surprise. Her crutches clanged together while she held tight to Sawyer's arm.

"Easy, Tina. I've got you. I won't let you fall," he assured. "You're doing great, sunshine."

After settling the girl onto the front portion of the saddle, he helped her out of her crutches and slid them into a specially designed leather sheath behind him. With one arm, he reached around her and unwound the reins from the saddle horn before handing them to her.

"Take us away, Tina."

"Me?" she squawked in a small voice.

"Yes, you."

"Oh, wow," she whispered. She clutched the reins in her bony fists. "Giddyup."

Sawyer lightly tapped the heels of his boots against Thunderbolt's sides. The horse reared its head and let out a loud whinny. Tina giggled, before Thunderbolt began slowly moving toward the pasture entrance.

"I got it," Nate called. Jogging toward the galvanized metal gate, he swung it open wide. As Sawyer and Tina passed him, Nate doffed his Stetson. Bowing deep, he raised his head and winked at the little girl. "Your pasture awaits, my queen."

Tina covered her mouth and laughed. It was the second sweetest sound Sawyer had heard all day. Brea's sultry timbre was the first.

CHAPTER FOUR

WITH HER DUFFLE bags stowed in the back of Jade's truck, Brea rode shotgun toward Barbara's house. When they pulled into the driveway, she fell instantly in love with the Victorian gingerbread-style home. It looked like an oversized dollhouse. As they climbed the stairs and onto the white wraparound porch, she sighed. Ivy climbed the multicolored spindles and white lattice panels. Brea couldn't wait to spend a month in the beautiful house…

Until Barbara opened the screen door and Ozzie, a massive black and tan Doberman, raced onto the porch, nearly knocking Brea on her ass. After circling her legs, Ozzie stopped. He drove his nose between her thighs, furiously sniffing her crotch. Her face caught fire as she tried to shove the beast's muzzle away.

"And you thought you were through with men," Jade giggled.

She shot her bestie a steely glare. "You are *so* not funny."

Jade laughed harder.

"Sorry about that," Barbara sheepishly groaned. "Ozzie! Leave it."

At her command, the dog jerked his head from Brea's crotch and padded over to nuzzle his mistress's hand. Barbara sent her an apologetic frown. "Crazy beast. I swear he's part Alabama crotch-hound. Please, come inside."

With a wary eye on Ozzie, she followed Jade and Barbara into the house. To Brea's relief, the cooch-sniffing mutt kept his nose out of her business while his mistress took them on a tour of her magnificent home. It had a warm, welcoming vibe, and Brea was charmed with the walnut pocket doors and glossy hardwoods.

But it was the detailed crown molding and bull's-eye-trimmed windows framed against crisp white walls that took her breath away. The craftsmanship was astounding, and the intricate carved spindles surrounding a grand staircase were icing on the cake. It wasn't going to be a hardship to spend a month in such architectural splendor.

After the tour, they waved good-bye to Jade, who promised to stop by often. Then Brea and Barbara spent the next several hours going over everything from breaker boxes to bird feeders and how to care for the massive flower and vegetable beds in the backyard. Ozzie ran wild, barking and chasing birds, while Barbara and Brea sat at a marble-topped outdoor dining set. Relaxing under the wide umbrella, the women talked and sipped ice tea.

Ozzie lifted his leg and relieved himself on the chain-link fence separating Barbara's yard from her neighbor's.

"Oh, I almost forgot. If something breaks…the dishwasher, garden hose…anything, my neighbor, Neville, is a natural-born repairman. He's great with his hands."

Brea nearly spewed tea out her nose. Coughing and sputtering, she finally cleared her throat and sent Barbara a suggestive grin. "Oh, really?"

"Not like that. Heavens no." The woman, all flustered and embarrassed, blushed wildly. "He helps me with house repairs from time to time. That's *it*."

Brea glanced at the chestnut-colored two-story craftsman over the fence and wondered why Barbara hadn't enlisted Neville to watch her dog and house. Then again, with a name like Neville, he might be hours away from moving into the nursing home. Or worse…he could be buckets full of crazy like Emmett, the scary Bigfoot hunter.

Brea was quickly learning that while Haven was a quaint town, some of its occupants were pretty strange.

Back inside the house, the women prepared an early dinner. Brea realized how much she'd missed the company of another female. The time she'd spent with both Jade and Barbara had been more relaxing than a day spa. Brea didn't have to worry about interrupting some amazing punt return on TV or being hounded about clean socks and reminded that the milk was all gone. It was like a breath of fresh air, a vacation, and she was enjoying every single second. She was even aware of the strange sense of peace growing inside her.

Like old friends, she and Barbara sat talking and laughing. The woman had a dry and biting sense of humor that Brea enjoyed. It wasn't long after the sun went down that Barbara thanked her once more for coming to the rescue, then said good night and good-bye.

As darkness closed in, Brea snagged a romance novel from the bookshelves and climbed the stairs. Halfway through the first chapter, she zonked completely out.

The sounds of birds chirping and a lawn mower churning in the distance tugged her from yet another sinfully erotic dream featuring none other than Sawyer. Brea tossed back the covers and moaned. Her girl parts still ached from the numerous nocturnal sexcapades that'd had her coming in her sleep. Ozzie's toenails clapped across the wooden floor. As she sat up, the dog padded to the bed and dropped his muzzle on the mattress beside her. With sad brown eyes, he peered up at her and whined. It was obvious that the crotch-sniffing hound was mourning the loss of his mistress. Reaching down, she stroked his head and ears.

"It sucks not being with the one you want. Trust me. I know. Don't worry. Your mommy hasn't abandoned you forever. Me, on the other hand…yeah, well…that's a sad story even your big, brave puppy-dog heart doesn't want to hear."

The pup issued a heavy, pitiful sigh. He stared up at her with an even sadder expression and Brea's heart melted.

"All right. I can see I'm going to need to declare this a no-moping day. Let's go get you a treat. That ought to cheer you up…it always does me. Of course, my treats walk on two legs and do things with their tongues that…" Brea let out a low growl.

Ozzie quirked one ear and cocked his head at her. With a

laugh, she pulled off her wrinkled T-shirt and tugged a clean one on. She'd been so exhausted last night she'd fallen asleep fully dressed.

After feeding and watering the dog, she gave him his promised treat, then made a pot of strong coffee. Leaning against the kitchen counter, waiting for her caffeine infusion to brew, images of Sawyer's face and all the wicked things he'd done to her in her dreams plowed through her brain. Her skin tingled and her body hummed.

"Oh, get a grip. You're not sixteen anymore. Stop pining over him like you did Luke Perry. You're a grown woman. You can't go around with your head in the clouds. Mr. Wet Dream, who kept you up all night, has character flaws like all the rest. The only difference is you haven't discovered them yet…and you're not going to. Because you're going to stay far, far away from that sinful side of beef, even if it kills you."

Talking to herself did little to sway Sawyer from her thoughts. Of course, her brain cells were still pulsating from the numerous orgasms he'd given her—in her dreams. She needed to find a way to turn off her subconscious to keep from torturing herself and get a good night sleep. Besides, she was there to take care of things for Barbara, not fixate on her own over-imaginative libido.

After a shower and a light breakfast, Brea called her boss, Charlie, and tiptoed around the debacle with the cops, Weed, and the drugs. Bless his understanding heart, Charlie was only concerned about her welfare and told Brea to take as much time as she needed, that her job would be waiting when she wanted to come back.

Relived to her toes, she then plucked the card Detective Estes had given her and called the station. She checked in with the desk sergeant and supplied him with Barbara's address and phone number, then stepped out onto the deck with Ozzie. The beast ran around chasing an occasional brave squirrel who dared to scurry over the thick green grass. She opened the book and began reading the story she'd started before passing out last night.

Barbara's story collection leaned a little more to the kinky and erotic side than Brea would have ever suspected. She was sailing into chapter three when sweat began to roll down her brow. Either the scorching sex scene she was reading or the heat was getting to Brea, probably a combination of both. She needed to cool down.

"And you thought last night was rough. You keep reading this shit and you're going to need to buy new sheets." Brea tossed the book aside and stood.

As she unwound the garden hose and turned it on, Ozzie raced toward her. Dancing around, he bit at the water. Brea laughed at the dog's zany antics as she supplied drinks to the foliage and one crazy, lovable mutt.

By the time she was through, both she and Ozzie were soaking wet. Brea put the hose away before woman and dog lay on the deck letting both clothes and fur dry in the afternoon sun. Closing her eyes, Brea let out a happy sigh. She hadn't been this stress-free in years. The rest of the day, she did absolutely nothing and it felt good for a change.

When the ten o'clock news was over, Brea climbed the stairs and tossed on her pajamas, a short, nearly threadbare T-shirt. The thing was practically see-through and didn't quite cover her ass, but she didn't care. It wasn't like anyone but Ozzie was going to see her tonight. She washed her face and brushed her teeth and was about to head downstairs when she passed the mirror in her room. A giggle bubbled off her lips. Homeless stripper came to mind what with her red lace thong peeking out from beneath the tattered hem of her shirt.

"Good grief. If there were ever a Bag Ladies of *Hustler*, I could be a centerfold," she said with a snort at her own reflection.

Back in the family room, Brea pulled the curtains and locked the doors before settling in on the couch. Scrolling through television stations with Ozzie curled by her side, she paused at the Food Network. The yellow-haired host observed a chef preparing grilled Tuscan garlic chicken that made her mouth water. She was about to get up and raid the pantry when her cell phone buzzed on the coffee table. Peering at the caller ID, she scowled.

"Give it a rest, Weed. I've said everything I want to you."

She issued a heavy sigh and ignored the call. Ozzie raised his head and gave her a look akin to sympathy.

"Just how smart are you?" she asked the dog.

He answered with a yawn, exposing his sharp, scary teeth before bounding off the couch and scurrying to the back door.

"All right, buddy," she chuckled as she headed his way. "I know dog code for *let me out or I'll pee all over the floor* when I see it."

Unlocking the door, she pushed it open as she flipped on the porch light. Ozzie sprang off the deck like he'd been shot out of a cannon. Rocketing across the lawn, he was in hot pursuit of a terrified rabbit, zigzagging maniacally across the yard. Brea's heart lurched to her throat as visions of Ozzie eviscerating poor little Thumper exploded in her brain.

Without thinking of her tacky attire, she raced off the porch after the dog.

"Leave it!" she scolded.

But the obstinate mutt ignored her. Chasing after the single-minded mutt, Brea waved her arms, screaming at him like a lunatic. She'd nearly cornered him twice, but Ozzie evaded her as he continued barking and trailing the nimble, frightened bunny.

"I said leave it, you bloodthirsty brute!"

The rabbit escaped through a gap under the fence as the door to the house slammed shut behind her. She slid to a halt in the grass, a wave of dread pouring through her. Turning, she sprinted up the stairs and gripped the doorknob. It was locked.

"Son of a bitch!"

AFTER STUDYING THE campers' activity schedule for the next day, Sawyer sat on the patio in his backyard, nursing a beer. Gazing up at the stars, twinkling like diamonds in the inky night sky, he wondered if Brea were looking at them, too.

"Damn, fucker, anyone finds out you're waxing poetic about stars and shit, they'll think you got your neutered at Troy's Animal Hospital."

Even the thought of total humiliation couldn't keep him from thinking about the sultry vixen. She'd invaded his thoughts more often than not during the day, and he couldn't stop thinking about the way the wind had tousled her dark hair that morning. Fuck. He knew exactly how she'd look after a night pounding her pussy raw. Just the thought turned his cock harder than a sledgehammer ready to bust up concrete all the way to the ranch.

Taking a long pull on the bottle, Sawyer tortured himself even more with visions of her plump lips wrapped around his shaft. They warred with the feel of her shapely legs locked at the ankle, behind his neck. His cock stirred once more as the light on his neighbor's back porch flipped on, partially spilling into his own yard.

Sawyer looked up expecting to see Barbara and Ozzie, but instead, he watched Brea race off the deck. Sawyer nearly dropped his beer when he took in the sight of her barely covered body glowing in the floodlights. His rousting cock stretched rigid and ready, instantly slamming against his zipper.

Rising to his feet, Sawyer drank in the sight of her milky, smooth ass cheeks jiggling as the curvy nymph chased after the dog, screaming like a mad woman. A slash of red between her legs had his mouth pooling with saliva. Swallowing tightly, he then pinched his lips together to keep from laughing at the comical sight, as all hell broke loose beyond the fence. After the chaos calmed, Brea sprinted back to the deck and wiggled the door handle before cursing.

Sawyer had finally found his damsel in distress.

"First day on the job, and I'm locked out," Brea spat. "Priceless. This is just piss-assed priceless."

Ozzie loped up beside her, panting and wagging his stubby tail while Sawyer sank back a bit farther in the darkness, grinning like a moron.

"You should be ashamed of yourself, running after a poor defenseless rabbit. Now look what you've done! We're locked out now because of you...you big goofy bastard."

Ozzie responded with a loud, taunting bark.

Sawyer slipped a hand to his pocket and fingered his keys, particularly the rubber-tipped house key Barbara had given him eons ago.

"Rule number one, never *ever* sniff my crotch. Rule number two, don't chase rabbits." She wagged her finger in his face. "Got it?"

Once again, the dog barked, and Sawyer could have sworn the playful pooch was grinning. When Brea darted a glance toward his house, he froze like a statue.

"Just my luck, there's not one light on over at old man Grayson's house. The dusty, fossilized fart probably passed out after the six o'clock news and is sawing logs in his recliner."

Old man? Dusty, fossilized fart? Sawyer wasn't sure if he should feel insulted or laugh at her inaccurate assumption.

Brea continued talking to Ozzie as if he were human. "I'd go over and see if he has a spare key, but not dressed like this. What if the decrepit dude has a bad heart? I might make him stroke out or something."

You'd make me do something, all right, darlin', but the only stroking I'll be doing is with my tongue...up and down that pretty red-lace-covered cunt of yours.

Sawyer's erection grew impossibly harder.

Brea darted another furtive glace his way before releasing a heavy sigh. She looked down at the dog and pouted. "All right, you little troublemaker. Let's hope I can find a window that's unlocked, or I'll be replacing some glass in the morning."

Sawyer remained in the shadows as Brea tugged on several window frames. The time had come to lend his fantasy girl a hand...or rather a key. He stepped off his deck and moved silently between the two houses. When he unlatched the gate, Brea cried out, "Score!"

By the time Sawyer had rounded the corner, he saw her trying to launch herself through a partially opened dining room window. Ozzie came barreling toward him, tongue hanging out and tail wagging frantically. Sawyer scratched the dog behind his pointed ears as Brea slid back to the ground with a hiss.

"Shit! That stings," she hissed, pressing a hand to her chest.

Peeling up her shirt, she peered down at the red welts that marred her ivory flesh. He wanted to call out to her but couldn't; he was too busy trying to keep from swallowing his tongue at the sight of her luscious breasts.

Undaunted by her failed first attempt, Brea gripped the base of the window frame once more. Pushing off with her legs, she launched herself forward, like a rocket. Well, partially, anyway. Suspended, half in and half out of the window, she teetered on the casement.

He rushed toward her. Those smooth, lily-white ass cheeks glowing in the moonlight called to him like the beacon of a lighthouse calls to a lost sailor. He was lost, all right, lost in lust. His cock expanded even more, and Sawyer knew there was no hope; his dick would wear the imprint of his zipper until he was ninety. He raised his hands, and his palms itched to grip and squeeze her supple orbs that lay out before him. As he clenched his teeth to keep from biting the ribbon of lace wedged in the crack of her ass, his nostrils flared. He could smell the rich, pungent scent of her pussy. Every muscle in his body tightened.

Suddenly Brea started to laugh.

"Oh, god. I'm stuck. I'm fucking stuck. This is not happening."

Sawyer inched in closer, ready to grab her by the waist and help her down, but Brea started to wiggle. He bit down on his tongue to keep from groaning. He could see...naked, her on her hands and knees, shaking that sexy ass from side to side as she backed that ass onto his ready cock. Sweat broke out over his brow as he stood like a statue...staring, dreaming, longing, with his dick throbbing like bitch.

"Ozzie, I hope you're enjoying the full moon I'm shooting you. But I swear to all that is holy, if you stick your wet, cold nose up my ass, you'll never get another treat. Are we clear?"

"What if it's a dry, warm nose? That's all the treat I want." Sawyer's deep voice rippled as he held back a laugh.

Brea screamed so loud she nearly punctured his eardrums. As she lurched upward, her arms spun like pinwheels. With a loud thwack, she cracked the back of her head on the windowpane above her and started to slide backward. Sawyer wrapped his hands around her waist while the sound of her blood-curdling scream nearly drowned out the fabric ripping from in front of her.

Peering over her shoulder, he found a piece of white fabric stuck in the base of the frame. It was at the same time that he realized his hands were burning with the heat of her bare flesh. Though she was still screaming, he closed his eyes and sighed. She was soft like velvet, and he slid his palms up and down her beguiling curves. And that's when she started kicking and punching for freedom. She'd traded in her screams for curses...curses that might possibly offend a Marine. All the while, Ozzie was playfully barking and running in circles around them. Sawyer nearly laughed at the chaotic uproar.

"Let me go, you crazy cocksucker!" Brea screamed. "Bite him, Ozzie. Bite his fucking balls off."

Her heel connected with Sawyer's shin, sending an arc of pain to shoot up his leg.

"Brea! Stop, goddammit!" he thundered as he released her.

Spinning toward him, her eyes were wide with both shock and terror.

"You! What are... Are you stalking me?" she breathlessly demanded.

She was oblivious to the fact that her shirt had ripped in two or that her cock-stiffening breasts were exposed. But Sawyer wasn't. The lightly welted scratches down her stomach didn't distract from her dusky-pink nipples drawn up tight and hard. Like sweet, ripe cherries, those tempting twins were all but begging to be sucked, licked, nibbled, and pinched.

Following his gaze, she looked down at her chest. With a feral screech, she gathered the edges of her shirt and fisted them closed. The movement lifted the fabric and revealed a pretty red, frilly lace thong that barely covered her pussy…the pussy he was ready to devour right there among Barbara's cabbage, green bean, and tomato plants.

Swallowing tightly, he dragged his gaze to Brea's face. Her cheeks were stained crimson. She looked disheveled, wild, and so temptingly fuckable. He probably would have tried taking here there in the backyard if humiliation weren't swimming in her caramel-colored eyes. Trying to temper his overzealous lust, he gently brushed back a strand of silky dark hair from her face. An insane arc of electricity careened up his arm.

Sliding two fingers under her chin, he tipped her head back and delved deep into her turbulent eyes. The nighttime sounds of crickets and bullfrogs fell silent as he studied the contours of her beautiful face. Her feminine nectar, now sweetening the air with a tart, spicy scent, called to him on an animalistic level while wreaking havoc in his brain. The air between them grew thick. The sexual tension hummed. He watched her rapid pulse throb at that sweet spot along the base of her neck. God, he wanted to lay his flat tongue against that fluttering spot and lave his way all down to that enticing scrap of cloth between her thighs.

When, not if, he finally got Brea beneath him, they'd burn the fucking house down.

"Why are you stalking me?" she spat.

"I'm not stalking you."

"Then what are you doing here?" Brea demanded.

"I live next door."

"Liar! Neville Grayson lives next door."

He wanted to grin but clenched his jaw and pinned her with a steady stare. "I'm Neville *Sawyer* Grayson."

"Oh, god." Her face flamed a brighter shade of red.

"What's your full name, gorgeous?"

"Lacking."

Sawyer blinked. "Lacking?"

"Yes. Lacking dignity."

A low, wicked laugh rumbled up from deep in his chest before he flashed a feral smile. "Trust me, Lacking. The things I want to do to you don't have an ounce of dignity in them."

A LAZY SMILE slid across his face. Brea prayed the earth would just open up and swallow her whole. A combustible mixture of embarrassment, need, and desire swirled and suffused in her blood. Her cheeks were on fire. She didn't know whether to kick him in the balls or slam her mouth over his and kiss his lips off. His hungry stare that promised hours and hours of carnal splendor wasn't making the decision easy for her. Lord, he was eating her up with his eyes. But Brea wanted a whole lot more than his gaze…she wanted his capable calloused hands touching every aching, throbbing place on her body. Imagining the feel of his fingers probing deep sent her stomach tumbling in crazy little somersaults.

No. No. No.

She couldn't succumb to her cravings. Sex equaled need. Need warped into reliance. Relying on a man to give her love only led to heartache and pain…every fucking time! She didn't want or need to take another emotional nosedive. Honestly, how many more relationships had to crash and burn before she grew a pair and broke this vicious cycle? She had to fight her driving desire to rip off his clothes and ride him like a banshee. But the only way she'd win the battle of her rebellious lust was with sarcasm and anger.

Taking a step back, she raised her chin and pinned him with a brittle smile. "I'm sure the single women of Haven know all about the undignified things you're capable of. Sorry to burst your bubble, Romeo, but I'm not interested. So either help me through the window or go home and let me do it myself."

"So you're locked out huh?"

"No. I have latent circus performer tendencies. Here's your sign," she drawled in her best Bill Engvall imitation. "Yes, I'm locked out, Einstein! Why else would I be standing here in my pajamas trying to climb through a freakin' window?"

"Those are your pajamas?" Sawyer's eyes grew wide and his lips twitched as if holding in a laugh.

"Who are you, the pajama police? What do you sleep in, mister?"

A wicked flame danced in his eyes. "Nothing. Not. A. Single. Fucking. Stitch."

She instantly wished she were his sheets. All the air sucked from her lungs—no doubt the molecules of oxygen were busy fanning the flames now incinerating her libido. Sawyer was definitely not what she needed right now, but dammit if she didn't want him with every needy cell in her body.

As she corralled her sexual distress, her smile turned caustic. "Well, if your house catches fire, I'll be sure to bring a blanket with a warning sticker that small objects are enclosed."

Sawyer laughed. "Darlin', you're going to need one labeled *choking hazard*." He leaned in, still wearing that erotic grin. "You need to be taken over my knee so I can spank the sass out of you."

Brea sucked in a startled gasp, but instead of being appalled at his humiliating comment, a shudder of arousal ricocheted down her spine, and heat pooled beneath her clit. Her overwhelming attraction to Sawyer had quickly convinced Brea that she needed mass quantities of psychotherapeutic drugs and a high-dollar shrink. But even that combo probably wouldn't save her from skipping down the familiar road to disaster.

She had to try and put the brakes on her out-of-control cravings. Thrusting out her chin, she strained for the most intimidating glare she could muster. "You try…you die. Go home, Sawyer. I can take care of this myself."

"I'm sure you can, but why scrape up all that pretty, soft skin when you can use this…" He reached into his pocket and pulled out a ring of keys. "I have a spare."

The dangling saw-toothed collection, clanging in front of her face, only mocked her predicament. Anger spiked. She clenched her jaw so hard her teeth throbbed. "Why didn't you offer to unlock the door in the first place?"

He shrugged. "I thought maybe you might make it through the window. But after your first attempt didn't go so well, I decided to come over and help."

First attempt? He'd been watching her? For shits and giggles, no doubt. What a prick!

Brea wanted to scream. "So, exactly how long had you been observing me, *Neville*?"

"Don't call me that. Call me Sawyer. I hate my given name."

"How long?" Brea barked.

He arched his brows and cleared this throat. "Only a few minutes. I was sitting outside on my porch when you and Ozzie started chasing that rabbit."

"*I* wasn't chasing the stupid rabbit. *I* was chasing the brain-dead dog before he killed the thing," she corrected.

Ozzie whimpered.

"Aw, look. Now, you've gone and hurt his feelings."

Sawyer's patronizing tone had her seeing red…vibrant red with flashes of hot white light. "He's a dog! He'll get over it. You're lucky I'm only calling you *Neville* at the moment and not a whole lot worse," she growled.

"Is that so? Just what are you doing here at Barbara's anyway?"

"I'm house and dog sitting for a month, Mr. Nosey."

"My, my, darlin'. For someone who needs a knight in shining

armor with a magic key to unlock your castle, you're sure not acting like a proper damsel in distress."

It took all the control she could manage not to slap the derisive grin off his too-gorgeous face. "First of all, I'm not your *darlin'*. Secondly, I'm more capable than a stupid damsel in distress."

His expression hardened. Heat flared in his golden-emerald eyes. "That may be. All I know right now is that you're sexy as hell when you're all riled up."

"Argh," she fumed. "Fuck this. And…and fuck you!"

Brea spun on her heel and stomped to the window. Bracing her palms on the bottom frame, she was determined to make it through the window this time…come hell or high water.

"Whoa. Whoa. Stop!" Sawyer gripped her shoulders. When he gently turned her to face him, compassion softened his face. His voice dropped to barely a whisper. "Please don't try that again, Brea. I'll unlock the door for you. Come on."

About fucking time, you asshole!

"Thank you," she managed to bite out with a hint of civility.

Sawyer raked a slow, hungry stare up her body before that lazy smile—the one that made her wish for all the things she couldn't have—crawled across his face. "Will you invite me in for a cold beer, too?"

Was this fuck-monkey for real?

Brea narrowed her eyes. "I don't have any."

"How 'bout a drink of water, then?"

"The sink's broken."

With a lopsided grin, he shook his head. "Now you're just lying to me, darlin'. All you had to say was no."

His heated breath sent a sensual thrill to clash with her fury. And when he reached up to rub his finger and thumb over the ends of her hair, his compelling stare lifted Brea's rage toward the stars. She truly wanted to remain pissed at the man, but his easy style of seduction made it an impossible feat.

Fuck!

"Mmm, soft as silk. Just like I knew it would be," he murmured.

He held her in a foggy haze of desire with his hypnotic stare. And the timbre of his whiskey-smooth voice sent quivers shooting through her limbs.

Thankfully, Ozzie barked, breaking the spell Sawyer had cast upon her. Swallowing tightly, Brea inched back. The much-needed space she put between them generated a look of rejection to flash across his face. Suddenly solemn, he nodded. Without a word, he walked to the back door and unlocked it.

Sawyer sent her a weak smile. "Don't forget to close and lock that window. I'll sleep better if I know you're safe and sound over here…alone."

His concern about her put another chink in Brea's armor. The anger had bled from her veins, and in its place, something else was seeping in. Something warm and reassuring. Something highly dangerous that threatened to crush the sense of peace she was struggling to find.

Brea felt as if she were living on a fault line and sensed a catastrophic earthquake was on the horizon.

"I will. Thank you."

He held her with a delving gaze for several long seconds. Finally, one corner of his mouth lifted, and he gave a nod of resignation, then turned and walked away. As she watched Sawyer's retreating back, her gaze locked on his fine ass. Teetering on a precipice far more treacherous than a windowsill, Brea ached to call him back…back for far more than just a beer. The lonely, horny woman inside prayed he'd turn around. If he did, it would all be over but the screams of ecstasy.

Thankfully he kept on walking.

Grasping how easily he could topple her over into familiar but suicidal territory exposed how truly weak and vulnerable she really was. Clearly, Brea was ill prepared to reinvent herself. Still, she had to find a way to keep from lighting the fuse on that stick of dynamite known as Neville Sawyer Grayson or risk being blown to smithereens.

Maybe she was stronger than she gave herself credit for. After all, she wasn't upstairs, ripping off his clothes and feeding on him like a sex-starved piranha. Brea had actually overthrown her hormones. She'd passed her first monumental test with flying colors. So why was her prize a mountain of frustration and not a bright, shiny trophy?

Ozzie let out a soft woof as he sat at her feet, wearing a cheesy dog grin. The metal gate snicked shut on the far side of the house, and the furry beast whimpered sadly. Brea nearly let out the same pathetic sound.

"All right. Inside, butt head," she scolded. "You've caused enough ruckus for one night."

Brea shut and locked the back door before securing the window in the dining room. After making her way upstairs, she changed her shirt, with Ozzie following behind her like a shadow. Back in the kitchen, she made herself a cup of tea while the dog promptly sprawled out on his bed in the laundry room. With elbows resting on the kitchen table, she laid her chin in her palms and watched the steam rise from the cup.

"This is going to be a long, mind-fucking month with *Neville* living next door. Sawyer is Neville… Damn, I didn't see that one coming."

Her epic and embarrassing window escapade spooled through her head like a horror movie. Brea didn't want to know what Sawyer had thought when he'd happened upon her, hanging out the window in her homeless-hooker attire. With all that bare ass and hail-damage beaming in the moonlight, she'd probably scarred him for life. She easily envisioned him back home right now scrubbing his eyes with bleach.

"Oh, god. I'll never be able to face that man again."

With a long-suffering moan, Brea dropped her head in her hands. Mooning the fantasy man of her wet dreams was one performance she never wanted to repeat. Her vivid humiliation began to wane as the memory of Sawyer's raw and hungry stare consumed her. She suspected, by the promise reflected in his eyes, that he was more than capable of making the kind of love that made the ground shake beneath her feet and the flippin' stars collide. Brea had never experienced something so epic, not with her trail of inept lovers. There wasn't a solitary thing inept about Sawyer. No, that man would leave her run-of-the-mill orgasms in the dust and easily ruin her for any other man.

Unfortunately, Brea would never know any of the spine-bending skills he possessed or how thoroughly he could rock her world.

"A fact equally depressing and regretful."

Ozzie softly yipped as if in agreement with her.

"Don't rub it in, fuzzy-butt," she drawled.

Lifting the mug to her lips, Brea sipped the warm tea. The heat reminded her of Sawyer's strong hands and hot, solid body.

"I need to buy more batteries…lots of them."

While her toys could provide sexual relief, they didn't do squat in offering what she wanted most…love and protection, companionship and trust. Brea longed to find a good man, one who wanted to settle down and raise a family with her. Someone she could grow old with.

She wanted the fairy tale, dammit!

But none of the men she'd aligned herself with in the past had been her prince. Watching Weed being hauled off in cuffs had ripped the blinders off her. She finally comprehended how utterly useless the man had been. His pea-sized brain couldn't remember the combination to the dishwasher; the sink was forever piled high with dirty dishes. He'd never learned the recipe for ice either; the trays sat empty in the freezer all the time. While his fingers worked perfectly on the remote control to his game system, they couldn't put the toilet seat down…ever. It was a wonder the man could wipe his own ass without Brea's help.

She'd been more of a mother than a girlfriend to every man she'd ever lived with.

Not anymore. She was on her own now. That reality brought

every insecurity and vulnerability within to float to the surface.

Ozzie rose and stood beside her. Brea scrubbed him behind the ears.

"I'm not totally alone, am I? You'll protect me from rapists and homicidal maniacs, won't you, boy?"

The dog cocked his head and looked at her as if she were crazy.

Yeah, she probably was.

Haven was a safe and quiet little town. As long as she didn't don an ape suit and prowl the streets at night, Brea would be perfectly safe. Poor Emmett. The man was a few dates short of a fruitcake. But she knew most everyone had demons to conquer; she'd simply steer clear of the old man's shotgun.

Draining the last of her tea, she rinsed the cup and tucked it into the dishwasher. Sensing his bedtime, Ozzie trudged to his doggie mattress once again and stretched out. Bidding the mischievous mutt a good night, Brea extinguished the lights in the kitchen, grabbed the steamy novel from the coffee table, and headed upstairs.

After completing her nightly beauty regimen, she crawled beneath the covers and opened the book. Only a few pages into the steamy story, she had to flip back the covers to cool off her scorching hormones. The nasty things hero Ramón was doing to Natasha had Brea's pulse racing and her body throbbing. Rolling out of bed, she retrieved her vibe before easing onto the mattress again. She peeled her shirt off over her head and dragged down her thong before settling back on her pillows once again, and started reading.

The story was raw and wicked. But Brea's mind was no longer filled with images of a swarthy Spaniard and a blonde aristocratic heiress. She envisioned the sexy, crimson-haired cowboy next door. Growing wetter by the second, Brea cupped her breasts. She rubbed and toyed with her nipples…pinching and plucking the taut, sensitive tips. She pretended Sawyer's fingers, lips, teeth, and tongue were the ones driving her demand.

As she aroused herself, heat enveloped her body. Her pulse quickened, and her empty tunnel hungrily clutched at nothing but air. She fantasized of Sawyer's hard shaft stretching and filling her slippery core…driving inside her with deep, steady strokes. Back and forth, dragging the crest over her inflamed and throbbing nerve endings.

Panting, she rocked her hips in slow, restless motions and closed her eyes, the story now long forgotten as Brea's own imagination and creativity took over. Sawyer's hands and lips were touching, licking, and sucking every inch of her flesh. His scent—that intoxicating mix of leather, sweet grass, and springtime—filled her senses. Dizzy with need, her mind unfurled a passion so real…so hot, feral, and raw, Brea whimpered and moaned. Turning on the vibe, she danced it over her swollen clit. Thunder rolled across her body. Lightning exploded behind her eyes. Her limbs tingled. An animalistic roar of ecstasy tore from her throat. Her body jerked and muscles tensed. Spasms quaked her pussy, and Brea was rolled beneath a wave of ecstasy as the intense orgasm consumed her. Riding the rippling aftershocks, the sounds of her soft mewls, panted breaths, and clamoring heartbeat echoed in her ears. And as she slowly floated back to earth, she lay quivering and covered in a light sheen of sweat.

CHAPTER FIVE

Returning to his house alone was hands-down the single hardest thing Sawyer had ever done. The sexually tormented cells inside his body snarled to turn around and push his way inside Brea's bedroom and her silky, soft body.

And that's what's known in a court of law as rape!

While he didn't want to spend the rest of his life in prison, the rock-hard part of his anatomy was willing to accept incarceration for a night of unbridled fun with Brea.

"Down, boy," he ordered his impulsive appendage. "She's not ready for that yet. She's skittish and fearful…of what? I have no idea. But I aim to find out, and soon."

Sawyer had studied the emotional gambit that played across Brea's face. She'd gone from embarrassment to lust, desire, and need. Then she'd slammed up a wall around her as fear, anxiety, and anger appeared.

She was torn, that much was clear. Her behavior only reinforced Sawyer's suspicions—she'd been hurt, but he now knew the wounds were still fresh and raw.

After climbing the stairs to his room, Sawyer looked at his empty bed. He scrubbed a hand over his face. Sleep would be hard-won knowing Brea was next door. She was probably naked and in bed.

"Why the fuck did I have to go there?" he groaned.

Why the hell has she got you tied in knots?

That was the million-dollar question. He didn't understand the insistent, searing, and all-consuming attraction she stirred inside him. No stranger to bedroom games, he'd slaked his lust with women in ways most men dreamed about. But Brea stirred something deeper. He didn't want to just fuck her—though it might get the insatiable attraction out of his system—Sawyer wanted to make love to her until he'd turned her inside out.

"Stop right there!" he halted his own thoughts with a warning.

Sawyer wasn't the *making love* kind of guy. Not anymore. Besides, he didn't know a thing about Brea. They'd only talked twice.

Like that matters? You've fucked women only to find out their name when you were through.

"That only happened one time," Sawyer corrected the derisive voice in his head.

Brea was far different from any other woman he'd known. She intrigued him. Turned him on like a light bulb, but he had no idea why.

Last night at Toot's, Brea had been introverted, polite, and almost shy. But earlier in the backyard, she'd cursed like a sailor and unleashed a shocking defiance that took him by surprise. He could still see her cheeks, stained the color of merlot, with embarrassment. What was she hiding beneath that tough-girl exterior? Sawyer sensed a fragile, sensitive woman…a woman he wanted to explore. Or was he just imagining it?

Maybe he was crazy.

Maybe *she* was as well.

She'd shown him two totally opposite sides so far. Maybe Brea *Lacking Dignity*—whatever her last name was—suffered multiple personality disorder. She might be the most complicated woman Sawyer had ever met.

"Complicated? She's more like a goddamn Rubik's Cube. I suck at solving that stupid puzzle."

But unlike the toy, Sawyer didn't plan to give up trying to align the beautiful colors of Brea's soul. The drive to see what other parts of herself she'd reveal was far too dazzling.

Stripping off his clothes, Sawyer's cock, having accepted the fact that a happy ending wasn't in its future, hung toward the floor in mourning. He climbed into bed and laid his head on the pillow, then closed his eyes. But all he could see behind his lids was Brea, wedged in the window's opening. Like a wicked enchantress, her tempting, ivory butt cheeks lured him. He wanted to stroke, knead, and claim her supple flesh…slide his teeth, and scrape his tongue over every glorious inch on display.

His cock jerked to life, eager and ready.

"Go back to sleep, dammit."

Forcing himself to focus his attention on the kids at the ranch, Sawyer was able to block Brea from his mind…for half a minute, at least. Every word they'd exchanged in Barbara's backyard rolled through his memory banks. Her comedic retort of "Here's your sign" had him fighting like mad not to laugh in her face. Being bested by a woman in a banter battle might emasculate some men, but Sawyer enjoyed her quick and sassy quips. It felt natural. Hell, he and his brothers had grown up—even to this day—slinging one-liners at each other.

Don't go getting your hopes up, fool. After you embarrassed the bejesus out of her tonight, she'll probably never speak to you again. Best find a way to rid yourself of this ridiculous attraction now. She's only going to be here a month.

Yeah, but there was a lot Sawyer could do with her…to her in that month.

Like a bloodhound on the scent of an escaped convict, his cock jerked to life. The only way to assuage his relentless ache was a one-man show. With a frustrated sigh, Sawyer whipped off the bed sheets and gripped his swollen erection. In a steady, even tempo, he stroked with his fist, from stem to tip. Suddenly a wave of self-loathing tore through him. Releasing his leaking member, he sat up with a growl.

"What the fuck am I doing? I haven't had to jack off since eighth grade. I'm sure as fuck not doing it now."

After vaulting off the bed, he grabbed his jeans and jerked them on. Sawyer snagged his shirt off the dresser, buttoned it, then slid on his boots and clutched his keys. He was dressed and gunning the engine of his quarter-ton duely—leaving a trail of rubber on the pavement—in minutes. Heading toward the Hangover, he figured he might find slim pickin's, but he'd find a willing woman to ease his aching dick. She wasn't going to be the one he wanted, but at least he could take off the edge.

When he walked into the bar, Gina flashed him an overly enthusiastic smile. "Two nights in a row? You trying to turn into a regular here?"

"No. I just felt like a nightcap before bed," he lied.

Skimming an assessing gaze over the crowd, he spied a familiar trio at one of the tables. Sylvia, a divorced mother of three, Gretchen, the single dental assistant, and Annette, who worked as a secretary at the high school, were laughing and tossing back shots.

Bingo!

The open-minded women had made him lose a fair amount of sleep, discovering ways to satiate all kinds of sexual curiosities. Of course, he'd gone to great lengths to keep his three-on-one secret private. The small town gossip guild would have a heyday if they got wind of the debauchery they'd played out in his bed.

But the longer he stared at the twisted, titillating trio, the more the desire to relieve the pent-up pressure in his jeans evaporated. He didn't want the women. He only wanted Brea.

The realization told him he was in way over his head already.

"Hey, Sawyer," Annette called out, her southern drawl slurring a bit. "Wanna join us for a little fun?"

"Sorry, sugar. Not tonight. You all go ahead and knock yourselves out." He nodded to the three, whose hopeful expressions dimmed.

Taking a seat at the bar, he noticed Gina's hand tremble as she set a mug of beer down in front of him.

"Everything all right?" His brows furrowed. "LaCroix hasn't been back bothering you, has he?"

"Nope. Haven't seen him since yesterday."

"Good." Sawyer took a gulp of the cold brew before glancing toward the back of the bar. "I'm surprised the twins aren't here playing pool."

"Oh…um, they were in earlier." From the corner of her eye, Gina peeked toward the staircase leading up to her apartment, then clutched a cloth in her hand.

Sawyer caught a glimpse of something—embarrassment or maybe guilt—sliding over her face before she dropped her chin and began polishing the already spotless bar. He took another swallow of brew and wiped his mouth on the back of his hand. Gina was as nervous as a moth in a bug zapper.

"They didn't cause you any trouble while they were here, did they?"

"No. Of course not," she assured. Gliding the rag over the same spot for the third time, she diverted her eyes from his. "None of you Graysons ever cause any trouble."

Placing his hand over hers, stilling all movement, he whispered so only Gina could hear, "Is something or someone bothering you?"

She jerked her head up and her hand away. Guilt was written all over her face. Clearly, the woman was spooked, and it instantly put Sawyer on edge.

"No. Why do you ask?" Gina's voice wobbled.

"Just checking." Sawyer shrugged. Tipping back his glass, he emptied the contents in another long swallow.

"Want another?"

"Nah. I'm good. Thanks, Gina. If you need anything, call me. Got it?"

"Sure thing. Thanks, Sawyer. Have a great night."

Sitting behind the wheel in his truck, he gazed at the neon beer sign in the window. Lightly tapping his fingers on the steering wheel, he knew something wasn't right. Gina was totally out of sorts and ruffled in a way he'd never seen before. Sawyer decided to check the rear of the bar and see if anything was amiss. Pulling down the alley behind the buildings on Main Street, he slammed his foot on the brakes. The familiar red pickup with vanity plates: MELODY4 – his brother Nate's truck, told Sawyer everything he needed to know. Except for some very pertinent questions—where was his virtuous brother, and was he still in possession of his virginity? If Nate was inside the bar, why hadn't Sawyer seen him? Suddenly he remembered the nervous glance Gina had darted at the stairs toward her…*bedroom.*

"Nate, you stupid son of a bitch! Guess you're not saving your cherry for marriage any longer, but Gina? Really?"

Sawyer's subtle pride at his little brother's leap into manhood was short-lived when a wave of worry coasted through him. Surely his idealistic brother didn't actually think he and Gina would be exchanging *I do's* now, did he?

"Oh, fuck. This has all the markings of epic heartbreak written all over it," he groaned.

He wanted to take Nate aside and find out if his brother's head—the one with a brain—was lost somewhere in the clouds or if his feet were, hopefully, still planted on the ground. Unfortunately, Sawyer wasn't about to go waltzing back into the bar in case the family bullheaded gene came out in all its glory and caused an ugly scene. People loved to talk, and he'd do whatever it'd take to keep their focus off the Grayson family.

Staring at his brother's truck, Sawyer had an idea that would force Nate to reach out to him. With a covert eye on the back door of the bar, Sawyer plucked a pair of pliers from his toolbox before popping the hood open on Nate's truck. After disconnecting the battery, Sawyer closed the heavy lid in place and hoisted the abducted battery into the bed of his own truck. Leaving Nate stranded at the Hangover, Sawyer drove home to wait for his brother's call. He'd demand ransom to be paid with a heart-to-heart conversation. But as the minutes turned into hours, he drifted off to sleep while his cell phone remained silent on the nightstand.

THE MORNING SUN bathed Brea's room in a hue of golden corn silk. Her covers were everywhere, even wrapped around her legs. A low groan reverberated from the back of her throat. Even after taking the edge off, she'd still had a screaming good time with Sawyer last night…at least in her dreams. The man had invaded her every waking thought and cloyed his way into her sleeping subconscious. She was in a world of trouble.

Closing her eyes, she focused on clearing her mind and appreciating the fact that she'd awakened to blissful silence. It was a welcome reprieve to Weed's constant barrage of head-banging metal music. She didn't miss that, or him, one bit.

"If only life came with a do-over button, I'd be hitting that sucker like a slot machine," she murmured aloud. "Starting with last night. Ugh!"

In an excruciating slide show, humiliating images of last night flashed through her brain. No matter how badly she wanted to, she couldn't scrub her shame away. All Brea could do was avoid the hunk next door and chalk up her window escapade as another train wreck in her tragedy called life.

She glanced at the clock radio on the nightstand and groaned. It was only six forty-five in the morning. While she normally woke at the same ungodly hour for work, her internal clock hadn't gotten the memo about her leave of absence. After rolling out of bed and tossing on her clothes, Brea met Ozzie at the bottom of the stairs. He danced around for a couple of seconds before racing to the back door. Sending him a look of warning, she waggled her finger at his muzzle. "No more chasing bunnies. Are we clear?"

Ozzie barked and wagged his nubby tail. Brea opened the door and let him out. Not only did she disengage the auto-locking mechanism this time but she also propped the sucker open with a heavy cast-iron stopper before stepping out and onto the deck.

"Wanna join me for breakfast?" Sawyer called out to her.

Blanching, Brea turned to see the sexy stud seated at a modern, glass-and-wrought-iron patio table. A massive plate of food lay out before him.

"No thanks," she replied.

"Aw, come on," he continued. "You're not still angry about last night, are you?"

"Why would I be angry? You unlocked the door and kept me from climbing in the window like a cat burglar."

"True." Sawyer nodded. "I thought maybe I'd embarrassed you or something."

"I embarrassed myself."

Rising from his chair, Sawyer strode toward the chain-link fence. Brea swallowed tightly as the long, thick muscles of his thighs bunched and flexed beneath his faded jeans. Ozzie let out a welcoming bark and raced toward the man, who reached over the fence and rubbed the dog's head.

Wearing a cocky smile, Sawyer winked. "No need to be embarrassed, darlin'. I'm not a monk. I've seen—"

"I'm sure you've seen and done all sorts of things. But I'd rather you spare me the lurid details."

A look of challenge twinkled in Sawyer's eyes. "Oh, I wasn't going to do that. I'm not the kind of man to kiss and tell."

"I'm sure your bounty of bed bunnies appreciates your chivalry."

Sawyer's golden brows slashed and he pursed his lips. "Is it just me, or are you this grouchy with everyone?"

Grouchy? You haven't seen grouchy yet, mister.

"No. Just you."

"Good to know."

"Why is that?"

"Because I can focus on ways to sweeten you up."

Brea rolled her eyes. "I don't need sweetening up. I don't need you pestering me."

"Pestering you? Now when have I ever done that?" His smooth voice melted over her flesh like soft butter on hot pancakes.

Humor skipped in his eyes.

"Look, *Neville*."

"Ah, ah, ah. Call me Sawyer, remember?"

Brea bit her lips together. The man unnerved her to the point that she wanted to call him a host of things…rude and insulting things. Instead, she nodded curtly, dragging her eyes to the snug-fitting T-shirt clinging to his wide chest.

"I appreciate your help last night, *Sawyer,* but I'd rather be left alone."

Liar.

"Oh, that's right. You're on a man ban. I'm assuming some prick hurt you badly. Why else would you go and shove all men into the doghouse?"

Though her expression remained blank, Brea was irked at how he so effortlessly he could read her.

"I guess what I'm asking is, since I helped you out last night, do I get a pass or does the fact that I have a penis include me, too?"

She lifted her gaze. "All men, including you," she bit out. "Come, Ozzie. It's time for breakfast."

With her back to Sawyer, Brea waited as the dog ran inside the house. Just as she began to step through the portal, he called out, "I'm going to remove that pesky man ban, darlin'. You just wait and see."

A tremor slid through her.

"That's what I'm afraid of," she whispered, and closed the door.

Filling Ozzie's bowl with fresh water, Brea peered out the window. Sawyer remained at the fence. His gaze fixed on Barbara's house and sparked with a challenge: *let the games begin.* Dammit, she didn't want a war. It was struggle enough to find the willpower to shy away from him. Why did he want to make that exponentially harder?

While Ozzie chomped his breakfast, Brea opened several windows on the first level. The morning temperature was delightfully cool, and she welcomed the breeze. Though by afternoon, she'd have to close up the house and let the air conditioner save her from the blistering Texas heat.

Sitting at the kitchen table, she scribbled out a grocery list. If Jade wasn't too busy—or sore from riding Colton, and could still walk—Brea planned to beg a ride to the grocery store. Reciting the list to keep from turning green with envy because of her friend's sex life, Brea heard voices being raised out front.

"Why are you such an asshole?"

"No. You're the asshole. What the fuck were you thinking?"

She knew *that* voice, all too well. It was Sawyer. Dropping her pen, she rushed to the living room window and peered next door. She found her neighbor all bowed up, as if ready to throw down, standing toe-to-toe with a guy who looked to be a younger version of him.

"You have no right to decide what I do or who I do it with, you interfering prick."

"I have every right!" Sawyer thundered. "You're my brother, and you're making a monumental mistake."

His brother...no wonder they resembled one another.

"Did I ask your opinion?"

"No," Sawyer barked. "But I'm giving it to you, anyway. It's never going to work out, Nate. Gina is a tough woman, she runs a bar, but more than that, she's way too old for you."

"You've got some big balls, but they're not crystal ones. You can't tell the future. And if you insult her again, I'll beat your ass into the ground."

"You wish." Sawyer rolled his eyes. "What about kids? You've always wanted to be a dad."

"We can have all the kids we want! She's not ninety."

"No, but she's old enough for it to be a risk to her health and the development of the child. Use your head, and I'm not talking about the one in your pants. Obviously that one thinks it's a fucking genius already. I'm talking about the one on your shoulders."

"That's ripe. Coming from you. How many women in town have you fucked? Or have you lost count?"

Brea's stomach took a nosedive. How many women had he been with? Were Sawyer and Colton buddies because they shared the same man-whore DNA?

"We're not talking about me."

"No. Your track record speaks for itself. Guess since you've already ruined your own life, you think you have the right to go and fuck up mine? Well, you can suck a bull's cock, 'cause it'll be a cold day in hell before I let you screw up my relationship with Gina!" Nate spat.

Sawyer's expression crumpled as if he'd been sucker-punched. The raw, visible pain wrinkling his face broke Brea's heart. What in the world had happened to him to cause such anguish?

"Shit," Nate cursed as remorse lined his face. "I'm sorry, Sawyer. I didn't mean to—"

"Your battery is in the bed of my truck. Take it and leave." His voice was empty. Hollow. Brittle and as cold as ice.

"Come on, bro. I didn't mean that. I was talking out my ass." The younger man's tone was dripping with contrition.

"No. Every word you said is true. Not only have I fucked up my life but I fucked Nash and Megan's up as well. You already know that. And you're right to not listen to me, Nate. I've batted a negative thousand when it comes to love. I'm definitely not the kind of role model you or any of the others need." Sawyer shook his head in disgust.

Nate stood silently gaping at Sawyer's self-deprecating rant.

"Go on. Get in the truck," he instructed. "I'll drive you back to the bar, help you re-connect the battery, and follow you out to the ranch."

"Come on, Saw—"

"Don't, Nate. Conversation is over. Drop it," Sawyer warned. Fire blazed in his emerald eyes.

With his lips pressed in a thin, tight line, Nate nodded before climbing into the big black truck.

As his brother slammed the door, Sawyer raked a hand through his hair. With stiff, deliberate strides, he charged inside the cab, gunned the engine, and sped down the street.

Stunned, Brea stood at the window replaying the heated exchange in her mind. *Your track record speaks for itself. Guess since you've already ruined your own life, you think you have the right to go and fuck up mine?*

Nate's words had reopened some type of mortal wound in Sawyer's heart. It was little comfort she and Sawyer shared a ghastly track record. Brea shook her head and grimaced.

"I'm a hot mess and evidently he is, too. We're a match made in heaven!"

AFTER SEVERAL AWKWARDLY silent, tension-filled minutes, Nate's battery was reconnected, and Sawyer was on his way to the ranch alone. Alone with his thoughts and alone with the sound of his brother's words swirling inside his head. He'd alienated two brothers in the span of two days. Sawyer was on a roll…a roll downhill through a pasture of cows fresh from a colon cleanse. The shit coating him wasn't pretty or fun.

Nate was right, he didn't have a crystal ball, but dammit, his kid brother was delusional if he thought Gina would marry him. Of course, Sawyer was probably being just as delusional lusting after a woman on a goddamn man ban, and one entrenching her heart behind walls so thick a bulldozer and a case of C-4 might not free it.

This was setting up to be a truly fucktastic day!

At the ranch, his sour mood had Sawyer keeping his distance from his family. Thankfully, they'd given him his space while he found a bit of peace working with the kids. He was still riddled with anxiety and a restlessness that left him feeling raw and exposed. By the end of the day, Sawyer was ready to go home.

"We're heading to the Hangover. Wanna join us?" Noble

asked.

Sawyer darted a glance at Nate, who dropped a stare toward the ground. "No. You all have fun. I'm going home. I'll see you in the morning."

Without looking back, he climbed into his truck and left. He gnashed his teeth all the way home, and couldn't keep from glancing next door when he pulled into his driveway. Colton's truck sat in front of Barbara's house. Like a horny teen, Sawyer wanted to knock on the door and say hi to his pal just to hopefully catch a glimpse of Brea. Instead, he cut the engine and cursed the one thing he wanted most but couldn't have—her.

In his room, Sawyer stripped off his clothes and glanced at the bed. Bending, he tore off the linens with a growl. It irked him that the prickly princess next door was haunting his dreams so vehemently that he'd laid an oyster in his sheets last night. Something he hadn't done since he was fourteen.

Last night, he'd had the nastiest dream of his life, and Brea held the starring role. He'd gotten so hard and hot he'd ejaculated all over himself. Obviously his unconscious mind hadn't been sated, because he'd still woken with an erection so hard he could have split a walnut tree.

After changing the sheets, he took a hot shower and tugged on his clothes. He snagged a cold beer headed outside to relax on his porch. The minute he stepped from the house, the mouth-watering aroma of seared meat assaulted his senses in a smoking haze wafting from next door. His stomach growled loudly.

"You wish." Colton barked out a laugh over his shoulder as Brea followed him onto the deck.

She wore a smile that dimmed the sun. "You are so full of shit. The only reason he was pouting was because I told him the playground between my legs was forever closed."

The sound of her laughter warmed Sawyer like smooth brandy, and her shameless confession made him grin.

"So you dumped the poor kid and sent him home to play with his own monkey bar?" Colton taunted. "You were a mean teen, Brea."

"I was not! Besides, Allen Wilson needed all the practice he could get. He had no idea what to do with his monkey bar…none of them did, I might add."

None of them? Christ, how many were there?

Brea's comments led Sawyer to believe she'd entertained a whole clown car of boys in high school. But unlike her past buffoons, Sawyer was fully competent with his equipment. The fact that she spoke as if she'd never had a capable lover made him want to teach her what *real* pleasure felt like. He'd like to educate her on how to provide it, too. Sawyer had no trouble picturing her full, pouty lips stretched tight around his monkey bar. Reaching down, he adjusted his reawakening cock.

Colton lifted the lid on the grill. A wave of billowing smoke rolled Sawyer's way, blocking his view but not hindering the couple's conversation.

"We were a pair, weren't we? One thing's for sure…neither one of us had to worry about being voted most likely never to get laid. What with you educating all the boys and me teaching the girls," Colton aid with a snort.

"*Some* of the boys," Brea corrected. "My number pales in comparison to yours. Hell, if we compared bedmate to bedmate, I'd come out practically a virgin against you."

Colton howled with laughter. "You? A virgin? Maybe we should call you Sister Mary-Brea."

Sawyer felt a little like a voyeur listening to the couple banter about their sexual prowess, but he enjoyed discovering yet another side of the fascinating woman. She was relaxed, revealing a carefree, happy openness with Colton that stabbed Sawyer with jealousy. He wanted Brea to be as candid with him. A part of him feared the chrysalis morphing before his eyes might unfurl her wings and fly away before he ever got the chance to earn her trust, let alone kiss her.

"No. I'm far too jaded to become a nun, though I did think about it…briefly."

The smoke had cleared, and Sawyer saw a lopsided smile curl one side of Brea's mouth.

Colton shook his head. "Looking back, I have no idea what I was trying to prove in high school. I'm just glad those days are over and I finally found Jade. And I'm damn glad you called *me* to spring you out of jail, sweetheart. Though I'm not happy about what that low-life prick put you through, I'm glad you're here with us."

Sawyer straightened. His brows slashed in confusion. *Jail? Brea was in jail? What fuck-nugget sent her to jail and why? What crime had she committed?*

Brea's happy expression faltered. "I don't want to talk about him or jail or the endless years I've fucked up my life. Let's just stick to resurrecting demons from high school. I can forgive myself for being young and stupid a lot easier than I can for being adult, desperate, and stupid."

Colton slung his arm around Brea's shoulder. Drawing her into a hug, he placed a kiss on the top of her head. "You're not stupid, sugar. You never have been. I promise not to mention that worthless sack of angus-puss again if you promise to stop beating yourself up. Isn't it better to have loved and lost than never loved at all?"

Brea shrugged. "I don't have a clue. It took me till going to jail to figure out I've never really been in love before. Not the kind of love you and Jade share. Someday I'll know that kind of completeness flowing off the two of you."

"It's more than love, sweetheart. We're soul mates."

"I've known that since freshman year." She poked Colton in the ribs. "But I'm afraid the only S-O-L-E mate I'll find is on the bottom of a shit-covered shoe."

"Yes, you will...one day."

Colton closed the lid on the grill and spied Sawyer across the fence. Smiling, he raised his hand and waved. *Shit. He'd been spotted.*

"Hey, man. What are you doing sitting there all alone? Get

your ass over here and join us. We've got four steaks and tons of food."

Sawyer watched Brea blanch at their friend's invitation. A refusal sat poised on the tip of his tongue, but he couldn't find the willpower to turn down the chance to spend time with her.

"You want me to bring some beer?"

"No need. There's plenty. Just haul ass over and join us, man."

At Colton's insistence, Sawyer hopped up and jogged next door. When he reached the deck, he clearly saw the look of horror on Brea's face and started second-guessing his decision.

"Are you sure I'm not imposing?" He delved into her caramel-colored eyes.

"Imposing? Uh…no. Not at all," she replied nervously. Forcing a smile that didn't quite reach her eyes—because they were packed with panic—Brea shook her head. "Like he said, there's plenty of food."

"I'll pop in and ask Jade to set another place at the table," Colton announced with a grin. "Steaks will be ready shortly."

Once he was alone with Brea, an uncomfortable silence settled around them. She lowered her lashes, averting her gaze to the wooden floor at their feet.

"Hey," he whispered. She snapped her head up, and Sawyer saw a million questions roll across her face. "I didn't mean to crash your dinner party. I can leave if you're uncomfortable."

"No. I-I…I'm fine. I mean, you're fine," she stammered.

A pretty pink blush blossomed over her cheeks. He wanted to reach out and cup her burning face but feared one touch and he'd be flash-fried clear to his boots. As he gazed into her tumultuous eyes, his need to kiss her outweighed the risk of turning to ash.

"Darlin', you're a million ways better than fine," he assured in a roguish whisper.

Inching in closer, Sawyer slid one hand around her lush waist and cupped his other to the back of her neck. Leaning in close to her mouth, he inhaled her startled gasp while her body tensed.

Dammit. She was as guarded as a newborn colt.

"Easy, gorgeous. I only want a little taste."

When she didn't stop him, Sawyer brushed his mouth to hers. Brea's lips were soft and supple, exactly like the heated flesh leaching from beneath her clothes and singeing his hand. He slid his tongue across the seam of her mouth, lingering patiently, waiting for her to open and let him in. Slowly, her timidness vanished, like wax under a flame, she melted against his body.

Thank fuck!

She wasn't immune to the invisible attraction between them after all. As she parted her lips, he deepened the kiss. Her silky moan vibrated over his tongue, and Sawyer issued a primitive mental howl.

He'd had every intention of keeping the kiss light and gentle, but one taste…and demand went off the chain. Like a freight train with rusty brakes, there was no stopping the momentum. He slid his hand up her spine, then he slowly dragged it back down her side, branding every lush, feminine curve to memory.

Brea had cast all her reservations aside as their tongues swirled and danced a hungry tango. He reveled in the delicious thrill of exploring every slick, wet dip and crevice of her sultry mouth. Reaching up, Brea threaded her fingers behind his neck, holding fast as he devoured her, and Sawyer felt a shiver ripple through her, matching the magnitude of demand sizzling through him. Melding her heart and the sweet slickness of her mouth with his, Sawyer knew that after this one amazing kiss, he'd never be the same again.

As he skimmed his palms down her ribs, savoring the swell of her breasts…the slope of her hip, his cock stretched hard as stone. Dropping both hands to her luscious butt cheeks, he gripped her there and pulled Brea in tight against his ready erection.

She mewled softly, a sound that sent liquid fire rolling up his spine. The kiss turned raw, savage, and unrelenting. Her heart pounded furiously against his chest and kept time with his own thundering beat.

Sawyer was lost…drowning in the sublime thrill Brea summoned inside him. Never before had a single kiss obliterated him to such degree. Neither had the need to drink in every drop of her soul. The blistering passion surging between them made the air crackle with the promise of a carnal storm.

A tendril of fear broke loose and snaked through his brain. Tumbling with the heated desire flowing through him, the two divergent emotions stumbled over one another as if vying for first place. Sawyer reluctantly lifted from her lips and pressed his forehead to hers. Their panted breaths mingled. But it was simply the sight of her that eased the anxiety swirling inside him. Her eyes were dark, smoky umber. Her lips were wet, red, and swollen. She screamed fuckable sex kitten. It took every ounce of resolve not to toss her over his shoulder, haul her across the yard, and race to his bedroom with her.

"Oh, my…" she said in a trembling whisper.

"Indeed." He softly chuckled. "I knew tasting you would be heaven, but that was like kissing the moon and the stars."

Brea swallowed tightly. Tensing, she inched back until she was free of his hold. "I-I'm sorry. I shouldn't have—"

"Don't," Sawyer warned. "Don't say you shouldn't have kissed me."

"But I shouldn't have,"

"Why? You going to try and tell me you didn't enjoy it? I know better."

"I did. That's the problem."

Before he could open his mouth to convince her that it really wasn't a *problem,* Colton and Jade stepped from the house.

"Glad you could join us, Sawyer," Jade welcomed with a smile. Turning toward Brea, her joy dimmed. "What's wrong? Are you all right?"

Sawyer's heart leapt to his throat when he saw the fat tears filling Brea's eyes.

"We'll be right back," he announced.

Wrapping his arm around her waist, he whisked Brea to the

side of the house. Placing two fingers beneath her chin, Sawyer lifted her face toward his. "I've never kissed a girl and made her cry before. You're demolishing my ego."

Her watery grin made Sawyer smile.

"Talk to me, Brea. Why are you crying?"

"Because I failed," she sniffed.

"At what? Your man ban?" A crooked smile curled one corner of his mouth.

"It's not a joke," she angrily spat. "I *have* to give up men, and I can't do that when you're… so…everything!"

"Why? Why do you have to give them up?" He'd purposely bypassed her *everything* remark, aiming to dissect the fuck out of it later.

"Because I always pick the wrong ones. I'm a loser magnet."

Sawyer blinked at her confession. "I doubt it could be that bad. We all make mist—"

"I'm not talking about one or two guys, Sawyer. I'm talking dozens." Brea's lips curled in revulsion. It was plain to see she might have joked about her past with Colton, but she truly wasn't proud of it. "I'm cursed! Just forget I exist, okay?"

If it hadn't been for the sincerity in her voice and the pain etched on her face, Sawyer would have laughed. He brushed a knuckle down her cheek and sent her a ghost of a smile.

"That's never going to happen, darlin'."

"Why not?"

"Because I'm deeply attracted to you."

"Great. That's just great!" She tossed her hands in the air and groaned. "You can't be. The only men attracted to me are ones so desperate to get into my pants they'll say anything. And the happy moron in me always believes them."

God, she was cute. Of course he, like all the rest, wanted in her pants. But Sawyer wasn't going to fill her head with false promises in order to accomplish it. The fact that she'd been with so many men stung a bit, but he didn't care as long as *he* was her last.

Where the fuck had that come from? Slow down, cowboy, before you step in something you can't scrub off your boots, his conscience warned at his reawakened thoughts of monogamy.

"You're a beautiful woman, Brea. I'm sure they were attracted to more than your..." Sawyer nodded toward her crotch and his cock throbbed.

Fuck! Wrong place to focus. Way wrong!

He quickly dragged his gaze back to her face and reminded himself not to act like the douchebags of her past. He understood what she'd said to Colton about being jaded. Sawyer had *married* his biggest mistake. Still, it hadn't left such a sour taste in his mouth that he'd flushed the whole female race down the septic tank...just the notion of exchanging vows with one of them again.

"You're selling yourself short with your man ban, baby."

"No, I'm not." She adamantly shook her head. "Until I can find a man who's not looking for a whore, a mother, or a scapegoat, I'm done looking...done trying."

Sawyer reached up and wiped the tears from her cheeks. "Not all men are leeches or pigs. Some of us are quite charming."

"They're only charming until they get what they want," she groused.

He decided to try a different tactic. Slapping a palm to his heart, Sawyer's face wrinkled in pain. "You wound me, woman."

Brea choked on a tiny laugh, then quickly sobered. "Do yourself a favor, Sawyer. Stay away from me. I'm nothing but bad luck. You're a nice guy, well, when you're not withholding house keys from me."

Though Brea was trying to make light of the situation, her self-reproach clanged like a gong, sending fury through him. He hated the fact that Brea couldn't see her own beauty. He'd simply have to open her eyes.

Cupping her cheeks, Sawyer gazed at her ripe lips. "I'm not staying away from you, darlin', because I can't. I want to learn everything about you. The good, the bad, and even the things you think are ugly. And when the time comes, I'm going to uncover all the naughty fantasies you have hidden inside that pretty little head of yours. Then I'm going to make them all come true."

Her eyes grew wide as a tremor shook her body. "You can't."

He flashed her a wicked grin and arched his brows. "Wanna bet?"

CHAPTER SIX

BREA SO WANTED to take that bet…wanted to dare him to bring her every deviant desire out from the shadows. Excitement, hope, and a metric ton of fear squeezed her chest with a pressure so intense she feared she might explode. Of course, his impressive erection nestled against her sex wasn't helping matters. The familiar throb of demand pulsed low and deep. Her nipples were as hard as pebbles and her stomach coiled in knots.

It was all she could do not to climb him like a spider monkey.

Her entire body mocked her stupid vow to give up men. It more than mocked; her hormones were hell-bent on casting her into a realm of self-induced torture as they screamed, *Do him! Do him! Fuck him senseless!*

But Brea knew if she caved and made love to the man, her soul would shatter along with her heart. Unfortunately—or thankfully…she hadn't fully decided—Sawyer pulled away before she had the chance to drag him to her room and test his earth-shattering sex skills. The man seemed more than capable of registering an eight-point-nine on the Richter scale. She knew, because her lips were still tingling from his mind-bending kiss a few minutes ago. And dammit, she wanted more…a lot more. More of his soft, talented lips…more of his tongue…sweet jesus, the things he did with that wicked tongue sent her imagination into overdrive. And more of his hot, rugged body pressed tight against hers.

God, she was losing her ever-loving mind. She didn't need more of him, she needed to find a way to silence the restless hunger he provoked. It was the same stupid-assed kind of lust that always fucked her in the ass later. Not literally but figuratively.

But Brea couldn't let go. She clung to Sawyer's wide shoulders as he held her in a possessive and unrelenting hold. The decisive and determined expression he wore told her that even if she tried, he wouldn't let her walk away…at least not easily.

"Damn, darlin'. That kiss we shared? I don't think I've ever had one as hot or sweet before."

"Ahem." Colton cleared his throat.

Brea jolted and jerked out of Sawyer's arms. When she took a big step backward, the commanding warmth of his body was replaced by a cold, empty void.

Colton curiously raised both brows and smirked. "Sorry. I didn't mean to… Ah, dinner's ready."

A part of her wondered if Colton's interruption had been coincidence or divine intervention…like some higher power was giving her a swift kick in the ass. Either way, Sawyer's kiss proved one thing. It was going to take a chainsaw to cut the strings that tied her to her old and familiar bad habits.

"You got lousy timing, man," Sawyer groused mockingly.

Colton shrugged with a crooked grin. "How I was I supposed to know the war was over and you two were making up?"

A blush set fire to Brea's face. "I'm going inside. I'm sure Jade needs help with something. I should have been doing that all along."

Turning on her heel, Brea stormed off. She hated how prickly and combative she became around Sawyer. But she couldn't help it. She didn't know how else to fight the losing battle raging inside her.

"She's doing fine…got it all under control." Colton's voice faded as Brea stormed into the kitchen.

"Hey, can you grab the potatoes out of the oven for me?" Jade nodded toward the stove as she tossed the salad.

"Of course. I feel terrible," Brea began as she donned a pair of oven mitts. "I invited you guys over for dinner, and you've done all the cooking."

"Oh, please. I love to cook. It's the cleaning up after that I can't stand."

Brea set the pan of twice-baked potatoes on the stove. "Then I'll take care of that when dinner's done."

"You have yourself a deal." A knowing smirk formed on Jade's face. "That was some kiss you and Sawyer shared on the porch."

Brea touched her fingers to her mouth and dipped her head.

Jade chuckled. "I'm guessing your man ban bit the dust?"

"No. I-I… It was an accident."

"Oh. So you two *accidentally* tried to kiss the lips off each other. Got it. I suppose you were only holding on to the back of his neck for safety reasons, huh? I mean, god knows if you hadn't found an anchor, he might have *accidentally* sucked your tongue clean down his throat." Jade giggled.

"Shut up." Brea sent her friend the stink eye, which only made her friend laugh harder. "I'm glad you find humor in my suffering."

Jade snorted. "Yeah, sharing a hot, steamy kiss with that hunk of cowboy must have been excruciating."

"It will be if I don't put a stop to it from here on out."

"Uh-oh." Jade frowned. "Okay. Take a deep breath and find your Zen."

"I can't!" Brea cried. "It just flipped me off and caught a flight to the Bahamas. It knows a lost cause when it sees ones."

"Then grab a beer. Your chickenshit Zen can't hold a candle to alcohol."

"Unfortunately neither can I."

Jade sent her a sympathetic smile, the kind a bestie shares when your emotions are too raw to speak. Seconds later, Colton and Sawyer came waltzing in through the back door. Jade held back whatever she was going to say next and placed a steak on each plate, while Brea silently followed, dishing out the potatoes.

"What a feast. I haven't eaten like this since last Thanksgiving," Sawyer stated. "Thanks again for inviting me over."

"Glad you could join us." Colton smacked Sawyer on the back before taking a seat next to Jade, leaving the chair next to Sawyer empty.

Butterflies dipped and swooped in Brea's stomach when she sat down beside him. Not only did the scent of clean soap and woodsy cologne tickle her senses but also the heat of his body enveloped her once again. The man unhinged her and saturated her brain cells with so much lust. Brea wondered how she'd manage to choke down dinner.

"I saw Nate walking toward your place this morning. I stopped to offer him a ride, but he said he wanted the exercise. He seemed a little ticked off. Is he okay?" Colton asked, carving into his steak.

Sneaking a sideways glance, Brea felt Sawyer's body tense. The silverware in his hands stilled and hung poised above his plate.

"Yeah, he's fine."

"I was surprised to see him. I thought your folks had a new group of guests at the ranch."

"They do. Usually everyone but Ned and me stay out at the house with them while the guests are there, but Nate had some business in town last night."

Jade perked up. "Oh, really? What's her name?"

Sawyer quickly banked a flash of guilt, then lifted his shoulders with a careless shrug. "My prodigal virgin brother was probably going to or from Bible study, or something."

Brea tensed. The man was lying! He and Nate had argued…she'd heard and watched them from the living room! Maybe Sawyer was trying to protect his brother's reputation and that of the older bartender, Gina? It didn't matter…whether big or small, a lie was a lie. Brea was well versed in that form of deception. And she'd just discovered Sawyer's Achilles tendon. He was as flawed as all the rest.

"Actually, that's not true," Sawyer softly confessed. "He's seeing someone I don't approve of."

Okay, so she'd obviously judged him too quickly…the man had a conscience! Shit. But how arrogant could he be, judging the woman as too old or wrong for his brother. Nate didn't think so, and he certainly didn't give two shits if Sawyer approved of his love life or not. Nate had driven home that point with a damn pitchfork, and Brea could still see the aftermath of the wounds etched on Sawyer's face.

She was desperate to know what had happened in the past…what skeletons were rattling around in Sawyer's closet. But if she wanted him to open up and share, she knew she'd have to do the same. Yeah, that was incentive enough for her to keep her big, inquisitive mouth shut.

"He's not sniffing around Deanne, is he?" Colton asked with a shudder of revulsion.

"Good god, no!" Sawyer barked.

"Who's Deanne?" Brea asked.

"The town slut," Jade enlightened.

"How do you know? You've only been here a month." Colton gaped.

"It's a small town, baby. People talk." Jade shrugged and then leaned in close to Brea. "Rumor has it, Deanne's tumbled more sheets than a box of fabric softener."

The whole table burst out laughing, then Jade abruptly sobered and shot Colton with a jealous glare. "You've never bumped bellies with Deanne, have you?"

"Hell no!" Colton adamantly shook his head before quirking a brow at Sawyer.

"Don't look at me. I wouldn't tap that without a court order…then I still wouldn't. They'd have to throw me in *jail*." He darted a knowing look at Brea and her heart sputtered.

Did he know she'd been in jail? How? She snapped her head Colton's way, but he was busy chomping on a piece of meat.

It was just a joke. You're being too sensitive. Chill.

Brea licked her lips and forced a smile. "Well, looks like we're dining with the only choir boys in town."

Jade rolled her eyes and scoffed.

"Maybe not choir boys, but we're not man-sluts either," Colton proclaimed.

"Not *anymore*," Jade teased dryly.

"So, how many are at the ranch this week?" Colton's redirection of the conversation was blatantly obvious. She and Jade shared a knowing grin.

"Twenty-four. Twelve girls and twelve boys," Sawyer answered before taking a bite of salad.

"What kind of ranch is it?" Brea asked.

She envisioned a 4-H youth farm program but was amazed and deeply moved when Sawyer explained the heart of Camp Melody. The pride in his words and the glow on his face told Brea that he was part of a rare breed. Not only was he living his dream but also helping bring happiness to the lives of weak and dying children. He was handsome and sexy, and nearly a Saint as well.

Seeing him in this whole new light made her feel guilty for the insults and defiance she'd subjected him to. His beauty was equally distributed on the inside and out. She clung to his every word, forgetting her food.

"It sounds amazing. I would love to see it sometime. I mean, if visitors are allowed."

"Of course they are. I'd be happy to show you around and introduce you to some of the campers, especially Tina." A sheepish grin crawled across his lips. "That cutie wrapped me around her little finger the minute I saw her."

"You've always been a sucker for a pretty face," Colton taunted.

Sawyer raised his head and stared pointedly at Brea. "Yeah, I know."

And just like that...lightning struck her girl parts, setting them ablaze. She was unconsciously responding to him in ways she couldn't control. Lowering her chin, she stared at her plate, wishing she were a strong, self-empowered kind of woman. But she wasn't…at least, not yet. She was still starved for affection and stupidly wanting to fill that void with her body.

"Eat up, sweetheart," Colton urged as if sensing she was sliding down a slippery slope to nowhere.

Forcing the food into her mouth, Brea tried her best to enjoy the remainder of the meal. Though she joined in on the various conversations, she was hyperaware of Sawyer's every breath and word. She knew she was in deep shit when she sat admiring the movement of his Adam's apple as he gulped his beer. It was pathetic that every sinful inch of him turned her on. Her heart and head both finally agreed…Brea was in for one hell of a fall.

When dinner was through, she handed everyone a fresh bottle of beer, then shooed them out the door to clean the kitchen. Sawyer held back while Colton and Jade stepped outside to the deck with Ozzie in tow.

"Let me help you with that." He picked the plates off the table and carried them to the sink.

"Thank you, but you don't need… Go on outside and relax."

"Not until you go with me." His wide smile made her knees go weak.

Yeah, she was toast. It was only a matter of time before Sawyer laid her out and spread her like butter.

Colton stuck his head inside. He was wearing a strange expression. "Ah, Sawyer…you might want to come out here for a minute."

Wiping his hands on a towel, he strolled out the back door. Curiosity had Brea following him. As she breached the portal, feminine giggles tinkled her ears.

"There you are, Sawyer!" A beautiful blonde with giant boobs waved from between two equally stunning women. All three were sitting in a bubbling hot tub on Sawyer's porch. A hot tub Brea hadn't taken notice of until now. In tandem, they all stood and wave, wearing different colors of string bikinis. Brea couldn't help but notice none of them had a ripple of cellulite to mar their perfect, skinny bodies.

"We tried waiting for you, sugar, but got so impatient we had to start the party without you," the blonde continued to explain.

Brea's stomach twisted. The knife of jealousy burst the bubble of hope she'd foolishly fashioned after Sawyer's kiss. The man of the hour, wide-eyed and mute, stood like a statue before darting a glance over his shoulder at Brea. Sawyer swallowed tightly before a look of panic tightened his face.

Jade moved in beside Brea, in support and solidarity.

Colton let out a long, low whistle. "Looks like you've got company."

Jade sent an incredulous glare Sawyer's way. Brea could all but hear her bestie internally yelling at the man to, *fix this shit, or die a slow, painful death!*

"Uh…yeah," he stammered. "I-I guess. I should…"

Brea's heart sank. She'd known she'd be taking a fall; she simply hadn't expected it to be quite this soon. But it was a minor drop, like skinning her knees. Besides, it was better to take a little bump now rather than later. At least she knew that Sawyer's kiss meant absolutely nothing. Brea was nothing in his eyes but another easy conquest…or so he had hoped.

"What are you doing over there?" Sawyer's voice held a hint of annoyance.

"We wanted to play in the water, but the pool's closing soon, so we crashed your hot tub instead," a pretty, petite brunette explained in a seductive tone.

The woman was so transparent. Brea didn't know if she wanted to gag or laugh. The three pool-time playmates hadn't shown up to swim. They'd showed up to fuck Sawyer…fuck him three times over, at least.

"You were a bad boy last night and blew us off." The third centerfold beauty, with glossy, auburn curls, scolded, pushing out her lip in an overdramatic pout. "We came over so you could make it up to us.

"I was busy. I still am," Sawyer bit out angrily.

"Aw, come on. We just want to have a little fun with you again," the blonde begged. "Get wet with us. There's plenty of room."

"Again?" Colton choked on a chuckle. "Damn, man. You must have the stamina of a race horse."

"Colton!" Jade spat as she slapped him on the shoulder.

Brea stood silently trying to work down the slew of ugly emotions lodged in her throat. What did she care if three bikini-clad playmates were brazenly soliciting the man who'd just kissed her? But dammit, she did care. Struggling to come to terms with the fact that her competition was staring her in the face, Brea was losing the war badly. She was an ugly duckling next to three beautiful, confident swans who were ruffling their feathers, preening, and coaxing the man Brea ached for with an invitation he wouldn't refuse.

Foolish tears stung the backs of her eyes, but she quickly blinked them away. Yes, Sawyer was funny, handsome, and had a heart of gold when it came to innocent children. But when it came to women, he was still a typical man…being led through life by his dick.

It doesn't matter! He's nothing but a temporary neighbor.

God, she wanted to believe that…convince herself he meant absolutely zilch to her. But the tightening in her chest, squeezing the air from her lungs, told her that Sawyer meant a whole lot more, at least to her heart.

As the flawless females continued to coax and cajole Sawyer, Brea's ears felt as if they were going to start bleeding. She wanted to shove his ass over the fence just to make the whiny bitches shut the fuck up.

Allowing anger to override her ridiculous jealous pride, Brea painted on a tight smile.

But Sawyer wasn't smiling. A look of embarrassment and anger lined his face.

It surprised and confused her. Why was he stalling? Why

wasn't he hurdling the fence, stripping off his clothes, and racing toward the sex-starved trio? He wasn't, and Brea couldn't figure out what he was waiting for.

An unwelcome flutter of hope broke loose inside her, but Brea swiftly crushed it down with a hammer bigger than Thor's. It was time to end this ridiculous attraction to Sawyer here and now. If he wasn't going to make a move...Brea would.

"Glad you were able to join us for dinner. Have fun with your friends," she announced dismissively.

Sawyer blinked and gaped at her, arching a brow in question. She forced her smile wider to still her quivering lips.

"You're a terrible liar," he whispered. "If you want me to go, just say so."

It was Brea's turn to blink and gape. "I-I... You don't want to keep your ladies waiting, do you?"

"First of all, they're not *my* ladies. Secondly, I didn't invite them. As far as I'm concerned, they're trespassing."

Of all the things she expected him to say, that certainly wasn't one of them.

"You're going to turn them down?" Colton asked in disbelief.

"Why? You want to go over there and join them or something?" Jade snapped, visibly pissed.

"No!" Colton adamantly shook his head. "Hell, no."

"Umm hmm." Jade pressed her lips in a tight line. "I'm going inside."

"I'll join you," Brea volunteered.

As she and Jade turned, Sawyer muttered a curse.

"I'll be back in a minute," he announced.

"Let's hope it takes you longer than a minute," Brea tossed over her shoulder.

"Yeah, or you're in serious need of some little blue pills," Colton snorted.

"Ha ha. My shit works just fine, thank you very much."

"Evidently it does if you can satisfy three at once," Brea bit out snidely.

Jade hissed out a laugh as the two women entered the house.

Irked that the green-eyed monster had sunk its ugly teeth into her flesh, Brea stormed into the living room and began to pace.

"If Colton even thinks of going over there to join those three hookers, I'm going to kill him!"

Her bestie's unwarranted fears stopped Brea in her tracks. "Oh, honey. He's not getting near those sleazy bimbos."

"He'd better not!"

"Relax, Jade." Brea drew the other woman in for a hug. "He loves you more than life. He's not going to let some YouTube video waiting to happen screw that up. Don't even go there. He's been in love with you since Moses was in diapers. Knock it off." Brea sent her friend a pained expression. "Who are those women anyway?"

"Their names are Sylvia, Gretchen, and Annette, but I lovingly refer to them as the linoleum sisters 'cause they're so easy to lay." Brea cracked a smile while Jade rolled her eyes. "They scope out fresh meat at the Hangover. They'll pick up any guy…married, single, they don't care. As long as he's got a pulse and can get up his dick, they're ready to fuck him."

"Do they pick up Sawyer often?" Though Brea truly didn't want to know the answer, the question rolled off her tongue before she could stop it.

"Hell if I know. I was as shocked as you were to find them in his hot tub. Maybe they really did come over to just relax."

"And maybe I'm a virgin," Brea said with a snort. "Bitch please."

"If you and Sawyer ever get between the sheets, you make sure his shit's wrapped up nice and tight with latex."

Brea arched her brows. "You don't have to worry about that. He's not getting anywhere near my kitten."

"Maybe not, but he sure wants to." Jade grinned. "I've seen the way he's been looking at you all night. That boy wants to get up inside your girl, all nice and deep."

Her words sent a wicked thrill racing through Brea's system.

The thought of Sawyer being *up inside her all nice and deep* made her heart sputter and oxygen freeze in her lungs. A strangled moan seeped from her lips.

"Aw, girl. Like I said before, you don't have to move in with a man…just fuck his brains out. Of course, you might need to give Sawyer a little time to recuperate after tonight, but it'll do you a world of good."

"God knows I need my brains fucked out, to the level of a lobotomy. It's been forever."

"You mean, you and Weed didn't…?"

"When he lost his job, months ago, he lost interest in me."

"Months? Ouch!" Jade wrinkled her nose.

"But that doesn't mean it's okay for me to fall in bed with Sawyer…even if he wanted me, which he doesn't. I'm clearly not his type. Besides, one taste of that man, and I'll want him all. And let's face it, he is definitely not a happily-ever-after kind of man."

"No. He's not. That's why he's safe." Jade winked.

The sound of male laughter came wafting in from the back door. "Where's my woman?" Colton's deep voice reverberated through Brea's chest like a bass drum.

"I'm in here, you twisted pervert," Jade hollered back.

A huge grin spread across his face as he strolled into the living room and wrapped her in his arms. Sawyer stood a few feet back, looking embarrassed and as guilty as Weed had the night he'd been arrested. For Brea, the flashback was chilling.

"You love that about me, sweetheart, and we both know it," Colton proclaimed. Jade simply sent him a droll stare. "Let's go home. You can put on that little pink bikini you keep in the bottom drawer and we can—"

"Oh, we'll go home, all right," Jade huffed. "And when we get there, I'll toss you a bottle of lotion and hand towel, and you can knock yourself out."

"Oh, I plan on grabbing the lotion, for sure." Colton sent her a wicked smile. "But I'm going to use it starting at your toes until I work my way up your body. Then I'm going to rub you in all the right places until you're—"

"TMI," Brea interrupted, holding up her hand. "Stifle the raunchy details, please."

Jade sent her a look of sympathy, while Colton grinned.

"They don't have to be the only ones having fun tonight."

Brea jumped and yelped as Sawyer's warm breath and deep voice caressed her ear. She opened her mouth to reply, but Colton quickly cut her off.

"I'm taking my jealous little hellcat home. Seems I need to prove she's the only one who trips my trigger. Thanks for a wonderful dinner, ya'll. Next time you two will have to come to our place for barbecue."

"That sounds great." Sawyer smiled and clapped Colton on the back.

"I'll call you in the morning," Jade whispered as she gave Brea a hug.

"You two kids play nice now." Colton grinned before closing the door behind him.

AN AWKWARD SILENCE fell between them. Brea nervously wrung her hands as Sawyer struggled to explain the unexpected hot tub episode. Up until the three women arrived, it had been an almost perfect evening. He wanted to taste Brea's soft lips and delve into her silky, hot mouth again, but damage control came first.

"Would you like another beer?" Brea asked, already heading toward the kitchen.

"That'd be great. Thanks."

Following her, he was unsure what to say in order to recapture the light he'd seen in her eyes during dinner. It would be a sad day indeed if he never again caught a glimpse of that pretty caramel-colored sparkle.

"When would you like to see the ranch? I can take you with me in the morning if you'd like." *After I roll you over and make love to you for the seventh or eighth time.*

She sat down across the table from him. As if stalling, she took a sip of her soda. "I don't know if it's such a good idea. I mean, you'll be working and…and I don't have a car or anything. Besides, Ozzie shouldn't be left here alone all day."

"If it will make you feel better, I can put you to work, and we'll take Ozzie with us. He loves the ranch and the kids love him."

Brea sent him a puzzled look. "Ozzie's been to the ranch before?"

"Yep. Since he was a pup. Barbara brings him out three times a week when she comes to volunteer."

"What does she do there?"

The tension seemed to slowly bleed from between them. Being separated by the expanse of the table was driving him batshit crazy. Rising from his chair, Sawyer extended his hand. He'd tried to reassure her with a laid-back style but held his breath until Brea took it. Her guarded expression returned, but he couldn't ignore the current racing up his arm. He sent her a tender smile as the energy flowed through their limbs.

"I'll show you."

Sawyer threaded his fingers through hers. Leading her past the kitchen and into the mudroom, he reluctantly released her and flipped on the light. He pulled the door open on one of the tall cabinets opposite the washer and dryer. Sawyer withdrew a stack of tiny plastic pots and a bag of potting soil.

"You probably didn't notice, but Barbara has several rows of seedlings growing on the east side of her vegetable beds. They're pumpkins, well…starter pumpkins, anyway. She grows them from seeds, then puts them in these." He held up the miniature square seedling pots. "The kids paint and decorate the outsides, then she gives them each a starter plant and teaches them how to care for them once they get back home."

"That's wonderful." Brea smiled brightly. "They get to take back a piece of the ranch with them and watch it grow."

He sent her a timid nod. "Sometimes."

"Why only sometimes?"

"A lot of the kids have to go back to the hospital after they leave us and can't take their plants with them."

"What happens to their pumpkins?"

"Well, let's just say the fall pumpkin harvest is huge." Sawyer smiled sadly. "We plant the ones left behind and attach a ribbon with the child's name to a stake and tend them. During the fall festival, the folks in town buy up every one of them. My mom takes photos of the folks who purchase the special pumpkins and sends them to either the child or their family if they've lost their battle and passed away."

Tears glittered in her eyes and Brea quickly swiped a fat drop as it rolled down her cheek. Sawyer's heart clutched. She wanted the world and everyone around her to see her as such a strong-willed, capable woman. But inside she was just as broken and vulnerable as he was.

"Hey." After brushing away a second tear, he cupped her chin. "I didn't mean to make you cry again."

Brea sniffed and sent him a watery smile. "It's just so sad. Those poor, innocent kids. They're fighting and I…and I…"

"You what?"

"I've super-glued my ass on the pity pot, whining about all the stupid mistakes I've made, while those kids take every day as a blessing instead of a curse, like me. God, I'm nothing but a waste of space."

"You're not a waste of space." It irked him that she thought so little of herself.

Brea brightened his life with every new thing he discovered about her, but Sawyer wanted to learn more. Starting with why she'd been in jail. The only crime he thought she could have ever committed was being too fucking beautiful.

"Sometimes all we can do is learn from our mistakes and move on," he continued.

"I've definitely learned. That's why I'm changing my

ways…or trying to."

"And coming to Haven will help you do that?"

She softly scoffed as if in doubt. "I don't know. I didn't have anywhere else to go,"

Sawyer lifted her chin and forced her gaze again. "Why don't we move to the couch and talk?"

"No." She stiffened as if he'd asked her to strip and pole dance for him. Not that Sawyer was opposed to the idea, but yeah…the timing was way wrong. "I want to help at the ranch, the way Barbara does. But I'll need to do some research."

Sawyer bit back a curse. Digging into Brea's past was like climbing up a mud-soaked mountain—one step forward to find he'd slid five steps back. Clearly she didn't trust him. But more concerning was the fact she didn't trust herself.

Turning, Brea raced from the mudroom. With a heavy sigh, Sawyer paused, then followed her to the living room. He watched as she scoured the bookshelves.

"She's got to have a book on gardening somewhere in here, I just know it."

"What is it you're trying to learn? Growing pumpkins is easy."

Brea lifted her head and shot him an incredulous stare. "For you maybe, but not for me. My thumb is so black…I kill fake plants."

Sawyer chuckled and strode toward her. "How can anyone kill a fake plant?"

"I don't know, it just happens. I buy some pretty silk flowers, arrange them in a vase, and poof…two days later they start sagging like an old woman's butt."

He laughed. "That's…a visual. Tell you what, I'll teach the kids how to feed and water their pumpkins. You help them decorate their pots and plant the seedlings. Deal?"

"How do I do that…the planting part, I mean?"

"You are a city girl, aren't you?"

"Just because I'm not a poster child for *Better Homes and*

Gardens doesn't make me a bad person."

He wanted to kiss the sass out of her and move on to a whole lot more. Sawyer wondered how far he could take her before she slapped that asinine man ban in his face.

No time like the present.

Sawyer slid his hands up the sides of her neck and cupped her cheeks. Brea's little inhalation told him she knew his intent. But she didn't stop him. In fact, she leaned in ever so slightly until their breath mingled, moist and hot. Even though the high-voltage current arcing between them was urging him on, Sawyer kept his touch soft and reverent.

"There's a different kind of bad I want to experience with you."

When he dipped his chin and brushed his lips to hers, the zaps of electricity surged. Brea gripped his biceps and held on as the energy around them crackled and hissed. This strange kinetic draw he felt with her both fascinated and frightened him. It was the reason he'd sent the women in his hot tub packing. Sure, they'd had some good times, but since tasting Brea, Sawyer's desire for any other woman had flown out the window. His attraction to her was spellbinding light-years different from anything he'd ever felt before. She was special in ways he couldn't put into words. All he knew was that something about her made him want to toss all caution to the wind and chance another heartbreak, because he could easily fall in love with Brea.

Deepening the kiss, Sawyer barely held on to his sanity when she opened for him and wrapped her slick tongue around his. It felt as if the heat of a million suns were singeing him alive. Eating at her like a man possessed, he cupped her nape. Brea clutched his shirt, both of them gripping and holding on to one another like an anchor...like salvation.

He trailed kisses down her neck and along the edge of her jaw, then claimed her lips once more. Brea's soft whimpers and mewls made his pulse leap. Losing himself in the warm texture of her mouth, his skin grew tight. Nerve endings pulsed in animalistic awakening.

Doing nothing but letting him kiss her, Brea single-handedly shredded his control.

Warning bells, buzzers, and foghorns warned he was moving too fast…falling in too deep. But Sawyer blocked them out and sank further into the soul-stealing nirvana of her mouth, racing headlong with wild, reckless abandon.

She skimmed her fingers up his arms, leaving a trail of liquid fire. His muscles tensed, rippled, and quivered. Then she scraped her fingernails into his hair, and Sawyer's testosterone yelled like a heavy metal band.

Then without warning, Brea tensed. A string of curses erupted in his head as he physically felt a consciousness shift inside her. Easing from her mouth, he dropped his forehead while the sexual energy enveloping them dissipated like a vapor of smoke. Sawyer wanted to punch his hand through a wall but figured he'd need it later, alone, in his own bed.

Brea panted, her breath short and ragged, while a ghostly dark shadow passed over her eyes. He didn't need to see the tiny frown settling between her brows to know what was coming. Still, he didn't want to accept being shut down and clenched his jaw.

"I-I can't do this." Her words raked his flesh like a caress of broken glass.

Unable to even make it to first base, he couldn't lift his hands from her body. Studying her red swollen lips and half-lidded and unfocused eyes, he wanted to block the demons of her past and convince her to enjoy the here and now. But the pragmatist inside him knew playtime had come to a screeching halt. A pink hue crawled up her cheeks. The last thing Sawyer wanted was for her to be embarrassed. Flashing her a playful wink and the most dazzling smile he could muster, he brushed one last feathery kiss over her lips.

"I'll pick you and Ozzie up at seven in the morning. It's a ranch, so wear something old that you won't mind getting dirty."

Or come to the door naked, and I'll make you twice as dirty right here on the living room floor.

His aching cock screamed in rebellion, but Sawyer couldn't grant it relief. Not yet. Gripping her round, lush ass, he pulled Brea against his pelvis. Hoping to assuage some of the pain down south, he also didn't want her ever doubting how much she turned him on.

Brea's eyes grew wide at the feel of his erection, and a disgruntled moan seeped from her throat. "I'm sorry. It's just…"

Placing a warm finger to her quivering lips, Sawyer shook his head. "No apologies and no regrets."

Dragging his thumb over her bottom lip, he drew in a less-than-steady breath and forced himself to take a small step back. There was so much more he wanted to say…to do, but he sensed her walls were paper-thin at the moment. Sawyer could shred them in an instant, but he didn't want to be added to her list of assholes. He'd wait until Brea stopped fighting this ungodly hunger between them to keep her from diving headfirst into an ocean of guilt.

"Eight o'clock," he reminded.

"Come over at seven thirty, and I'll feed you breakfast." She looked startled, as if the invitation had randomly rolled off her tongue. "I mean…you can't work on an empty stomach. You need to fuel your body, right?"

Sawyer couldn't help but smile at her sudden nervousness. Tracing a soothing finger down her soft cheek, he nodded. "Seven thirty it is."

He turned and started for the front door.

"Wait!" Brea cried. Sawyer froze in place, then turned as she raced toward him and launched herself in his arms. Burying her face in his neck, she pressed her lips to his throat. "Stay. Please?"

Shock pinged through him as he eased back and studied her expression. A nanosecond passed before he urgently dropped his mouth to hers. Her lips were lush, warm, and so damn inviting he wanted to growl. He didn't know if she meant for him to stay five minutes or all fucking night. He could usually read women like a book, but not Brea. She gave him more mixed signals than a dyslexic football coach. But she'd given him secret passage to her fortress of towers and turrets, and Sawyer had every intention of storming her luscious castle, but only *if* she was truly on board.

"Tell me what you want, Brea."

"You." Her breathless answer held a hint of question, as if she feared he might turn her down.

Not in this lifetime, or the next.

"You sure?"

Stop trying to talk her out of it, dumb ass! the voice in his head implored.

Sawyer held his breath. Though the walk home was short, it would be a challenge of biblical proportions with a raging case of blue balls throbbing inside his jeans.

"Yes. I'm sure."

As if sealing the deal, she slid her fingers into his. Then, without another word, Brea led him to the stairs. Sawyer could feel the palpable war raging inside her. Though not what he wanted, he mentally prepared himself if her courage faltered and he had to bow out and leave.

Brea led him to her room, waffling slightly before breaching the portal. Sawyer gently squeezed her hand and bent in close to her ear.

"You take the lead…take what you want, darlin'."

CHAPTER SEVEN

THE MINUTE SHE yelled for Sawyer to wait, a devil popped up on one shoulder and an angel on the other. The two began fighting like an old married couple in the throes of divorce.

What are you doing? Have you lost your damn mind? the angel scolded.

Get some! You know you want to. You deserve it. Weed and the rest of those losers never gave you free rein to take the lead. It's about time you got some satisfaction for once, instead of always giving, giving, giving! Giving head. Giving money. Giving your ever-lovin' soul to douchebag after douchebag who only used you to bust a nut, then rolled over and started snoring. Sawyer's nothing like those dipshits, and you damn well know it.

Don't do it! You'll be sorry. He'll break your heart. Oh…this can only end in catastrophe.

Aw, don't listen to her. It's just sex. You won't fall in love with him. He's too perfect. He doesn't need you. But by the feel of what he's packin' in those jeans…he wants you. Just think how that huge cock is going to feel, stretching and filling your poor neglected pussy. It's time to get down and dirty with that grade-A hunk of beef! Or would you rather wake up in the morning sticky and aching from another night of wet dreams?

The devil's cajoling had rendered her opposing angel speechless. And while she'd bravely asked him to stay, now that she was alone with Sawyer in her room, tendrils of doubt wound like vines through her veins. The swell of uncertainty and panic had her feeling strung out like a junkie. She'd have laughed at herself if she weren't so busy trembling.

As if sensing the manic emotions cresting inside her, Sawyer cupped her cheeks and pressed a light, chaste kiss upon her lips. "Darlin', if you don't want to do this, it's okay."

"No. I do…it's just…"

"Feeling guilty about blowing your man-ban to hell, again?"

"Partly, yes. But that's not the problem…I mean, there isn't a problem, not really. It's just that, I-I…" Lord, she was stammering like a loon. Swallowing tightly, Brea yanked up her big-girl thong. "Do you love me?"

Sawyer's eyes widened. His face paled as if he'd seen a ghost. His mouth opened and snapped shut as if she'd proposed marriage to a priest. "Love you?"

Brea nearly laughed at the squeaking terror in his voice.

"Yes. Do you love me?"

"I…I…I'm sorry. I-I mean, I don't even know you very well yet." His voice quivered as if merely mentioning the L-word would leave him dismembered in a bloody carnage of claws and teeth. "No, Brea. I'm not in love with you. Listen…maybe this isn't such—"

"No. Wait. I only have one more question." She nervously licked her lips. "You won't ask me to move in with you after we…do this, will you?"

"Move in with me?" His expression was total bewilderment. He was probably thinking she'd escaped from a psych ward and was in desperate need of some Thorazine. "No. I prefer to live alone. Look, Brea…I'm not sure what you think, but…I'm not looking for—"

"Good," she cut him off and lifted to her toes. Biting back a grin at his puzzled gaze, Brea kissed him. "Please forget all the questions I asked, and tell me I haven't ruined the mood, because I really want you to stay and fuck me to oblivion."

Brea was certain he thought her a total nutjob, but unbeknownst to Sawyer, he'd guaranteed Brea couldn't slide back into her old destructive habits. He didn't love her and she wasn't moving in with him. She could now have the most amazing sex of her life with the man of her fantasies and walk away unscathed.

She felt strong, brave, and incredibly free.

Leaning in, she cupped his nape and kissed him. But Sawyer's lips were like iron, his body rigid as steel. He was probably trying to process if she was crazy or not. Then, as if nudged with a cattle prod, he melted against her lips and body while taking full control of the kiss.

His forceful command had her heart pounding double time. Their tongues swirled and circled while his copper whiskers prickled her face. She was enveloped in the heat and scent of his rugged body, and he filled the dark, empty places inside her. Tossing aside her inhibitions, Brea drew his hand to her breast. Covering his fingers with his palm, she squeezed, coaxing him to knead her heavy orbs. He didn't disappoint.

"Mercy." His voice was strained and hoarse. "I'm going to do a whole lot more than fuck you into oblivion, darlin'."

Mischief glittered his gold and emerald eyes. Brea wanted to pinch herself to make sure she wasn't lost in the splendor of another wet dream. She wasn't. Sawyer was real. There. Standing in her bedroom with his capable hand wrapped around her breast.

"And just how do you intend to do that?"

"Watch and feel, darlin'…just watch and feel," he drawled with a wealth of self-confidence.

Her body tingled in anticipation. With one hand lingering on her left breast, he raised his other hand, paying equal attention to her right, kneading them in tandem. Her body temperature soared while Sawyer held her in a hypnotic gaze. Moaning softly, she palmed his cheek. The prickly scruff scraped her flesh. She could easily imagine the feel of those whiskers gliding up between her thighs. Sawyer strummed his thumb over the fabric on her pebbled nipples. Brea closed her eyes and purred.

"You've got too many clothes on," Sawyer whispered.

"So do you," she murmured.

"I think we should remedy the situation, don't you?"

"Oh, yeah," she agreed in a sultry drawl.

Brea reached for the buttons of his shirt as Sawyer's jaw clenched.

"Is something wrong?"

"Yeah," he groaned. "I'm trying like hell not to rip your clothes to shreds, toss you on the bed, and mount you like a Brahma bull."

Brea's nerve endings lit up like a laser show. "What's stopping you?"

"Like I said, I'm going to do a whole lot more than fuck you." His voice came out strangled and the muscles of his neck bunched. "I'm going to crawl deep inside your pretty little soul."

No. No. No. That wasn't part of the deal.

She opened her mouth to argue, but Sawyer simply stole the words from her lips with a passionate kiss. Burnishing the tips of her breasts, each agonizing stroke promised endless, blissful torture. Her hormones cheered like the pep squad at a University of Texas homecoming game.

"Undress me, Brea," Sawyer whispered. "I need to feel your hands on me."

Her fingers trembled as she began freeing the buttons of his shirt. When she finished, the fabric fell open and she stilled, drinking in every ridge and plane of his sculpted chest. His faded jeans hung low on his hips, and her eyes were drawn to his cinnamon-colored hair disappearing beneath the waistband.

Butterflies fluttered and swirled in her stomach. She grew light-headed knowing all this male splendor would soon be hers. Well, at least for one night. As she pressed her palms against his firm, velvety, hot flesh, his muscles quivered beneath her fingers. He drew a quick intake of air through his mouth as she moved her hands over every ridge and valley.

Brea was reading his body like a book of braille, taking great pleasure in memorizing the story of Sawyer.

He plucked and rolled her throbbing nipples as she grew restless and frustrated with the fabric separating bare flesh.

"I need." she panted, "you to get these damn clothes off."

"When I'm ready," he chuckled.

"But I'm ready now," she whimpered.

He simply smiled and slowly shook his head. "I'm warming you up proper."

"You warm me up any more and I'll be nothing but flames."

"I like the sound of that…burn for me, baby," he murmured in a rough and gravelly voice. Seemingly content right where he was, he mercilessly teased and tormented her aroused peaks as he laved his tongue over her neck, ears, and lips.

Brea couldn't take it anymore. She was melting from the inside out.

"Dammit, Sawyer. What are you waiting for? I'm dying! Get off my nipples! Strip out of those jeans, and shove that slab of wood you've got between your legs inside me."

He stopped kissing her; he was laughing too hard to continue.

But she wasn't joking. If he didn't lay her down…or shove her up against the door soon, Brea was going to spontaneously combust—for sure.

He wanted to ride her like a bull? Well, sometimes you had to take the bull by the horns. Gripping his shoulders, she leaned in and flicked the tip of her tongue over one of his tight bronze nipples.

Sawyer stopped laughing. In fact, he tensed and growled as Brea savored his salty taste tingling on her tongue.

"What are you doing, trying to kill me, or just have your way with me?"

"Turnabout is fair play, cowboy."

As she paid homage to his other nipple, Sawyer sucked in a hiss. Hearing him suffering too had her smiling against his flesh, but only for a second. Her patience had reached its end. The rate Sawyer was moving, it would be sunrise before she had the chance to lay eyes on all his naked glory. Oh, how she planned to drink in every bare inch, too. From the tops of his copper hair all the way down to his masculine toes.

Lifting onto the balls of her feet, she peeled the shirt off his wide shoulders. Sawyer grudgingly released her throbbing nipples and allowed the material to flutter to the floor before taking her breasts in hand again.

Brea suddenly didn't care how long he wanted to strum her buds; she was lost in awe at the sight of his decadent torso. He'd been pussy-tingling sexy with his shirt on, but now? Holy hell! The man was a work of art. She wanted to weep at the sheer perfection of his rugged sun-kissed skin and sculpted, chiseled muscles.

If his top half looked this stunning, she couldn't wait to see what was under his jeans.

Unable to keep from touching him, Brea traced her fingertips over the swells and dips along his shoulders and collarbones, dragging them lightly down the center of his chest, delighting in the feel of his body quivering. Sawyer wasn't any more immune to her than she was to him.

Growing bolder, Brea swirled the tip of her tongue around his flat nipple. He let out a low growl, then bent and repaid her torment by nipping at one bud. An arc of pain-mixed satin spread outward, the feeling so surreal and sublime. She captured his nipple between her teeth and lashed it with her tongue.

Crying out a curse, Sawyer pried her from his chest and reared back. Sparks of need flashed in his eyes. His nostrils flared like a rabid bull.

Oh, yeah. She'd gotten his attention, all right, maybe more than she needed.

"Are you *trying* to make me lose my head?"

"No." She flashed him a saucy smile. "I'm just returning the favor."

"And what favor is that?" He smirked.

"You've made me suffer for days now."

"Oh, I have, have I? In what way…exactly?"

"In every way. Everything about you is…decadent, delicious, and tempting."

"I can say the very same about you." A cocky grin speared his lips. "Maybe it's time we do something about this mutual suffering. What do you say?"

"Well, I thought's that's where we were headed, but you're moving so cotton-pickin' slow I doubt we're ever going to make it to the bed."

"Slow? I'm moving too slow?"

Brea nodded. Her lips started to curl at his incredulous tone.

"Relax, darlin'. You'll be begging and pleading soon enough. I promise."

"I sure hope so."

He arched his brows and grinned. "You doubt my abilities?"

She shook her head. "Not one bit. That's why I'm so damn anxious."

A low chuckle rumbled up from deep in his chest. This playful bedroom banter was all new to her, but Brea liked it. She liked it a lot.

"Settle your sexy ass down. I'm going to make you shatter so hard and so often your hot little body will be quivering for days…weeks…months even."

The prospect of death by orgasm made her start quivering already. Biting back a grin, she jerked up her chin and looked him square in the eyes. "Prove it."

His confident grin screamed, *challenge accepted*. Without a word, Sawyer shucked her cotton tee off over her head and tossed it toward the door. His gaze locked onto her pink bra, trimmed in white lace, and he licked his lips. As he intently focused on the demi-cups, Sawyer's breath grew ragged. She skimmed a gaze at the bulky package beneath his jeans and knew he was equally ready to get this provocative party started.

"Do you want me to take my bra off, or would you rather—"

"Bite it off with my teeth?"

"Or…there's that way, too." She giggled.

Her laughter brought his attention back to her face. He flashed her a clit-throbbing grin.

"On second thought…you take it off for me, darlin'. Take everything off. One piece at a time…nice and slow."

Good grief. That certainly backfired on her. She'd never stripped for any man before. Usually her clothes were pawed off her in a rush. Revealing herself, for his eyes only, felt sharper and more intimate than sex itself. Brea wasn't quite sure how or what to uncover first. As she slid one strap of her bra to the elbow, she felt as if she were peeling away her own layers of protection. And when she had finally worked the garment free and sent it puddling at her feet, Sawyer held her gaze. He didn't fixate on her tits or grab and stuff one in his mouth like a slobbering dog. He simply delved deeper into her eyes, drawing out every vulnerability, weakness, and fear inside her.

Brea had never felt more naked or unsure of herself.

But then Sawyer did something that replenished her courage and restored her faith in a sliver of the male species; he smiled and opened his arms. As she thrust herself against his steely chest, he wrapped her in his protective arms. Then all of a sudden, Ozzie started barking. Not the usual sound when a squirrel infringed on the dog's lawn. No, these were loud, frightening, rip-your-jugular-open kinds of barks that made the hair stand up all over her body.

"What is he—"

"Something's wrong. Stay here," Sawyer commanded.

Reaching down, he scooped his shirt off the floor and hastily pulled it on. She wasn't going to stand there like a stump while Sawyer faced the lurking potential danger down below. After scooping up her bra, Brea hurried and retrieved her shirt, putting them both back on as if the house were on fire. Sawyer crept toward the door, his head cocked as if listening for signs of an intruder. When he reached for the knob, she bent in close to his ear.

"I'm coming with you."

"No! Stay up here. Lock the door behind me and don't leave this room until I come back for you. Got it?"

"No. I'm not a helpless little—"

Before she could finish her sentence, a thunderous explosion rocked the house. Like a mighty earthquake, the floor shook and creaked beneath their feet. The sound of breaking glass blended in an unholy cacophony of chaos so loud and unexpected that Brea screamed. Sawyer tucked an arm around her waist and rolled them both to the unforgiving floor. Ozzie's frantic barks grew louder as he began clawing on the other side of the bedroom door. The blood-chilling sound of his claws gouging into the wood made her heart slam faster and harder against her ribs.

"What the hell happened?" she gasped.

"Gunshot."

"Gunshot? That sounded more like a goddamn cannon." Brea thrashed beneath his body, struggling to get up.

"What are you doing?" he growled. "Stay still."

"I need to check on Ozzie. He might be hurt."

"I'll get him. You stay put. Don't move," Sawyer demanded as he stood.

"Why would anyone want to shoot at Barbara's house?" Ignoring his order, Brea sat up.

Sawyer shook his head, clearly at a loss for words. When he opened the bedroom door, Ozzie came bounding in—hackles up and teeth bared. He looked downright chilling. She knelt, and the snarling dog rushed to her, sniffing her arms and face, as if taking inventory to see if his human was all right.

"Come back here, you dirty, no good, sum'bitch!" came a man's bellow from the front yard.

"Oh, for fuck's sakes," Sawyer hissed as he stormed to the window and threw back the drapes.

"Get back here, you coward. I know I winged 'ya. Dagblast it. Now I gotta hunt you down to finish you off."

Checking Ozzie over for injuries he might have sustained from the mêlée downstairs, Brea tipped a quizzical gaze up at Sawyer. "Who is that?"

He didn't reply, simply jerked up the window and stuck his

head out into the darkness. "Goddammit, Emmett."

The crazy Bigfoot dude. Priceless.

"What the hell are you doing?" Sawyer scolded. "Trying to kill us?"

"Not you, Neville. I was trying to put Bigfoot down," Emmett called out. "I caught the smelly, fuzzy bastard peeking in Barbara's window down here."

"He was looking in the window? Bigfoot or someone…like a man?"

"You know, you should be thanking me for saving your life and that new girl who's staying here. Bigfoot could have had her as an appetizer…or worse, and you for dinner. Instead of asking a bunch of foolish questions, you should be thanking me."

No longer in protect mode, Ozzie started licking Brea's face and wagging his tail, until she pushed him away and stood. "Enough, brave boy. I'm fine."

Moving alongside Sawyer, she peered out the window. Emmett stood in the middle of the yard, cradling a giant shotgun.

"So why didn't you kill it?" Sawyer yelled, clearly pissed.

"I tried. That crafty, sum'bitch, turned tail and ran 'fore I could get off another shot."

"One that would have finished taking down the house, no doubt," Brea mumbled under her breath.

In the distance, a siren screamed. Ozzie whined and cocked his head. Brea stroked his ears, wanting to calm him.

"Sounds like Jasper's on his way. Stay there. We're on our way down, and whatever you do, *don't shoot.*" Sawyer closed the window and sucked in a deep breath. "We'd better go see how much damage that crazy fucker's done."

"He needs to be committed to a mental hospital. That man is certifiably insane." Brea slapped her hands on her hips with a huff.

But Sawyer managed to wipe away the lingering fragments of terror as his eyes raked a slow, wistful caress down her body. Regret lined his face.

"No argument there. The man definitely doesn't have all his cornflakes in the box."

As she watched Sawyer button his shirt, the consequence hammer came crashing down, hard, on Brea's head. Obviously, her cornflakes weren't all in the box either. She'd been minutes—okay, maybe an hour at the rate Sawyer had been moving—from spreading her legs and all but shoving his dick inside her body.

But he said he didn't love you, and he liked living alone. You're safe. Or so the same delusional brain cell that had convinced Brea to call Sawyer back wanted her to believe. She wasn't feeling quite so gullible at the moment. More mortified.

If mentally unstable Emmett hadn't tried to blow the house down, Brea would have succumbed to Sawyer's charms. Like a kid in a candy store, she would have gorged herself on every inch of his big, hard cock.

Not only did she lack backbone to stick to her convictions, she had zero willpower to boot. She closed her eyes and swallowed a long, mournful groan. How many more times would she lay her heart out to be trampled and stomped before she stopped being so weak around men?

The feel of Sawyer's fingers lightly skimming over her cheeks had her opening her eyes. A miniscule second later, his mouth thinned into a tight, angry line. So much for masking her emotions.

Shit!

"Don't. We'll talk this through after we deal with the aftermath of Emmett."

That was one invitation she desperately wanted to decline. She'd much rather send Sawyer home…for good. But she held her tongue while the police siren shrieked outside, and red and blue strobes danced off the walls. Taking her hand, Sawyer led her downstairs.

The siren fell silent as she blinked at the carnage of what used to be Barbara's living room. The plate glass window now had a gaping hole in the middle. Shards of glass, like jagged teeth, refracted prisms from the squad cars lights. They danced around the room like a seventies disco ball. Warm night air rushed inside while the curtains that framed the window softly billowed and swayed.

Fragments of glass littered the hardwoods in front of her, and to the right, along the wall that separated the living room and kitchen, were holes where buckshot had peppered the drywall.

"Oh, god," she gasped. "Look at this mess."

"Drop your shotgun, Emmett." came a command from outside.

"Aw, for crying out loud, Jasper. You know I 'ain't gonna shoot ya," the crazy bastard drawled.

Praising him for his protection, Brea quickly sequestered Ozzie in the mudroom to keep him from cutting his paws. When she joined Sawyer in the living room, she found the men from outside had brought their party inside. Emmett wore his usual curmudgeon and sour expression. The officer, who she assumed was Jasper—a round, middle-aged man who looked to live off donuts—wore a slightly bored, dispassionate expression. Sawyer, on the other hand looked totally pissed off as the men inspected the damage.

The cop's badge glimmered in the recessed lights overhead and brought an oily rush of déjà vu. She could still smell the stench of urine and stale sweat that surrounded her in that damn holding cell. Logically, Brea knew she'd likely never see that hellhole again, but it didn't keep her anxiety from spiking or the bile from rolling up the back of her throat.

Staring at the cop, she sank to the couch, wrapped her arms around her middle, and tried to stave off a total freak out. Interrupting her view of the cop, Sawyer ate up the distance between them in three long strides. Kneeling down in front of her, his brows slashed in concern, he gently cupped her chin.

"Don't worry. I'll have the house fixed up long before Barbara returns."

"I'm not worried about that."

Brea couldn't mask the quiver in her voice or keep herself from glancing back at the cop. Sawyer followed her gaze, then shifted slightly and barred her view of everyone and everything except his face and wide shoulders.

"Why is Jasper upsetting you? Are you wanted for something?" Suspicion slathered his tone.

She shook her head and clenched her teeth. The guy she'd nearly banged ten minutes ago thought her a fugitive. A new kind of misery invaded her soul. While she'd climbed in bed with strangers who'd probably thought worse of her, Sawyer's opinion mattered to Brea. She didn't know why. Maybe some self-respect had been jarred loose inside that godforsaken holding cell. Or maybe foolishly rushing into so many meaningless relationships had finally made her wise up.

In reality, she didn't know shit about Sawyer. Oh, she knew liked steak, beer, and bringing joy to sick kids. On the other hand, he also enjoyed kinky sex with three women at the same time...three skinny, gorgeous women. She couldn't fault him for that, especially since she'd managed to carve a shit-ton of notches in her bedpost, too.

In many ways, they were amazingly similar. Maybe Sawyer used his body to connect with women the way she did with men. It would explain his desire to seduce her, but Brea ached for something more. But she knew she'd never find it in the mesmerizing stare of Sawyer Grayson. The man was as big a player as she. Or rather she *used* to be.

"I don't believe you," Sawyer softly whispered. "Jasper has you freaked out. Why were you in jail?"

Colton! You son of a bitch!

"What else did Colton—"

"He didn't say anything, Brea. I heard you two talking about it when I was on my porch. Tell me what happened."

"Nothing. I didn't do anything, and I don't want to talk about it." She stiffened and dropped her gaze to her lap.

"There's a whole lot you don't want to talk about, but we're going to…soon."

"No. I-I need you to leave and—"

"Dagnabbit, Jasper. I told you it was Bigfoot!" Emmett stomped his foot. "You 'ain't taking my gun. I gotta protect this town from that big, hairy ape."

"That's my job. And I *am* confiscating your gun." Jasper pulled off his hat and ran a hand over his thinning salt-and-pepper hair. "Call me if Bigfoot comes back. I'll shoot him for you."

"He ain't gonna wait around for you to decide to show up. He's a slippery cuss," Emmett argued. "He was bent over, yonder…peeking in the window. I seen him with my own two eyes."

"Are you sure it was Bigfoot and not some peeping Tom?" Sawyer asked.

"Well…" Emmett pondered the question. "I'm not rightly sure."

Brea's pulse leapt. "Someone was looking in the window?"

"That might explain why Ozzie came unglued right before the gunshot," Sawyer grimly stated.

A look of worry filled his face, sending a veil of fear to engulf her.

"Ain't you been listenin' to me? I done told ya that twice now, missy." Emmett scowled. "You youngsters don't pay attention these days. Y'all got your noses in your fancy computer tablets, cellular phones, and spend all your time taking selfless."

"They're called selfies," Jasper corrected.

"I don't care what they're called," Emmett huffed. "You all need to put your electronics away and open your eyes. There's a big ol' world out there."

The old man raised a gnarled finger and pointed at Brea. "And you…you'd better be keeping the lights on and your doors locked up tight, little lady. Someone's watching you. It might be Bigfoot or some twisted maniac wantin' to defile you."

"Emmett!" Sawyer barked. "That's enough."

But it was too late. The seeds had been sown. Panic sent her stomach pitching. Her mind filled with images of a faceless sicko raping, torturing, and murdering her. Tremors assaulted her body, and all Brea wanted to do was grab Ozzie and run back to Colton and Jade.

As if summoned by ESP, the couple barreled through the front door.

"Who got shot?" Jade's eyes were wide with panic, her face pale with fear. The second she spied Brea, Jade raced to the couch and wrapped her in a tight hug. "Oh, thank god. I was so scared you were dead."

"I'm fine," Brea whispered as they both trembled. "No one's dead or shot. But that crazy Bigfoot hunter guy blew the shit out of Barbara's house."

"Emmett...really?" Colton chided with a long, heavy sigh.

"Pfft. You're all gonna be thanking me one day when I save your hides from that ugly beast."

"Yeah, yeah," Jasper drawled. "Until then, you need to see that Barbara's house is set right. Pay for the damage you've done, or she's liable to shoot you herself."

"I ain't one to shirk my responsibilities. Don't you go accusing me of such, neither. I ain't never let no one pay my way. My momma taught me better than that."

"Too bad she didn't teach you common sense," Jade mumbled so low that only Brea could hear.

"There ain't nuthin' wrong with my hearing, you little tart." Emmett scowled at her.

"Did you just call my woman a tart, old man?" Colton bellowed. "I ought to kick—"

"Jasper! Get him out of here before we *all* lose our temper," Sawyer ordered.

Colton sent a weak smile to Jade before kneeling alongside Sawyer. "Brea, sweetheart...are you all right?"

She didn't respond, simply watched Jasper lead Emmett outside. Once the zany old fart was gone, she nodded. "I was until that lunatic started talking about peeping Toms and rapists."

"Oh, sugar. Ignore him," Jade lamented. "Emmett's nuttier than a squirrel turd."

Brea chortled. "It's a little hard to do when he's shooting the damn windows out."

"I know…I know." Jade patted the back of Brea's hand.

"How did you two hear…?"

"Lucy called us. Her sister, Lottie… Wait. Let me start at the beginning. Francine, the town dispatcher, beautician, and florist got the nine-one-one from Maynard Pierce. He lives across the street from you." Jade pointed toward the jagged window. "Anyway, after Maynard reported the gunshot, he called Jeff—"

"No, sweetheart, his name is Jed," Colton corrected.

"Oh, right. Sorry. Anyway, Maynard called Jed, who is married to Lottie…who called Lucy…who called us since Lucy knew we were friends. So, we jumped in the truck and came back over to make sure you weren't dead!"

Jade flopped against the back of the couch and took a deep breath.

Brea shook her head. "Wow. High-speed Internet is like dial-up compared to the way news travels in this town."

"You have no idea!" Jade rolled her eyes. "At least a photo with you engaged in a torrid lip lock on Main Street hasn't graced the front page of the newspaper."

"Not yet." Sawyer grinned and winked.

Brea turned a guarded gaze on him. The excitement tonight could easily make the front page, but she and Sawyer wouldn't ever be gracing the news. Brea wasn't letting the man near her pants, tits, or pussy again.

Her lusting days were over.

Finished.

Through.

Even if she had to bite the bullet and order a case of granny panties off the Internet, then find a convent that would take an overused virgin…she was done with men!

SAWYER WANTED TO lay Emmett out cold for interrupting what had been the start of a phenomenal night. Hopefully, if Colton and Jade left soon, he and Brea could pick up where they left off.

"You got any plywood we can use to board up that window?" Colton asked.

"Yeah. As a matter of fact, I do. In the garage."

Colton kissed Jade softly. "We'll be back in a few to take care of this mess. Why don't you and Brea wait in the kitchen…fix yourselves some tea…or toss back a few shots."

"No! Brea doesn't get booze." Jade blanched.

Colton cringed. "Right. Sorry, sugar."

"I never did find out…why you don't drink? Are you allergic to—"

Jade cut him off with a mischievous grin. "It makes her dance and lose her pants…literally lose her damn pants before she starts trying to fu—"

"Shut up!" Brea spat.

"Oh, really?" Sawyer chuckled. He'd file that tidbit of info away for later.

"We'll clean up the glass while you guys get the wood."

He grinned when Brea redirected the conversation. "No. You relax. You've been through enough for one night, darlin'." Sawyer patted her knee before standing.

"I'll do what I want," she barked. "Stop bossing me around. You've been doing it since Emmett shot out the window. I don't like it."

"Fair enough." He bit back a smile. It warmed his heart to see her feisty side return. It was a far better sight than the fear in her eyes when Jasper had arrived. "I wasn't trying to school you, just keep you safe."

He could tell she wanted to argue, but Jade stood and pulled

Brea to her feet before the two headed toward the kitchen.

Outside, he'd no sooner stepped off the porch than Colton rounded on him and stopped Sawyer in his tracks.

"What's this shit about a peeping Tom?"

"I don't know. Emmett first started ranting about Bigfoot looking in the window, but when pressed, he admitted it might have been a man. Someone or something was out there for sure. Ozzie went apeshit before the window was shot out."

"Was he in front of it, barking?"

"I don't know."

Colton's eyes narrowed. "Where were you and Brea?"

"Upstairs."

"In her bedroom?"

Sawyer hadn't defended his integrity for nearly a decade. He certainly didn't like doing it now. The disapproving expression and grilling tone of voice had him biting back a reminder that Colton wasn't Brea's father.

Sawyer yanked the garage door open and flipped on the light. "Yeah."

With arched brows, Colton bit out his next question. "Did you two—"

"Have sex? Not that it's any of your business, but no. Emmett…fucking blew that prospect away as well."

He watched Colton's jaw clench and tick. The air between them turned arctic. "Look, if there's some reason I should back the fuck off…I'm all ears."

Colton pursed his lips. "Not my place to tell you her secrets, man."

"Fair enough, but you obviously have an issue with my interest in her. Who are you protecting…me or her? And why the fuck was she in jail?"

Colton's mouth fell open. "She told you about that?"

"No. I overheard the two of you on the deck earlier tonight."

"Ah." Colton nodded.

"When I asked her about it, she didn't answer. So now I'm

asking you."

"If she doesn't want to tell you, then—"

"Dammit, Colton. What the hell did she do?"

"*She* didn't do anything," he spat. "The only thing she's guilty of is getting mixed up with another douchebag who treated her like shit and tried to throw her under the bus. But he didn't succeed. She's free and clear… They never even brought up any charges against her."

"Charges for what exactly?"

"When she's ready, she'll tell you."

"Is this douche the reason she's put that fucking man ban in place?"

"One of them."

"One? How many—"

Colton raised his hand. "Unless you want me telling her your secrets, don't keep pressing me for hers. Ask her yourself."

"Go ahead. Tell her anything you want about me." Sawyer shrugged. "The whole town knows all my shit, anyway."

"But they don't know hers, and I want to keep it that way."

Sawyer pinned him with a glare. "I'm not part of the gossip guild, and you damn well know it."

"True. Up to tonight your private life has been… How long have you been getting kinky with the twisted sisters?" A cunning smile spread across Colton's mouth. "Maybe you really don't want Brea finding *everything* out after all."

"She's not stupid. I'm sure she figured it out, just like you did."

"No, she's not, which makes me wonder why she was still willing to take you to her bedroom after all that. You must be one smooth-talkin' son of a bitch. Most women would've kicked you in the nuts and put a curse on your dick…made it shrivel up and fall off."

"Brea's not like other women," Sawyer whispered.

"No. She's not. She wants to find the good in everyone and believe that she'll eventually hook up with a man with equally good intentions. Problem is, the guys she finds wouldn't know a good intention from a sack of shit."

"So she took me upstairs—"

"Because she's still searching for Mr. Right." A grim expression settled over Colton's face. "I love you like a brother, man...but we both know...you're not him. I won't sit by and watch her go down in flames again. If you're just looking for another piece of ass, I'll tell her what you're up to. She'll shut you down faster than the health department in a burger joint swarming with cockroaches. Got it?"

Bristling, Sawyer opened his mouth to tell his well-meaning *friend* to go fuck himself. But Nash's words exploded in his head: *I should have left well enough alone instead of listening to your piss poor advice.* Then right on their heels were Nate's angry words: *You have no right to decide what I do or who I do it with, you interfering prick.*

There wasn't an ounce of comfort being on the receiving end of a meddling asswipe and his *good intentions.*

Swallowing back his rage, Sawyer held out the other end of the plywood to Colton. The man could bitch and lecture all he wanted. Sawyer had no intention of turning his back on Brea. "Let's get that window boarded up. I don't like the idea of someone watching her."

"You never answered me," Colton pressed.

"No. I didn't." Sawyer clenched his jaw and hoisted the sheet of wood against his shoulder.

"Fuck!" Colton mumbled under his breath and lifted the other end.

"Tell me one more thing. Where's this douche-canoe who sent her to jail?"

"Hopefully, still behind bars. I'll find out in the morning."

"If he's out, I'd appreciate a name and a description. I want her to stay safe."

"In or out of bed?" Colton jabbed.

Sawyer clenched his hands into fists. "Look, I'm not purposely trying to piss in your Wheaties. I know she's a little damaged. Christ, bro, do you think I'm blind? But I'm not backing off just because you want me to."

"Why not?"

"Because...Brea is different... She's special."

"You wouldn't know special if she was on her knees sucking your cock."

"Climb down from your cross, motherfucker. You and I are cut from the same cloth, or did you forget? You stood right next to me when I kicked the triplets out of the hot tub and sent them home. So shove your sanctimonious, disapproving father bullshit up your ass."

Colton shrugged. "Maybe you sent them home so you could sink your teeth into some fresh meat."

A blinding red rage engulfed him. "You cocksucking motherfucker! How would you like it if I referred to Jade as *fresh meat*?"

Colton's nostrils flared.

"Exactly! You have no goddamn clue what I feel for Brea, so back the fuck off."

"Do you hear yourself? You've known her...what? Two whole days?"

"It wouldn't matter if I'd known her two minutes. It changes nothing."

The adamant tone of his voice and words shocked Sawyer more than the look of disbelief crawling over Colton's face.

"What the... Are you trying to say you're in love with her?"

CHAPTER EIGHT

"I...I don't...know," Sawyer mumbled. "All I know is that Brea is different and unique."

"That's right." Colton moved in until they stood toe-to-toe. "She doesn't need another man fucking her over. What she needs is someone to love her. If you're not willing to do that, then keep playing hide the salami with Sylvia, Gretchen, and Annette. Or beat the priest, alone in your room. Just leave Brea alone. Got it?"

"I got it. You tell me again and I'll break your goddamn face," Sawyer barked.

His defiant Grayson gene came roaring to the surface. Things were about to run ugly. Colton's ultimatum ignited a living, breathing hot rage within. Sawyer knew exactly why Nash had made a mess of things with Megan—why Nate had unleashed his hurtful words, as well.

It was time for Sawyer to break open the bottle of honesty and stow away his pride. He'd likely ruin the friendship between him and Colton.

No. He wasn't in love with Brea, but Sawyer's feelings ran deeper than heavy like. She fascinated and aroused him. Colton's desire to protect her wasn't out of line. If the roles were reversed, Sawyer would do anything to protect her from one more dick-weed who might break her heart. He'd suffer a million root canals without Novocain before he'd bring an ounce of pain into her life. Sawyer wanted to heal her, and maybe along the way...if he was lucky, he'd heal himself, too.

"You'll need a goddamn army!" Colton challenged.

"Look, man. I don't want to hurt her any more than I want

to fight you. Let's get that window boarded up. We both have to work in the morning."

And you're taking Brea with you.

Sawyer still saw the excitement dancing in her eyes when he'd invited her to the ranch. Colton was right; Sawyer needed to slow this out-of-control wagon down. But he couldn't very well un-invite her...he didn't want to. The more time he spent with Brea, the stronger his attraction grew, and he liked it.

The two men carried the plywood to the front of Barbara's house. Sawyer could hear the women inside laughing, and he caught himself grinning. But the thought of someone stalking her, possibly wanting to hurt her or take away her bubbly spirit, sent him into cave-man mode.

Easy, Hercules! Remember what Colton said? She needs someone to love her.

Which he didn't.

Yes, he cared for her more than he should...more than he wanted, but the idea of falling in love again squeezed Sawyer's heart like a fist.

After securing the plywood, he and Colton cleaned up the glass.

"Would you hardworking men like a cold beer? There's a couple left in the fridge."

Sawyer turned to find Brea standing at the edge of the living room. Her panic was gone, but he could see tendrils of uneasiness still lingered. He wanted to wrap her in his arms, take away her anxiety, and lose himself in her sweet kisses. The ghost of her luscious curves pressed against him haunted his flesh. So did the salty essence of her skin on his tongue and her taut nipples on the tips of his fingers. But most of all, the scent of her heady, intoxicating pussy still branded in his brain made him want to mark her with his seed in every primitive and animalistic way.

She's still searching for Mr. Right...but we both know...you're not him.

Colton's words resonated in Sawyer's head. He swallowed a

growl of frustration and flashed her a quick smile. "No thanks, I'm good."

She quickly banked the ripple of rejection that fluttered across her face. He wouldn't have even noticed had Colton not shared a few of Brea's secrets.

"None here. We're done," Colton announced. "I'll come over in the morning and start patching up the drywall...order a new pane of glass. We'll get everything back to normal."

"Thank you. I appreciate you two doing all this." Brea nodded toward the plywood. "I wouldn't have slept a wink if that were left gaping open."

"No problem. I like working with my hands." Even as the words slid past Sawyer's lips, he wanted to call them back. Especially when a beet-red blush crawled up Brea's chest and settled on her cheeks.

"I think the ladies in the hot tub were hoping for more skills than just your hands," Jade drawled with a sassy, smartassed smirk.

Brea forced a smile that resembled pain.

Sawyer groaned. "For the last time, they just...showed up."

"Gives new meaning to meals on wheels, doesn't it?" Brea's zinger hit his heart like a bull's-eye.

Clenching his jaw, he didn't want her jealous or loathing him. He wanted her trust.

"All right...all right. You've busted the man's balls enough for one night, ladies," Colton intervened, holding up his hands. "Are you ready to head back to the ranch, my little troublemaker?"

Jade gaped at him in feigned innocence before a devious smile crawled across her lips. "If you suggest me putting on that bikini again, I'll show you trouble."

"Just remember, my tigress. I have rope and I'm not afraid to use it." Colton winked.

"All right. All you perverts...out!" Brea ordered with a chuckle.

Sawyer hung back after Colton and Jade headed to their truck. He dropped his lips close to her ear. "*All* the perverts?"

He didn't miss the shiver that rippled through her.

Brea inhaled and paused as if weighing his question. "Yes. Every last one of them."

Deep down, Sawyer knew it was for the best, but he couldn't keep from wanting her. The woman was like a drug.

"I guess," she began timidly, "since Colton's coming by tomorrow, I'll need to take a rain check on helping out at the ranch."

Her palpable disappointment made Sawyer frown, but he lifted his shoulder with a careless shrug. "It's okay. Come with me the day after."

"We'll see."

She was shutting down…closing doors in his face. He didn't like it. "If you see or hear anything suspicious, call me. Day or night. Barbara left you my number, right?"

"Yes." Brea nodded. "If Emmett decides to take out another window, I'll call."

He sent her a scolding glare.

"You'll call if you get scared. In fact, give me *your* number in case I need to get ahold of you." Sawyer pulled out his cell, storing her number as Brea rattled it off. "I'm serious. If you hear so much as a mouse fart, call me."

She nibbled on her bottom lip and nodded.

God, how he ached to latch on to that that plump flesh, pull it beneath his own teeth and feast until she whimpered. Instead, he pressed a tender kiss to her forehead.

"Good night, Brea."

"Night."

Sawyer felt her gaze burn into his back all the way across the yard. He put one foot in front of the other, but every cell in his body protested. The last thing he wanted was to go crawl inside his cold, empty bed. He'd much rather crawl inside her sinful body and stay up all night giving her dozens of screaming O's.

But Colton had made it clear, Brea needed more...needed the thing Sawyer couldn't give her...love.

Trudging up the stairs to his room, Sawyer cursed the pricks who'd broken her heart. Steering clear of his bed, he stripped off his clothes and stepped into a pair of shorts, then moved a chair toward the window. Yes, he'd be as useless as tits on a boar at work tomorrow, but he'd survive. A little sleep deprivation wouldn't kill him as long as he knew his girl remained safe all night.

Your girl?

"I'm so fucked!" he drawled woefully.

Refusing to dissect the Freudian slip, he opened his window and took a seat on the chair. While he didn't have a clear angle of the backyard, Sawyer would be able to see if Bigfoot or the peeping prick stepped foot at the front of the house. Easing back, he began implementing his own style of covert stalking.

Night sounds of crickets, bullfrogs, and an occasional owl surrounded him as humanity fell silent. Four hours later, he glanced at the clock and scrubbed a hand over his face. Several blocks away, he heard the faint sound of a dog barking and straightened in his chair. He craned his neck as he slowly scanned Barbara's yard and front porch. The only things moving were the leaves on the trees. All appeared quiet, but the uneasiness inside him still stirred.

Sunlight warmed his face and jolted him awake. Blinking, Sawyer backed away from the blinding rays, cursing himself for falling asleep. He rolled his shoulders to work out the kink in his neck. Thankfully, he'd not dreamed about Brea, because his jeans weren't stuck to his crotch in a gooey mess.

"Get inside, you wild beast, and I'll fill your bowl with kibble."

Though he couldn't see her, the sound of Brea's voice made him smile. Ozzie scampered across the yard toward the deck, and Sawyer blew out a sigh of relief. The woman next door was alive and well. Making his way to the bathroom, he showered and readied for work. By six twenty-five, he was pulling out of the garage.

Next door on the wide white porch, Brea stood, hands on her hips and brows arched.

"Everything okay?" Sawyer called to her.

She nodded and smirked. "You forgot about breakfast, didn't you?"

Fuck!

He had and felt like an idiot.

"No," he lied and turned off the motor and climbed out of the truck.

She rolled her eyes, saying without words what Sawyer already knew.

He was... *busted!*

Inwardly dragging out the backhoe, he was prepared to do whatever it took to dig himself out. Still, if he wanted to gain her trust, he needed to be honest.

"Actually, yes. I did," he confessed sheepishly. "I figured since you weren't able to come to work with me, the offer might not still be on the table."

"It is on the table...all of it." Brea giggled. "Inside, mister. I've been slaving over a hot stove all morning. You stand me up, and Ozzie will have to eat it all. He'll probably end up barfing everywhere, too."

"Why? Are you that bad of a cook?" he teased.

She gasped, then sent him a mock scowl. "Bite me."

Brea turned on her heel and stormed inside the house. Of course, he followed, unable to wipe the grin from his face. Quickly stepping up behind her, he leaned in close to her ear.

"You keep talking dirty to me, and we'll both bypass breakfast, 'cause I'll be devouring you instead."

Brea's stride faltered slightly before she corrected her gait. Her cheeks were pink when she nodded toward the table laden with pancakes, bacon, eggs, fluffy, big biscuits, three different jars of jelly, and two steaming cups of coffee sitting beside two empty plates. If he hadn't known better, he would have sworn she'd taken cooking lessons from his mom. There was enough food to feed an army.

Sawyer let out a low whistle. "Damn, Brea. You've outdone yourself."

"Thank you." She preened as she sat down across from him. "Dig in before it gets cold."

After loading his plate, he dove in and discovered she was as good, if not a bit better, at cooking than his mom. The old adage, *the way to a man's heart is through his stomach*, was true. He was in love with her cooking, for sure.

Toot would have some stiff competition if Brea decided to stay and open a restaurant. But the greedy little boy inside him didn't want to share her culinary talents with the rest of the town…or any of her other talents, for that matter.

When he drew the coffee to his lips, the heat of the mug warmed them…warmed them the same way her mouth had last night.

Don't go there, fucker. You'll be late for work and…

A knock at the front door pulled Sawyer from his burgeoning carnal thoughts.

Brea hopped up from her chair as Ozzie let out a bark.

"Hang on." Sawyer stood. "Let me answer it."

"Brea, sweetheart. It's me," Colton called from the porch.

"Stand down, soldier," Brea giggled. "It's not Bigfoot."

"You can never be too safe."

"In Haven? Please."

If she was worried about a stalker, she didn't show it. Good. He didn't want her worrying… That was his job. But all the worry slid from his brain as he watched the seductive sway of her hips as she walked toward the door. His palms itched to touch her there, and every other warm, captivating place on her body and in her soul. But *Daddy* Colton had arrived and would be watching Sawyer's every move under a parental microscope. He'd be lucky to steal a kiss before leaving. Yeah, he didn't much like being a dog on a leash and restricted from behaving badly.

THOUGH SHE WAS always happy to see Colton, his timing, once again, was lousy. Brea felt cheated that her breakfast with Sawyer had been interrupted. Not that she'd planned to offer him anything but food. She wanted to prove to herself that she could find happiness in his platonic company without bedroom gymnastics involved. It was a baby step, but one she needed to achieve.

She invited Colton to join them for breakfast and nearly laughed at the disapproving scowl he aimed at Sawyer.

"Lighten up, Captain America. I didn't spend the night violating her in every deviant way known to man," Sawyer drawled, then added under his breath, "but I sure wanted to."

Colton's intimidating mien lifted and a crooked grin tilted his lips. "Can't blame me for making sure her virtue stays intact."

Sawyer dropped his fork. It clanged on his plate as Brea choked on her coffee. Slapping a napkin to her cover her mouth, she nearly shot coffee out her nose. Bolting from his seat, Sawyer slapped her on the back, asking her over and over again if she could breathe.

Nodding, she coughed out on a hoarse whisper, "I'm fine…I'm good.'"

After she'd regained her composure, she widened her eyes at Colton. "Don't say things like that. You almost killed me! My virtue hasn't been intact since the eighth grade, and you damn well know it."

"Who was the lucky guy?" Sawyer grinned.

"Billy Franklin," Colton supplied. "A scrawny, pimply-faced—"

"Hush!" Brea covered his mouth with her hand. "We are not waltzing down memory lane this morning."

"Why not?" Colton asked with a chuckle after he'd pried her

fingers away. "I think it's a cute story."

"Not another word." Fire danced in her eyes.

"You can tell me later, bro." Sawyer grinned. He loved watching her squirm in the hot seat.

"Who was your first?" she challenged Colton. "I bet you can't even remember her name."

"Of course I do," he answered wistfully. "Billy's sister, Brenda Mae Franklin. She was my first older woman too."

"Brenda Mae? My god, Colton! How old were you, five?" Brea gasped.

"No. I was fourteen," he replied indignantly.

It was Sawyer's turn to choke, but thankfully it wasn't on his coffee. "Damn. You started young."

"Who was your first?" Colton asked.

All the laughter drained from Sawyer's face. "Sara."

"You mean you were a virgin when you married her?"

Brea's heart nearly burst in her chest. *Married? He was married? Where the hell was Mrs. Grayson? Did she know about the skanky triplets from the hot tub?*

To her horror, Brea had nearly behaved exactly like those skanky bitches. She'd almost slept with a married man, too.

"No! You asked who was my first," Sawyer defended.

"You're…you're…You have a wife?" Brea sputtered as anger rose inside her like an island-eating tsunami.

"I did. I'm divorced."

His words had her caustic surge rolling back out to sea, yet the ground beneath her felt slightly eroded. Sawyer had survived the dreaded *Big D*. The second most terrifying curveball life could ever throw. The first, of course, being never finding your soul mate among the masses.

"I'm sorry." Brea reached across the table and softly cupped his hand.

"No need to be sorry, darlin'." He flashed her a smile that didn't quite reach his eyes. "It was a miserable existence. I'm much happier being free."

After several long seconds of awkward silence, he glanced at his watch and stood. "I need to get to work. I'll drop by this evening and make sure you're doing all right."

Brea followed Sawyer as he headed toward the door. She was about to tell him he didn't need to bother, but the thought of seeing him again filled her with such anticipation she bit her tongue.

"Thank you. If you'd like to stay for dinner, I'd be happy to cook again."

"You don't have to try and seduce me with your mouthwatering cooking. You're mouthwatering enough for me."

A thrilling rush rose up from her toes. Brea nervously licked her lips. If Colton hadn't been within earshot, she would have tossed Sawyer's gauntlet right back at him. Instead, she simply sent him an innocent shrug.

He issued a barely perceptible growl before settling his mouth close to her ear. "Dammit, woman. I'm going to be thinking about you in sexy lingerie and cheeseburgers the rest of the day."

"Good."

"Why is that good?"

"Because my imagination won't be the only one suffering."

"You get rid of Colton, and I'll call in sick." He waggled his brows. "We can torture each other in every naughty way, all day long."

She'd passed her test with flying colors, at least until now. But Brea was well on her way to getting a big, fat F if she didn't find her spine and tell him…

"Have a great day, Sawyer," Colton called from the kitchen.

Yeah…what her overprotective, pseudo-big brother just said.

After Sawyer left, Brea hurried back to the kitchen. She didn't want to stand at the window as he walked away, watching him like an abandoned puppy. Painting on a smile purely for Colton's benefit, she sat down and sipped her coffee.

"Don't sit there farting out rainbows and unicorns on my account. Talk to me."

The look of concern on Colton's face had her heart fluttering madly in her chest.

"What do you want to talk about?"

"About your fascination with Sawyer. You do know he's not a settling-down kind of guy, right?"

"I might be a special kind of snowflake, but I'm not stupid." Brea waved off his concern. "I love you dearly. But I don't need a daddy or a lecture. What I need are the holes in the wall patched, a new pane of glass, and Emmett's gun—or at least all his ammo confiscated. If that crazy old fart decides to pepper this place with buckshot again, I'm going that shove his gun where the sun dosen't shine."

"You're changing the subject."

"Damn right I am. I want five minutes not talking, thinking, or fantasizing about Sawyer. All right?"

"Fuck!" Colton closed his eyes and exhaled a long, heavy sigh.

"What?"

"You're already *that* obsessed with him? That's not good, Brea."

"I'm not acting on it, am I?"

She wasn't. At least not that very second...well, not too much.

"Only because he left. What are you planning to feed him for dinner...muff pie?"

"Nope. I can't. I don't have any hair down there."

Colton groaned and slapped a palm to his forehead. "Dammit, Brea. You're like my little sister. I did *not* need that visual."

"You asked." She shoved her hands on her hips. "It's not my fault you can't handle the answers. Maybe you shouldn't be asking such personal questions, sugar."

"I'm just trying to save you from being hurt."

"Don't. If I fall off the wagon and land cunt-first in a field of hard-ons, I'll climb out again, when I'm thoroughly sated. But trust me. My heart will be miles away from that field of dreams...locked in a lead vault. Feel better now?"

"Not one iota!"

She threw her hands up in the air. "What do you want me to do…super-glue my thighs together?"

"Would you?" He sounded far too excited at the prospect.

"No!" she snapped. "Stop. Now. You're pissing me off. I'm a grown woman."

He stood and rounded the table before wrapping her in a hug. Obviously thinking he'd change her mind if he changed tactics, Colton was too transparent for his own good.

"I'm not trying to rile you up, sweetheart," he began. "I just don't want to see you hurt again."

Okay, so maybe it worked…the man was killing her with kindness.

"I don't either. But I'm not a china doll. Life is full of hurt and disappointment. I can't live in a plastic bubble until I'm old and gray. I'm going to have to risk a few bumps and bruises." Brea gave him a tight squeeze before easing out of his grasp. "I'm grateful for your concern, but I have to find my own way down this new road. If I decide to let Sawyer join me for a couple miles, so what. I know he won't be walking beside me when I reach the end of my journey. Satisfied?"

"How can you be so sure?"

"Because he doesn't love me, and he doesn't want me moving in with him."

"And you know this…how?"

"I asked him."

Colton's mouth fell open. "You *asked* him?"

"I did. See? This old dog *is* learning new tricks. Now close your mouth, eat your breakfast, and then call the glass company, will ya?"

Though a million questions were swimming in the man's pretty blue eyes, Colton did as she instructed.

He called in a team of contractors. Brea played hostess, offering iced tea and sandwiches to the crews, and by late afternoon, Barbara's house looked like new. If Brea hadn't been present during last night's destruction, she'd have never suspected the place had been blown to hell and back.

After thanking Colton and waving good-bye, she raced upstairs and took a shower. She dried her hair and curled the ends, giving them both volume and a softness to frame her face. After applying a thin layer of makeup, she pulled on a sundress and sandals and added a spritz of perfume. Sawyer had only seen her at her worst. Brea wanted to let him glimpse her at her best…well, her best out of bed.

Brea hurried to the kitchen. She pulled a package of pork chops from the fridge and just as she started mixing a honey-soy sauce marinade, Ozzie began to bark. When she peered nervously around the corner, she saw neither Bigfoot nor a psycho-rapist was looking in the new window.

Then the doorbell rang.

Glancing at the clock, she saw it was four forty-five. Brea smiled, assuming Sawyer had left work early. She hurried to the door and pulled it open. The smile fell from her face. Terror raced through her veins as a stocky bald man wearing an evil grin pressed a gun to her chest and forced her backward.

Ozzie's hackles were raised from his neck all the way to his tail. He barked and snarled at the man.

"Put dog away, or I kill it," the man demanded in a thick Russian accent.

"Down, boy," Brea said in a quivering command. But Ozzie didn't obey.

The Russian thug pointed the gun at the dog. Brea panicked. As adrenaline pumped through her at the speed of light, she stepped in front of Ozzie. "Wait. Don't shoot him. Let me put him outside. He doesn't have to die."

"Do it." The man gripped Brea's hair and Ozzie went berserk.

"No! Down, boy!" Brea yelled.

Boris or Vladimir or whatever the intruder's name was, pulled her in close to his ugly, too-flat face. "You try to run, I shoot you in the back."

"I-I understand."

The gun-wielding thug shoved her away. Brea bent and clutched Ozzie's collar. Sending up a silent prayer that the beast actually did possess some intelligence, she dragged the still-snarling animal to the front door. The crazed Russian followed behind her, poking his gun into Brea's spine.

"Outside, Sawyer. Go outside and be a good boy, Sawyer."

It was a long shot, but she hoped that imprinting his name into Ozzie's psyche, the animal *might* go next door. But then again, the Doberman might just tear down the street, forsaking her last few minutes of life on his newfound freedom.

Even if—by some miracle—he went next door, Sawyer was probably still at the ranch. It could be minutes or hours before he returned home. Instead of a candlelit dinner for two, he'd find Brea's body—bloodied, beaten, raped, and tortured, on Barbara's glossy hardwoods.

Oh, god. Help me! Help me, please.

She shut the door and inhaled a ragged breath. "I don't have much money, but I'll give you what I've got. Just please…take it and leave. Don't hurt me."

The man began to laugh. It was a vile, gut-churning, and menacing chuckle. "Hurt you? No. You have my merchandise. Get it for me. Now."

"Merchandise? What merchandise? I don't know what you're—"

He drew his hand back and slapped her hard across the face. "Lying *pizda*!"

Lights exploded behind her eye. Pain seared up the side of her face. Wobbling as fringes of darkness clouded her vision, Brea feared she was going to pass out. Biting back a howl of pain and a scream of terror, she tasted blood…her own.

The vile maniac continued to talk, but only bits and pieces registered through the chaos of panic and pain consuming her.

"Don't lie again. Weed…"

Brea jerked her head at the mention of her ex.

"The *gluppy ukolot* called from jail. He tell me you have the merchandise. Get it for me or die."

Brea swallowed the bile rising up in her throat. Tears burned the backs of her eyes, and a wave of dizziness threatened to take her to her knees. *Weed.* This sack of monkey-spunk was a friend of Weed's? Whatever *gluppy ukolot* meant, it wasn't close to the names she was inwardly calling her dickless ex.

You'll be going down with me, baby!

His haunting words from jail rolled through her brain. She wanted to scream. She'd stupidly believed Weed had meant she'd be going to prison with him…not this. The motherfucker had set her up. Not only that, he'd told the scary Russian son of a bitch that she had his merchandise…drugs. When the prick found out Weed had lied to him and she didn't have his precious drugs, the drug lord would kill her…fast and quick. Or she could only hope.

A slow, evil smile curled the scary prick's lips. "I see in your eyes. You know what I talk about now. Yes?"

With her heart in her throat, Brea's mind raced like the speeding bullet that would soon explode from the barrel of his gun. The complete and utter terror coursing through her veins was a living, breathing beast.

Stall… You've got to stall this lunatic…somehow!

Brea tried to think of ways to buy some precious time.

If she pretended to look for his stash, it might buy her some time. Yet she'd only be prolonging the inevitable.

Either way, she was going to die.

She thought of offering the sociopath some milk and cookies…or belting out in song, complete with a few quirky dance steps and gyrating hip thrusts. Brea knew then that the synopses in her brain could not cope with the promise of her impending death. She'd gone off her rocker…completely and utterly come unhinged. She'd just cracked the fuck up!

"Bring bags. Now!"

"Bags? I-I don't—"

Shoving the barrel of the gun against her cheek, the batshit-crazy meth-daddy stole the words from her brain and tongue.

"You bring bags with you…here…yes?"

"Just the ones from…"

The closet! But there weren't any drugs in them. Brea had opened them…shaken them out for Detective Nickel. Whatever bags Weed had hidden this monster's drugs in, Brea didn't have them. They had to still be back in Denton.

"Get them. Or I kill you. Then tear place apart with my bare hands."

She had no choice but to give him the empty bags and pray he'd kill her quickly. She didn't want to be raped or tortured. But Brea was fairly certain the drug lord didn't give a shit what she wanted, especially after he discovered Weed had led the man on a wild goose chase.

A flash of something over the Russian's right shoulder caught her attention. She wasn't sure if it was a leaf or maybe Ozzie had wandered back onto the porch, but something had moved. An ember of hope flickered to flame, but she kept it hidden behind the neutral expression on her face…well, as neutral as unmitigated looked. To keep from glancing back at the window and alerting the drug-demanding Russian, Brea lowered her lashes and held her breath.

"Get bags or get down on knees."

Hell no! She was not going to help this prick kill her execution-style by assuming the position. Fuck that!

"They're up in my room," she explained with trembling lips. "Do you want to come with me or should I bring them down to you?"

"I follow you."

Brea nodded and forced herself to take a step toward the stairs. Her legs shook like a big girl's booty at an all-night rave.

When a knock came from the front door, she froze.

The gunman lowered his weapon to her ribs and moved in beside her.

"Don't answer," he snarled.

"If I don't answer, whoever it is might walk right in. This is a small town."

The man scowled at her words. "Okay. But tell them to go away. If they don't, I kill you both."

Placing her trembling fingers on the knob, she felt the Russian place the muzzle to her head before stepping in beside her, between the door and the wall. With her only means of escape now nestled in her palm, Brea was too petrified to throw open the door and run away. Fighting back tears, she opened the door a few inches to find Sawyer standing on the porch. She knew this would be the last time she'd ever have the chance to lay eyes on him. He smiled, but it was like ice. And when he darted a barely perceptible glance to his belt, Brea dropped her gaze to see a gun tucked in the waistband of his jeans.

He knew. Thank god! Sawyer knew she was in trouble.

"Hey, baby. You ready to go see that movie?"

"I'm sorry. I have a headache." She tried to sound contrite, but she was too busy darting her eyes to the right. She hoped he would understand that the Russian prick was standing next to her with a gun at her head.

"That's too bad," he replied through clenched teeth.

Sawyer raised his hand, fingers extended, as if intending to stroke her arm. But quick as lightning, he wrapped his arm around her waist and pulled her toward him while simultaneously kicking the door open.

Everything began to move in slow motion.

Tucking her behind him, Sawyer slammed his leg out straight, pinning the scary Russian to the wall with the front door. Ozzie raced under Sawyer's legs and inside. The dog barked viciously at the drug lord before leaping into the air and sinking his sharp teeth into the man's arm that held the gun. A shot rang out and Brea screamed.

"Sawyer?"

"I'm fine baby. I'm fine," he assured before bellowing encouragement to the dog. "Rip his arm off, Ozzie. Good boy! Bite him. Sink those big teeth into him!"

The Russian's high-pitched wails filled the air. The badass drug lord was screaming like a bitch. Sawyer pressed his back against the doorjamb and lifted his other leg, ensuring the would-be assassin remained firmly wedged in place. Ozzie didn't relent as his low, menacing growls joined the cacophony. But no amount of noise masked the thud when the Russian dropped his gun to the floor.

"Get that gun, love," Sawyer instructed with a grunt.

As Brea crawled beneath his leg and plucked the gun off the floor, a loud explosion rang out from the back of the house. She jumped to her feet and snapped her head toward the kitchen as Detective Estes raced into the living room. Blinking in shock, she zipped around to see Sawyer lower his legs as dozens of officers—with guns drawn—swarmed in through the front door.

"Call off the dog," Estes yelled above the screams and growls.

"Ozzie! Leave it," Brea commanded. With a snarl, the fuzzy hero let go.

Brea took a step back. The dog followed and sat at her feet like a sentinel, poised and ready to protect her again. She turned her head to see Sawyer handing his gun over to one of the cops before he lifted his chin and looked her way. He appeared shell-shocked. No doubt she was wearing the same combo of terror and relief. Sawyer was right there, clutching her to his chest in a death hold. She clung to him, trembling. Determined not to fall apart, she blinked back tears and simply held him.

"Christ, baby. I thought I was going to lose you," he said, his voice cracking.

Sawyer buried his face in the crook of her neck.

"Look at you, Yuri," Estes chided with an icy smile. "Big, bad Russian crime boss, drug lord, pimp, and all 'round social deviant...you just got taken down by a man, a woman, and a dog. Guess you kinda underestimated all three, now didn't you?"

The man began spitting in a language she didn't understand,

but the hatred in his eyes told her Yuri wasn't rattling off his family recipe for chicken Kiev.

"Are you all right?" Sawyer's voice was stronger, but his breathing was harsh, like hers, and his body continued to tremble, like hers.

There was no way she could keep her emotions in check and talk, so Brea simply nodded.

"Guess you shouldn't have left your comrades sitting with their thumbs up their asses in that Hummer down the street, huh?" Estes continued goading the man. "Don't worry, your buddies are cuffed and ready for transport with their *new* friends…the DEA, ATF, and FBI. But I bet they're going to love the shit out of hearing how we found you…crying like a little boy."

Yuri's face turned red before unleashing a new string of foreign words in the same vicious tone. Estes dismissed the man with a wave of his hand before nodding to one of the officers. "Cuff him and get him out of here. The FBI can decide how or if they want to deal with his arm."

Brea had managed to keep her shit wired tight until she heard the snick of handcuffs. Knowing the monster could no longer hurt her, she felt a wave of emotions careening through her and sucking her down into an inky-black abyss.

She was shivering like a naked Floridian in Alaska as tears spilled from her eyes and mournful wails bubbled up from deep in her throat. Sawyer swept her up into his arms before cradling her like a baby on the couch. She buried her head against his chest, gripped his shirt in her fists, and fell completely apart.

"It's okay, my love. I've got you. You're safe. It's all over," he cooed as he gently rocked her back and forth.

Heart pounding like a herd of wild horses, she sobbed inconsolably against Sawyer as bits and pieces of conversations going on around her flitted through her head. Yuri Orlov, FBI's most wanted, methamphetamines, duffle bags, prison, Weed, Colton, Jade. The bits and pieces plucked from the air confused her even more. Brea pushed them away until the words melded to indecipherable static. Encased in the steely heat of Sawyer's protection, she closed her eyes and let his reassuring whispers carry her mind away.

When she lifted her eyelids again, Jade and Colton—wearing worried expressions—were kneeling on the floor in front of her.

Officers and plain-clothed detectives paraded through the house, sending a sickly déjà vu to crawl beneath her flesh.

"There's our girl." Colton sent her a weak smile.

"Welcome back, darlin'," Sawyer drawled, pressing a kiss to her head. "I'm glad you decided to come back to me."

As her terror-induced fugue began to clear, Brea lifted her head and frantically searched the room for Yuri.

"He's gone, on his way to Denton, then to a federal holding facility in Houston."

She found a wealth of comfort in the information Sawyer imparted, but a million times more simply wrapped in his rugged arms.

"Bingo! Found it, boss. They were hidden in a false bottom." The announcement came from a suited detective standing in the kitchen, next to the table that held Brea's duffle bags. With a knife in one hand, the man plucked packets of white powder from the totes with the other.

A strangled cry slid from her lips. Weed *had* hidden drugs in her bags. But worse, he'd sent a Russian drug lord to retrieve them. Her ex didn't give two shits whether Brea died or not. The miserable sack of shit had set her up.

She felt beyond stupid and totally used.

Suddenly, Sawyer's soothing arms were as painful as thousands of knives cutting into her skin. Logically, she knew he was nothing like her ex and probably never would be...

Probably.

That was the kicker. She wasn't positive, because she'd lost faith in her own judgment and didn't have a clue how to regain her confidence again. Brea wanted to crawl inside a hole and give up. Not on life but on finding her happy ever after. Trusting men with your heart was dangerous, but they never bothered to tell girls that…at least not in fairy tales.

CHAPTER NINE

THE MORNING SUN warmed Sawyer's back as he stood on Barbara's deck sipping coffee. Brea and Jade were still inside sleeping. Colton had taken off before dawn to care for his cattle but promised to return as soon as possible. The three of them had kept an all-night vigil in Brea's room, watching her sleep and gently waking her when numerous nightmares came calling.

Now, as Ozzie ran and marked several trees in the backyard, Sawyer's heart tightened. If it hadn't been for the smart mutt, Brea might have…

Stop! You've ripped your guts out thinking the same thing all night. Give it a rest.

But he couldn't.

The realization of what might have happened had he not spotted Ozzie running free and called him back to take him inside Barbara's had played in his head for hours. Sawyer's stomach knotted. His heart raced at the memory of seeing that Russian prick holding a gun to Brea's head. Seeing the blood on her lip and the bright red handprint where he'd slapped her blazing across her porcelain face. He'd wanted to raze the fucking house with his bare hands to save her.

Thank god, Weed—the prick-assed bastard—had decided to grow a conscience and call Estes after telling Yuri where to find Brea and his drugs. The fact that her *ex* had been tracking her via her cell phone fueled Sawyer's anger to a bloodthirsty level. Though he and Ozzie had managed to save her, the cavalry showing up when they had was a relief. Not because he wasn't planning to put a bullet through Yuri's head; he was, but now he didn't have to clean the man's gray matter off Barbara's walls.

When the danger was over, her soulful eyes filling with tears had told him she was sliding down into a bleak chasm. The only thing he could do was hold her and promise that everything would be okay.

Thankfully, it'd played out the way it had, but Sawyer couldn't stop thinking about what might have happened, had it all backfired and…

Again. Knock it off, asshole.

Yuri Orlov was now sitting at the Federal Detention Center in Houston awaiting trial. Brea was safe…or at least Sawyer hoped so. Weed was now out on bail, but God help the fuck-knuckle if he ever showed his face in Haven. It would be his last mistake, because Sawyer would make sure the prick's body was never found.

Of course, the only way he could truly keep Brea safe would be to keep her joined at his hip, or preferably, his cock. But he'd play hell convincing her of that. Especially after the heart-to-heart he and Colton had in the wee hours of this morning. Sawyer finally understood the reason for her bizarre questions the night Emmett had blown out the window.

That had only been two nights ago…when he'd sworn he wasn't in love with her. He couldn't make that claim today—he'd uncovered that morsel of honesty around four this morning. Knowing she might never share more with him than a one-night stand shredded his soul. It was either irony or Murphy's Law that he'd finally found a woman he'd risk waking up with every day only to discover a major roadblock in the way—Brea's journey of self-discovery was just beginning.

Somehow…someway, Sawyer had managed to piss the royal fuck out of Karma.

"Mind if I join you?"

Brea's soft voice surrounded him like a blanket of cotton. When he turned, she stood near the door, mug of coffee in hand as the morning breeze stirred her long, dark hair.

The woman was a fucking goddess.

A temptress.

And sadly, a lost soul so thoroughly broken he didn't know how to put her back together. But Sawyer would find a way. Yes sirree. Even if it took super glue, duct tape, and a soldering iron, he'd repair every splintered shard of her delicate soul. Because she was worth it...worth every painstaking, frustrating, perplexing, sassy-assed moment he shared with her.

Sawyer held out his hand. Brea hesitated and finally took it before he led her to a padded chair at the table. Ozzie, who'd been sniffing out every square inch of lawn, leapt to the deck and sat down by her feet. Brea reached out and rubbed his ears, praising the courageous Doberman once more for how brave he was and how proud he should be.

Tiny frown lines lay at her mouth and between her brows. She had something on her mind...something he suspected he wouldn't want to hear. Taking a seat across from her, he patiently waited for her to speak.

"I appreciate everything you, Colton, and Jade have done for me. Last night was rough. I'm not going to lie. It meant a lot having you all upstairs with me. Today is a new day, and I'm putting the events of last night and years of mistakes behind me. I'm ready to move on. I guess what I'm trying to say is that you all can go back to your regularly scheduled lives. I'm going to be just fine."

She was obviously trying to convince herself that, after one fitful night of sleep, she'd miraculously bounced back. That she could sweep her harrowing ordeal yesterday and every shitting game the fuckers before him had played on her right under the rug.

Sawyer certainly wasn't buying any of it.

"Is that so?" Keeping his eyes locked with hers, he let the question hang in the air and took a sip of coffee.

Brea grew nervous at his pointed silence. "Yes. You all have lives and can't hang around day and night watching Barbara's gardens grow, now can you?"

"That's not what we're doing, and you know it."

She ducked her head. "No. You're babysitting a grown woman whose perpetual reckless decisions finally came back and bit her in the ass."

"You had nothing to do with Wee—that fuck-monkey setting you up." Sawyer slammed his fist on the table.

Brea recoiled in her chair, causing Ozzie to jump to his feet and bare his teeth at Sawyer in warning.

"Easy, boy. He's not going to hurt me."

"That's the first honest thing I've heard you say since I met you."

Her incredulous look morphed into a glare meant to incinerate him on the spot.

"Name one time I've *ever* lied to you."

"It's not me you're lying to, darlin'… it's yourself."

"I have no idea what you're talking about." She tossed her nose in the air and studied the cloudless sky. Thank fuck Weed and Yuri hadn't destroyed her stubborn spirit…the one Sawyer loved bantering with. He couldn't help but inwardly smile.

"You think giving up men is going to automatically make your life nothing but rainbows and kittens." She opened her mouth to argue, but Sawyer simply held up his hand. "Let me finish. Men aren't the problem…the caliber of men you associate with is…excluding me, of course."

She rolled her eyes and scoffed. "Is that so? I wasn't aware you were a shrink."

"I'm not. But in the short time I've known you, I've seen a million different sides of you. Brea, you're like a diamond. I've never met a more multi-faceted, frustrating, and fascinating woman than you. And any man who can't see you in all your glory and beauty is either blind or brain-dead. Trust me, darlin'. I'm neither."

"I think that's the most backhanded compliment—well, I'm assuming it's a compliment—that I've ever heard."

"Let me put it another way. I was wrong to try and get in your pants, not because I don't ache for you...lord knows I do, night and day. But I want more than your body. I want to crawl inside your mind...until I know everything about you. Because when I get you beneath me, and I *will* have you beneath me, we are going to share the same air...body...and heart. Do you understand what I'm saying?"

Her little gasp was barely audible, but he heard it. Taking her breath away filled him with pleasure almost as much as the timid nod she gave him.

"Good. I have a little proposition for you." Sawyer leaned in and rested his elbows on the table. "I'd like you and Ozzie to come and spend a few weeks at the ranch with my folks."

"I can't do that."

"Why not?"

"I have to take care of Barbara's place...her gardens. Besides, your parents have enough on their plate with the kids. They don't need another woman and a dog under foot. No. I can't." She adamantly shook her head.

"They're the ones who suggested it."

"When?"

"Last night. Mom texted me. She was worried about—"

"Wait. How did your mom find out... Never mind, I know. Haven is an ISP all its own."

"Yes, it is. In fact, before they'd finished reading that scumfuck, Yuri, his rights, half the town had gathered outside the house."

"Oh, god," she moaned. "I wasn't paying attention to—"

"Anything but what you needed to be...the sound of my voice."

A flicker of recollection lit her eyes briefly before she snuffed it out.

"Thank you for that. I don't remember if I told you last night, but I'm grateful that you and Ozzie saved my life."

Her phrases were beginning to sound more and more like a

kiss-off. Sawyer wasn't about to sit idly by and let her shove him out the door. It was time to change things up a bit.

He flashed her his most dazzling smile. "All in a day's work for a superhero."

When the corners of her mouth kicked up, it was worth the price of such a cheese-dick line.

"So you secretly wear a cape and tights?"

"Cape yes, but no tights…they chafe my balls."

A throaty laugh rolled off her lips and sent his pulse skipping like a five-year-old down an uneven sidewalk. God, he wished he were still as guileless as a kid, especially where Brea was concerned. But life had left him with skinned elbows and knees. Sawyer had learned to tread more carefully now.

"So what do you think about packing a bag and letting my family put you to work? Ozzie will come with us and we'll drive back each night and water the gardens."

She didn't answer. Instead, she cocked her head and stared at him intently. "What does working on the ranch have to do with you crawling inside my head?"

Ah, she was a perceptive little wench.

"Well, if you come to the ranch, we'll be working together. Not only do I get to keep you safe but we can spend time together." He didn't want to mention yet that he'd be staying the nights there as well. "It'll give us the chance to do what we're doing now—get to know one another before we move on to bumpin' bellies."

There it was again, that sultry laugh that sent his testosterone surging.

"I've never done that…started a relationship off as friends, I mean," she shyly confessed.

Sawyer stood and circled the table. Taking her hand, he helped her to her feet as that crazy current she always roused zapped him clear down to his boots. In time, he planned to do more than bump bellies with this woman. He planned to rock her world clean off its foundation.

He pulled her against him and drank in the warmth of his freshly wakened kitten. "No time like the present to start. I aim to teach you what no man ever has before… how to love yourself."

And hopefully…eventually, how to love me back.

"I love myself," she protested. "I just make really bad decisions."

"Not anymore."

"Are you always so sure of yourself?"

"Most times."

Liar.

"Well, some of the time," he amended. "Mostly, I just do what everyone else does…muddle through this thing called life."

She nibbled her bottom lip for long seconds, then sent him a mischievous smile. "Only if you promise to wear the cape *and* the tights for me from time to time."

She stole the rest of his heart then and there. If she never loved him back, Sawyer was totally fucked.

Three hours later, his truck loaded with woman, dog, and a borrowed suitcase from Barbara's closet, Sawyer pulled down the gravel drive of his childhood home. The campers and staff didn't pay much attention to their arrival, but the family certainly did. His mom hurried to the truck wearing a warm, welcoming smile. Only Sawyer could see the depth of worry and concern shimmering in her green eyes.

"Brea, it's so good to finally meet you." Nola hugged the girl tightly. "I'm so sorry you had to go through such a horrific ordeal. Come…let's get you in out of this hot sun and up to the house, where you can relax. I'll get you both something cold to drink."

Ozzie barked, startling some of the children. But when Nola bent and rubbed his ears, his tongue lolled out, and the young campers wary expressions softened.

"And you…you good boy for saving the day…I'll get you a big bowl of water and some special treats," she gushed over the dog.

Sawyer plucked Brea's suitcase from the back of the truck and sent her a sheepish grin. "You'll have to excuse my mom. She's always like this with company."

"Don't go excusing me, young man," Nola scolded with a fake scowl. "I only aim to make Brea feel at home, something you should be doing as well."

The wind danced through Brea's hair as she nervously glanced between him and Nola. It was as if Brea had never seen mother and child playfully banter before. Maybe she hadn't. That curiosity only made him more determined to learn all he could about her.

"I'll meet you two in the kitchen," Nola announced before heading toward the house.

"Shall we?" Sawyer grinned.

Brea nodded shyly.

"You dog! You dirty, rotten, no-good, monkey-humpin' mongrel!" Noble bellowed as he jogged toward them. "How the hell did you already beat me to her?"

Brea blinked in startled surprise.

"You snooze, you lose, bro." Sawyer preened. He draped his arm around Brea's shoulders and drew her in close to his side.

"I should have known by the way you were stalking her that first night."

"Stalking?" Brea asked, brows arching up high.

"Yep. Old Sawyer here was scoping you out from across the street when you first came to town. Please, pardon my manners. I'm Noble...*I'm* the better brother." He bent in a ridiculously deep bow.

"Better at what?" Brea chuckled.

"Don't ask!" Sawyer warned before the conversation took a nosedive to the sexually awkward.

"Ditch this washed-up limp-noodled brother of mine, and I'll show you." Noble winked with a suggestive grin.

"Give it a rest, Noble." Sawyer moved in close and lowered

his voice. "You couldn't get laid at a clusterfuck."

"You son of a—"

"Ah, ah, ah," Sawyer interrupted. "Little ears are in camp. You know the rules."

"Do all you Grayson brothers look alike?" Brea chuckled.

"Which other brothers of mine have you met?" Sawyer asked.

Before she could reply, his father's deep voice speared the air. "Noble! A little help over here?"

"Don't get your heart set on this one until you get to know me." Noble sent Brea a playful wink.

"Go back to work," Sawyer grumbled.

Noble grumbled something under his breath as he turned and jogged away.

Relaxing at the kitchen table, sipping tea, Sawyer couldn't miss the shrewd looks his mom darted his way. Like a bloodhound, Nola had picked up the scent that he was more than just interested in Brea. He couldn't keep from grinning. Interrogation time would be starting real soon.

After settling Brea into the guest room, Sawyer took her on a tour of the ranch. He introduced her to the campers, especially Tina. The little sprite had done to Brea exactly what she had him…stolen his heart. Sawyer hoped that in moving his girl in with the family, the change of environment might lessen the emotional strain of Yuri and Weed. He hoped it would help ease his own fears as well.

It was well past midnight. Sawyer sat in the kitchen nursing a beer and warring with his increasing hunger for Brea when his mother came in and sat down beside him.

With a gentle smile, she patted the back of his hand. "How long are you going to wait, dear boy?"

"Wait for what?"

"To tell her you're in love with her?"

"Mom, I'm—"

"Don't try and lie to me, Neville. I see the way you look at her, and the way she looks at you."

He gave his mom a crooked grin. "I was going to say…I'm waiting."

"For what?"

"For her to trust herself and me."

"Oh, I see. Trust can be a booger. But don't wait too long. Life is short. Maybe she needs to believe she's found someone worthy of giving her trust to."

He chuckled. "She just might at that."

Three days later, Sawyer stood near the shelter house that served as the craft center. Brea was helping the campers pack their pumpkin plants into small paper bags. A trail of potting soil was smeared over her forehead. She was amazing. Not only had she taught the kids limited horticulture but she'd revealed yet another side of herself to him. Brea was patient and nurturing with the kids. It warmed his heart and other places—namely his dick. Both were growing increasingly restless and frustrated. Sawyer wanted more. Fuck, he wanted it all with Brea.

After dinner was through and the kitchen cleaned up, he left Brea at his folk's, playing a bawdy fill-in-the-blank card game. As promised, he drove back to his house, watered Barbara's gardens, then went inside his own house. Climbing the stairs to his room, Sawyer's mind was already fixating on spending another restless night at the ranch with his tempting woman across the hall. The only thing stopping him from sneaking into her room to live out all his deviant dreams with the girl was fear of being caught in the act by his mom.

Stripping off his clothes, he lost himself and his load fantasizing about Brea in the shower. Self-pleasure was nothing but a hollow, temporary relief that did nothing to lessen the lurid spell Brea had cast upon him.

Gazing at her as she helped the children, his cock stirred.

"What if my pumpkin dies?" Charlie, a little boy struggling with leukemia, arched a quizzical stare at Brea.

Cocking her head, she studied the young man. "Then we'll bury it near the creek and put flowers on top of its grave.

Everyone will remember how valiantly it struggled to live strong and grow old."

The boy sent her a solemn nod. "Just like me."

Brea clenched her jaw. Unshed tears glistened in her eye as she gave Charlie a resolute nod. Sawyer swallowed the lump of emotion lodged in his throat.

The family and staff grasped the children's struggles. Everyone dealt with the powerful emotions the kids evoked in their own ways. But for a novice—an outsider, like Brea—to grasp the gravity of their life-and-death battles, rocked him to the core. She didn't disregard or candy-coat their fears but met them head on with compassion and kindness. She gave each child the gift of dignity and promise—the embodiment of Camp Melody.

She glanced his way and he sent her a warm smile.

Fuck, how could he not love the woman?

IN BREA'S HEART, the past few days had been nothing short of magical. Sawyer's brothers were a rowdy bunch, ceaselessly busting each other's balls, but the whole clan thrived on happiness and shared a palpable love that Brea envied.

She'd barely given thought to her ordeal that had brought her to the ranch. But that was mostly thanks to Sawyer. He'd been a constant, supportive friend, and her feelings for him were growing in leaps and bounds. Of course, her sexual attraction to the man had increased as well. Every time their eyes met, he either undressed her with a carnal stare or fixed her with a look of trust and understanding. He was forever giving her a silent promise she couldn't ignore. And just when she thought he'd haul her to the barn and wreck her beneath a myriad of screaming O's, he'd simply wink and flash her that dazzling smile—the one that made her pulse race and her stomach cartwheel.

Her pent-up cravings for the man were driving her insane. She ached for him to touch her. Not like he'd been doing…not the gentle stroke of her cheeks or a rugged arm around her waist. Brea wanted him to get down and dirty in her lady garden and lay some damn seed.

As the guests began boarding busses to leave, she noticed Sawyer off to the side, sitting on the ground beside Tina. Tears spilled down the little girl's cheeks, and a look of sadness was etched on his face. Brea's heart squeezed as she watched him gently wipe the girl's tears away and place a tender kiss on her forehead. The poignant sight filled Brea with such emotion that she could barely breathe.

For a man who'd been nothing but a royal pain in her ass, conjuring embarrassment, anger, and a level of lust that singed her flesh, he was a steadfast protector. Sawyer had proved over and over again that he was a man she could count on. A man she'd grown to trust.

Trust? Have you gone completely insane? Every man you've ever trusted has ripped your damn heart out and stomped it in dirt!

Yes, indeed they had. Because she'd been foolish enough to arbitrarily hand them something they'd never deserved…never earned. Sawyer had gone above and beyond for her, and still, Brea lacked faith in her own judgment. Going from the frying pan into the fire terrified her.

"Brea!" Sawyer called. She turned as he and Tina walked toward her. "Someone wants to say good-bye."

The little girl's eyes were rimmed red, but she put on a brave smile and opened her arms. Brea dropped to her knees and hugged Tina with all her might. "You do as the doctors say so I can see you again next year."

"You mean…you'll be here next time I come?"

Will you? Or will you continue to run from one relationship to the next, becoming so jaded and cynical no man will ever want to waste his time with you?

Jade's words rolled through her head: *You should stay here in Haven. Find a job and settle down, close to Colton and me. It's not a bad thing to have friends around in case you need them, and we'll always be here for you.*

Brea darted a glance up at Sawyer. He wore a cocky quizzical expression, one that dared her to make a commitment. He'd donned that infuriating, royal-pain-in-her-ass attitude of his again. Brea wanted to growl. How any man could go from compassionate to infuriating in the blink of an eye, like Sawyer, boggled her mind.

She lifted her chin and sent him a smirk of her own. "I'm certainly going to try, Tina. If Sawyer wants to keep me…on at the ranch, that is."

Surprise gave way to a look of relief. "I plan on keeping you a whole lot more than you can imagine."

His unexpected declaration sent a ribbon of hope to unfurl inside her. A rush of something almost dreamlike blossomed in its wake. Anticipation hummed through her system. She felt as if something spectacular waited on the horizon.

She tried to bank the sensations. Expectation and trust were dangerous bedfellows, yet Brea couldn't shove away the sparkling sensations bubbling up inside her. A little voice in the back of her head told her that—this time—she didn't need to.

As the last bus pulled away, Sawyer sent her a proud smile. "You're amazing."

The heat of pride warmed her cheeks.

Newton called everyone to the deck for the weekly post-evaluation. Brea tried to focus on the man's words, but the enticing heat rolling off Sawyer beside her was more than a mammoth distraction. His sweaty masculine musk, laced with the sweetness of leather and hay, was more than a diversion. She couldn't think of anything other than sliding her tongue over his salty skin, and lower…to the much saltier treasure inside his jeans. Images of riding him harder than Thunderbolt at Churchill Downs careened through her head. Fuck booze. Being within five feet of the man turned her into a raving nymphomaniac. Sawyer was her own private tequila.

When the meeting was over, all but immediate family departed. "Y'all wash up. Dinner will be ready in twenty minutes."

"What are we having?" Nate asked.

"Roast."

"Hell yeah," Noble cheered.

When the family raced inside, Sawyer wrapped his arm around Brea's waist and pulled her to his chest. As he pressed his lips to her ear, his moist breath made her tingle. "What's got you so turned on? I can smell your spice and it's driving me crazy."

Heat flooded her cheeks. "You."

"Let's go."

"Where?"

"Home."

Brea pivoted and blinked up at him. "What about Ozzie?"

"He'll be fine. My family will spoil him proper."

"But your mom. She's expecting—"

"She won't mind. Dad and my brothers will be happy. It means more food for them."

He took her hand and pulled her behind him as they raced to his truck. The thrill cresting through her washed away the doubts as they tried to burrow their way inside her head.

Not a word was spoken until Sawyer stopped at the end of the long gravel drive. Turning, he stared into her eyes with a fire so bright it nearly sent Brea up in flames as well. "Your man ban is over, darlin'. We're going to put this fire out between us, even if it means we won't walk straight for a week. Understood?"

Her mouth went dry. Her heart hammered loud and strong. This was it. No more waltzing around the inevitable. Anticipation and anxiety merged in a kaleidoscope that short-circuited her brain. She was ready to *put this fire out* between them, too.

She didn't care if she was making a colossal mistake. Like she had with the others before, she'd learn to live with the consequences…if and when it came to that.

"Yes," she whispered softly.

She lowered her lashes, and the massive bulge of Sawyer's jeans had her pussy melting. Sawyer turned onto the paved road and Brea threw decorum out the window. Bending down, she began to work his belt buckle free.

"What are you doing?" Sawyer moaned.

"Getting this party started."

"Not yet." He gripped a fist in her hair and lifted her head. Glancing down at her face, he clenched his jaw. "We're going to start it in the shower with me soaping up every inch of your creamy, smooth skin. Then we'll move our way to the sink if we can't make it to the bedroom. I'm going to set you on the marble top and nibble on your hot little pussy, just like an appetizer. Then once I get you spread out on my bed, I'm going to devour you like Thanksgiving dinner…eat my fill of you until you're mindless."

A harder, more intense tremor shook her to the core…her dripping-wet and ready core. But Sawyer was out of his mind if he thought she was just going to lie back and take all that clit-throbbing pleasure. She was going to give as good as she got.

"Only if I can return the favor, cowboy."

Sawyer chuckled. "If you're able."

"Oh, I'm more than able. I'm going to rock your world."

"I don't doubt that for a second. But just remember, I'm going to rock yours, too."

"You already do," she confessed.

Sawyer pushed down on the gas pedal as Brea giggled. Like a bullet, they reached Haven in a few short minutes and were pulling into his driveway seconds later.

He hopped out of the truck and sent her a look of warning. "Don't touch that door handle. I'm a gentleman."

Brea blinked, then grinned. No man had ever opened a car door for her. But she was dealing with a whole new breed. It made her feel special…pampered. Definitely out of the norm.

They'd barely made it through the front door before Sawyer had her pressed up against the wall, lips latched on to hers, and his busy hands tearing at their clothes.

Suddenly, he reared back. "Dammit, I'm sorry."

"Sorry?" she gasped, then scowled. "Oh, no, you don't! You can't stop now."

"I wasn't going to. But I need to slow down. I didn't want to go at you, pawing you bare and driving inside you like some crazed animal."

"Maybe I like a little monkey sex," she teased.

"True, but I want to seduce you."

"You do that just by breathing!"

"Oh, really?" His voice dropped and a crooked smile tugged the corner of his mouth.

"Yes. I want to paw you naked every time you look at me the way you are now."

He cupped her face and slowly, methodically, he brushed her lips with his. Teased them with the tip of his tongue before nibbling on her mouth. His hands skimmed over her, leaving an arousing trail of fire. The heat rising inside her was almost unbearable, but she'd gladly suffer as long as he wanted to hold her to the flame.

Their kiss grew more urgent…more intense…more igniting. She couldn't protect her heart as Sawyer was stealing it from the inside out. A week ago she'd have been terrified and turned tail to run. But not now. Now she was determined to find a way to be strong and secure. Come heaven or hell, even if the cost was her heart or soul…or both, she was going to fuck this man's brains out.

He inched his hands down the front of her jeans and pulled from her lips. "Damn, you're wet."

Brea couldn't help but softly laugh. "And that surprises you why?"

"Not surprised, and not quite sure how it's possible, but it turns me on even more. Fuck, Brea…you drive me crazy."

"Good crazy or Emmett crazy?" she taunted.

She loved that he didn't try to hide the urgency inside him. She felt the very same.

After gliding his lips down her neck and up to her ear, Sawyer nipped the lobe as his ragged breath sent goose bumps peppering her skin. "If I don't get you naked soon, I'm going to make Emmett look sane, darlin'."

Brea lolled her head to the side, granting him more access. "We don't want that, now do we?"

"No, baby...I only want you."

Every syllable of his silky voice touched her soul like a soft caress. Her own breath turned shallow as hunger and need thrummed through her. As he teased her with his lips, teeth, and tongue, she made quick work of the buttons on her shirt. When she tossed it to the floor, Sawyer scooped her breasts from her bra. As he sucked one aching, hard nipple into his mouth, Brea arched, offering herself up to his every pleasure...and hers. He laved his tongue in slow, precise circles while his strong, calloused hands caressed her fiery flesh.

Sawyer was effortlessly drawing every ounce of pleasure from her body, and Brea wanted him to drain her dry.

She was awed by the reverent way he bathed her breasts and skimmed her body with such a tender and compelling touch, and the walls around her gave way and crumbled at her feet. Brea's fears and doubts...her past, her future...no longer existed. There was only here...and now—and each precious moment of time was measured by the sublime gift of Sawyer.

Gripping his head, she held on as he paid homage to her other breast with the same spine-bending attention. Laving, licking, and sucking, he spiraled her into another dimension of desire. And he was only at her breasts! God help her when he moved that talented mouth lower; she'd melt into a slick, gooey puddle on the floor.

Oh, but what a glorious way to go.

CHAPTER TEN

B REA'S RAGGED GASPS of pleasure were unmitigated torture. Her fingernails scraping his scalp had him nearly crawling out of his skin. But Sawyer was determined to take his time and bask in every succulent second even though his dick was stretched so tight it threatened to burst his flesh *and* the seam of his jeans.

He'd known the blazing attraction they shared would be combustible, but this…this was hotter than Satan's ball sweat. The fires of hell weren't as scorching as the blood bubbling in his veins.

Keeping his lust on a leash was like wrestling a man-eating tiger. He couldn't wait to sink his teeth into her and eat the living fuck out of her. But she was more than a willing victim to slake his carnivorous lust. This was Brea—the fragile and broken, sassy and combative, incredible and precious woman who'd sparked his cold, dead heart back to life.

Sawyer didn't want just her body, he wanted her soul…wanted to heal her scars and teach her how love was supposed to feel.

Dropping his hands to her hips, he gripped her tight against his rigid erection. A guttural moan slid from her throat, and Sawyer paused his attention on her perfectly pert nipple. Lifting his head, he drew close to her mouth, breathing in her blissful sigh. Then he kissed her with a rabid craving coiling so tightly inside him until she trembled in his arms.

He pulsed to be wedged balls deep inside her molten core, yet Sawyer couldn't break his claim of her soft, hot mouth. He wanted to spend weeks, months, and years exploring every slick, swollen inch of her. But he already knew, no amount of time would be enough to ever sate his fervent hunger for her.

Lifting one hand, he cupped her neck and tilted her head, granting him the right angle to delve his tongue deeper. He'd do the same with her hips soon and bury himself to the base of his stalk inside her.

As if sensing his thoughts, she lifted her leg and draped it around his thigh. In silent invitation, she opened herself up for him. Everything became more potent and real.

The demand to rip away the barrier of clothing between them grew urgent. It was as if their thoughts had melded as one as the sound of Brea's zipper coming undone echoed in his ears. His tenuous grip of control snapped. Tearing away from her mouth, Sawyer inched back. With both of them panting breathlessly, he stared at the flush of desire staining her flesh...watched as she wiggled the tight denim off her hips.

Brea sent him a quirky smile. "This is the part where you're supposed to strip, too."

"What...and miss this pretty show you're putting on for me? Not on your life."

"Good god, you *are* a perv, aren't you?"

"Oh, yeah," he drawled seductively. "And I plan to show you just how much."

"Then you'd better start using those lips for something besides talking."

"I'll happily oblige." The playful smile induced by their banter slid from his face. He reached up and gripped a fist in her hair. His voice dipped to a raspy whisper. "Get those jeans off and spread your legs."

Fire leapt in her eyes and he heard her swallow. She'd be swallowing every inch soon. He inhaled sharply, filling his senses with the heavy perfume of her cunt. Sawyer needed to quench his thirst before he'd let her fall to her knees. His gaze locked to the triangle of ivory satin barely covering her thatch of dark curls.

"Um, I haven't taught it to do any tricks if that's what you're waiting for," Brea chuckled.

Sawyer jerked his head up. "Huh?"

"My pussy…you know, the one you're staring at. It doesn't do any tricks. But my tongue knows a few." The playful light twinkling in her eyes made him grin.

"So does mine, darlin'."

"Thank god," she exhaled.

Sawyer meant to squat to the floor, but his cock was so thick and hard there was no more give in his jeans. Yanking off his boots, he shucked off his shirt, then made quick work of scrambling out of his pants. The second his erection burst free, he let out a sigh of relief.

"Oh. My. God." Brea's mouth hung open. Her eyes were glued to his dripping cock.

Yeah, he was blessed with a big dick. In fact, all the Grayson brothers had been. Growing up, they'd skinny-dipped in the creek behind the house. Sawyer never gave a thought about the size of his junk. Not until the first shower after gym class, in junior high. Compared to the other boys' hot dogs, his was a salami. So concerned and self-conscience, he'd sought out his older brother, Ned, to ask if something was wrong with them. The man had laughed and shaken his head, then assured Sawyer that someday he'd be damn glad the Lord had blessed them in such a way.

Today was definitely one of those days.

"Something wrong?" He grinned as her mouth remained agape.

"Where… How… Was that anaconda shoved in your jeans this whole time?"

"Yes, but it was rather painful."

"Oh, my," she murmured. "I'll have to kiss it and make it all better then."

Before she could inch down the wall to her knees, Sawyer splayed his palm on her stomach, anchoring her in place.

"Ah, ah. Not yet. My turn first."

"What happened to ladies first? I thought you were a gentleman?"

"I am. That's why you're first…the first to shatter."

When a tiny shiver slid through her, Sawyer felt her stomach muscles bunch beneath his hand. She was already contracting, clutching at nothing but air. Dropping to his knees, he gripped her thighs and spread them apart, ready to fill the void inside her. He pressed his nose against the scrap of satin and inhaled deeply. Her heady, moist heat surrounded him like a mask. As he snaked his tongue over the fabric's edge, Brea whimpered. When he teased her, drawing the tip up the middle of her thong, she moaned. The faint taste of her nectar teased his taste buds and invaded his system like a drug. He'd need detox and rehab before the night was through.

Snarling, Sawyer reached up and ripped the barrier away. Brea let out a strangled sound…something between a moan and a chuckle. "I'll buy you more panties."

His eyes were fixed on the shock of dark curls in his face. The heat of her core enveloped his fingers as he raked them through her soft curls. Using his thumbs, he spread her glossy lips open and groaned.

Wet.

Pink.

Swollen.

Mine!

Sawyer's mental claim of Brea rocked him to his core. Never before—not with Sara, and certainly not with the kinky trio—had the primitive necessity to possess a woman seized him in such a way.

"Oh, god. Please, Sawyer…" Brea's plea was but a whisper. "Your breath. it's…it's so hot. I'm going to die if you don't…"

"If I don't what, gorgeous?"

"Lick me…dammit. Stop torturing me before I lose my mind."

With his tongue poised at her center, he lifted his gazed up at her. He froze, awed at her raw beauty. A rosy hue stained her cheeks. Her eyes were half-lidded, glassy, and a bit unfocused. And the rise and fall of her breasts with each panted breath, well…Sawyer had never seen anything as exquisite in his life. A part of him longed to keep her here, suspended on that stunning edge of want and demand. Instead, he branded this stunning image of her to memory and blew out a gentle breath over her folds.

"Sawyer!" She screamed his name in a very unladylike growl.

"Shhh," he cooed. "Relax. I'll make it better than good…"

He plunged his tongue as far inside her as possible. Hot. Soft. Slick. Her silky spice coated his tongue, and Sawyer's eyes rolled to the back of his head. Lapping at her with strong, steady strokes, he suckled her warm cream and nudged her clit with his nose. Brea moaned and writhed, grinding her pretty little pussy all over his face.

"You win!" she cried mournfully. "Your tongue is way more talented than mine. Oh, god! Yes! Don't stop. Whatever you do…don't stop."

He smiled against her steamy center as he devoured her.

"Yes. Yes. Sawyerrrr. You're going to make me come so hard… Oh, god. Yes. Right there. Oh, fuck…oh, fuck. Your mouth is incredible."

He'd had women whimper and moan, but her words were like an aphrodisiac. Fuck, she turned him on.

Nibbling at her pebbled clit, he slid two fingers inside her. Her soft muscles clutched his digits as her nectar spilled into his palm. She was flowing like a damn river. He swirled his tongue through her juice, then wrapped his lips around her clit. Sucking her swollen nub, he found that magic bundle of nerves behind her pubic bone.

"Oh. Oh…ohhhh."

Brea responded as wildly as she had in his dreams.

Her frantic, escalating whimpers and the trembling muscles of her body told him he was doing everything right. As he watched pleasure play across her face, his cock wept, throbbed, and strained to ride her hard and dirty, all night long.

She gripped his head in her hands, rolled her hips, and clutched her velvet tunnel around him hard. Screaming his name, Brea bore down and shattered all over his mouth. Flutters of bliss consumed her and she screamed out his name. Lost in the splendor of her cries, he drove his fingers through her fluttering, quivering passage, lapping the sweetness spilling from inside her. No woman had ever looked more erotic. Nothing had ever tasted sweeter than her honey-soaked pussy.

When Brea's knees began to buckle, Sawyer swept her up into his arms and cradled her against his chest. She slung her arms around his neck as he carried her up the stairs to his room. Sawyer couldn't help but smile at her sated expression.

With her eyes still closed, Brea licked her lips. "Do anything you want to me, cowboy…I don't care. Just save enough steam to do that thing you just did with your tongue again. Okay?"

Her words were thick, almost slurred as if she were drunk.

"With pleasure."

She answered on a soft, contented purr. His ravenous cock jerked ready for its chance to send her to the stars again. After placing her in the middle of his bed, he took a step back and simply stared at her. Her glossy hair spilled over his white pillow and cascaded down her shoulders. She looked almost innocent. Her eyes were closed, and a tiny little smile tugged the corners of her mouth. Lying there all languid and boneless, she was the most alluring vision on the planet.

It seemed unfathomable that only a week ago she'd been a stranger, but now he couldn't imagine his life without her.

LYING IN THE middle of Sawyer's bed—at least she thought it was his bed—Brea's pores oozed satisfaction. Her body pulsed in pleasure, and lingering aftershocks rippled and twitched deep in her core.

Sawyer had summoned sensations she'd never felt before and bent them until they coalesced into prisms of white light. He'd detonated Hailey's comet and the Leonid meteor shower in tandem. And like a million shooting stars, he propelled her into orbit as a rush of tingling spasms consumed her. She'd never known such an onslaught of bliss existed.

And he'd done it all with his tongue!

Brea couldn't wait to see where his big, fat cock might send her.

And what a cock it was. Sawyer had a fine, F-I-N-E dick. Thick and long, with angry veins lining the shaft. Thinking about trying to squeeze every inch of him inside her made Brea's pussy clutch. Forcing her heavy eyelids open, she saw Sawyer standing beside the bed. He was wearing a cocky grin and a twinkle of promise in his eyes.

Oh, hell yes. Bring it on…bring it all on!

She thought his smug veneer cute—a little unnerving that he was well aware of his skills—but cute nonetheless.

"Look at you…all full of yourself and everything."

"You're the one who admitted I had a more talented tongue."

"I may have thrown in the towel a little early. You did catch me at a weak moment after all."

"Uh-huh, and who put you in that moment of weakness, darlin'? The man with the talented tongue, I believe?"

She couldn't argue that point.

He licked his lips, wrapped a fist around his impressive cock, slowly stroking himself up and down while inching closer to the bed. "So you threw in the towel too early, is that right?"

Brea grinned and nodded.

"Well, then I assume you have something you want to prove?" The raspy tone of his voice told her that playful bantering was over.

"You bet your beautiful, big cock, I do," she answered in a sex-kitten purr.

He crawled onto the bed like a hungry wolf, staring at her with such intensity it nearly stopped her heart. Goose bumps erupted over her arms as a shiver slid down her spine.

"Beautiful?" His brows arched in disbelief. Brea nodded as he straddled her waist. "No, darlin'…you're what's beautiful."

The levee around her heart gave way and a rush of emotions flooded her soul. Tears stung the backs of her eyes, but she quickly blinked them away. She'd never thought herself even pretty until Sawyer. But he made her feel beyond pretty; he made her feel alluring, desirable, and totally alive.

Still fisting his cock, he placed his other palm flush against the headboard. Rocking his hips forward, he brought his glistening crest to her mouth. Heat spiraled outward just as it had when he'd devoured her pussy. Inhaling a deep breath, she savored the robust scent of testosterone. She ached to taste the glossy beads leaking from the tip.

"Open those lush lips for me, darlin'." She complied as Sawyer sucked in a hiss. "Your hot breath fluttering over my cock feels like heaven. I can't wait to feel your sinful mouth wrapped around me."

Neither could she.

Anticipation spiked and Brea could almost feel his thick ropes of come splattering over her tongue and showering her throat. Reaching up, she covered his hand with hers, silently asking for control. When he released his shaft, she slid her fingers around him.

Hot as fire.

Hard as steel.

Yet soft like velvet.

She held him as he pulsed in her palm. Watching his features harden with strained delight, Brea fed inch after glorious inch past her lips. Dragging her tongue over his throbbing veins, she whimpered as his salty emollient burst over her taste buds. She gazed at the muscles in his arms, suspended above her, as they trembled and shifted beneath his tanned skin.

Tilting back her head, she took Sawyer's fat crest all the way down to the back of her throat, then softly swallowed. He growled out a strangled curse before threading his fingers through her hair. Holding her still, he slowly rocked his hips, setting the tempo he desired. Lips stretched tight, Brea stared up at Sawyer. Jaw clenched. Eyes sparking in a fire of green and gold. His gaze was fixed on her mouth, watching his cock vanish and reappear between her lips.

Sawyer didn't fuck her mouth, he made love to it, slow and gentle, with such tenderness she wanted to weep.

"Your mouth… Christ, Brea. I've never felt anything more incredible…"

Neither had she.

Cinching his fist more tightly, tingles exploded over her scalp, and she moaned in delight at the new and different sensation. Reaching up, she clutched the cheeks of his ass. Focused on her breathing, she coaxed him to slide deeper still with a gentle suction of her mouth.

Both her mind and body felt new. As if she'd never been properly introduced to the dormant sensations Sawyer awakened within her. Seeking an outlet for the fervor he roused inside her, Brea skimmed a hand between her legs. Sawyer peeked over his shoulder and watched as she stroked her clit.

Peering down at her, he flashed her a wicked smile. "That's it, darlin'…come undone for me when I shower that sinful mouth of yours."

As Brea rode the waves cresting inside her, she held on while Sawyer's slow driving kept her anchored to him. She was ready to erupt like a cannon but kept herself hovering on the cusp until he was ready to fly. She wouldn't have to suffer for long. His thrusts were growing quicker, harder, more demanding. His face contorted, lined in equal parts torture and pleasure.

Seconds later, he slammed forward and stilled at the back of her throat. His back bowed as he gripped her hair with both hands. Sawyer choked out her name on a bellicose roar. The sound of release raked over her skin like lava. Brea's blood surged. Demand screamed. She followed Sawyer over, bucking and jolting, nearly choking on streams of his hot, slick seed as he jettisoned down her throat.

The crescendo ebbed and Sawyer gently slid in and out of her lips as the last of his offering spurted over her tongue. His eyes were closed when he released her hair and blindly cupped her cheeks. He knew right where to place his hands, as if each contour of her face had been memorized. Her heart sputtered and a new kind of warmth filled her… It was the warmth of contentment.

Brea cleaned his shaft while intermittent twitches and jerks quaked his cock. Sawyer strummed his thumb along the hollow of her cheek in a wordless gesture of gratitude.

His touch evoked such strange and unexpected emotions. She felt treasured, adored…loved.

Gone was the hollowness…the empty void. But none so blatantly absent as the remorse that plagued her soul. Guilt had once been a constant. Guilt for allowing men to use her, like a donor cup at a sperm bank. Guilt for selling her body, to pay the price for companionship…really shitty companionship.

Reality splintered her reverie like a mighty oak struck by lightning.

Sawyer had spent days trying to prove—in numerous and subtle abstract ways—that she was worthy of happiness. All the hours they'd filled, talking, laughing, and zinging one-liners back and forth, had been for a reason. And all the little things he'd done, like seeking her out during the day to ask if she was doing okay. Or suggestive smiles and winks he covertly sent her while they worked with the kids. Every time he was near, Sawyer had touched her indirectly with reassurance and care. He bathed her in glorious attention and never once asked, or even seemingly expected, anything in return.

Because he's not asking you to pay a price for friendship or affection.

Sawyer slowly pulled from her mouth. A look of worry wrinkled his forehead.

"Hey. Are you all right?"

Brea nodded as she stared at his cock. Still swollen, straining, and glistening with her saliva. The loss of his heated body sent a chill to settle through her. But when he swept her into his arms and tumbled to his side on the mattress, pulling her to face him, that cold isolation within vanished.

His smoky emerald eyes delved deep. Sawyer reached up and gently brushed a strand of hair away from her face. "Your mind is racing like an Olympic sprinter who just bitch-slapped a bear. Talk to me, baby. You're not gnawing on a bunch of guilt now, are you?"

"No."

"Thank god. That's the last thing I want."

Surveying her feelings brought tears to her eyes and sent a squall of emotions to swell inside her.

"I suppose what I'm having is a moment of clarity."

"How so?" He lifted up on one elbow and narrowed his eyes. "You're thinking you just made another mistake, aren't you?"

No. But nothing in these postcoital moments felt familiar.

Satisfaction was pumping through her veins instead of her assessing her self-worth by the blow job she'd just given him. But the biggest puzzle piece missing was she didn't feel the desperate need to pack her shit and move in with him. Surprisingly, that wasn't even on her radar.

What she was felt was peace!

Since arriving in Haven, instead of fearing being alone with herself, she'd actually *enjoyed* it. Well, when windows weren't being blown out or her life threatened by a zealous drug lord. All the horrible, terrifying personality flaws she feared she'd discover about herself hadn't materialized. Maybe they never were inside her to begin with.

Where? When? How had such self-deprecating ideas taken root in the first place?

She didn't know, but she aimed to do some serious soul-searching and find out.

It wasn't any wonder her heart had been broken more times than a flasher's trench coat zipper.

Sawyer's lips tightened into a thin line as he stared at her in waiting silence.

"No. This wasn't a mistake."

"No. It wasn't. I'm glad you realize that." His expression softened. "When I met you a week ago, I had no idea what an unexpected surprise you'd be in my life."

No. *He* was the unexpected surprise…a huge one.

"I wowed you with my dazzling personality and easygoing nature, right?" God, she couldn't even say the words with a straight face.

Sawyer laughed…hard. "Not quite. You were like a rattlesnake, all coiled up and ready to strike, in the beginning. But yes, I suppose I was dazzled…dazzled by the glow of your sexy ass shining in the moonlight, teetering on that windowsill. You have no idea how I struggled to keep from grabbing hold of those milky white orbs and burying my tongue between your cheeks."

Even though she didn't want to be reminded of that embarrassing night, a dirty thrill zipped through her. Yanking the pillow from beneath her head, she smacked him in the arm. Sawyer laughed and knocked it away before shoving her back to the mattress and straddling her hips.

Brea was giggling, but her laughter slowly died as she stared at his gorgeous face. God, he was truly beautiful.

The smile slowly vanished from his lips as he studied the contours of her face. "You've taught me something over these past seven days, Brea."

"I taught you?" She was totally puzzled. "What? How *not* to climb through a window?"

Sawyer grinned and shook his head. "That, but no. You taught me that the past doesn't have to define the future. A lesson you need to teach yourself, as well."

His words slowly sank into her brain. She began to realize that by banishing men from her life, she'd simply traded in one set of blinders for another. Men weren't her enemy, she was, or rather her lack of self-esteem. But Sawyer had lifted the blinders and taught her something, too—besides what orgasms were supposed to feel like. He'd taught her something far more precious—that she deserved love and respect. He'd shown her the difference between a good man and a worthless, leaching loser.

Her stomach pitched. "Oh, god. This is great…just great!"

"What's the matter?" he asked, clearly confused.

"My parents…they've been right all along." Brea flung her hands in the air. "Oh, god. You have no idea the ass I'm going to have to kiss now. Shit!"

"Whose ass? Your parent's?"

"Yes," she hissed. "And it chaps my nipples something fierce! Aw, dammit!"

Sawyer blinked and then chuckled. "First of all, you don't have to kiss anyone's ass. Not mine and especially not your parents'. And I've got just the thing for your chapped nipples. Don't worry, I'll take extra-special care of them for you." He bent and flicked his tongue over her pebbled peaks, then raised his head and waggled his brows. His playful antics defused her irritation. "So tell me, what were your parents right about?"

Brea shook her head. "It doesn't matter. I'll call them and grovel later."

"No. Don't." Sawyer frowned. "If you can't trust them to be there for you through good times and bad, you don't owe them explanations. Keep the people who want the best for you by your side. People like Colton, Jade, and…well, me."

She hadn't turned her back on her parents; they'd turned their backs on her. That fact stung, but Brea was finding a new sense of courage taking root inside her.

"You're right. But we were close once. I think it's time I called and tried to remove the wedge that's between me and my folks."

A ghost of a smile curled his lips. "When something's important, it's never too late to change. After my divorce, I vowed two things. One was never to wake up with a woman in my bed. I'm changing my decision here and now. I want to wake up with you by my side in the morning, Brea."

He's a good man. Waking up with him isn't the same as moving in. He's not saying shit to get inside your pants...he's already done that. He cares about you and has feelings for y-o-u.

Her subconscious whisper sent panic and joy and hope and terror colliding inside her. She opened her mouth to laugh, or maybe it was to scream, but in the end, it didn't matter. Sawyer meshed his lips to hers, erasing all rational thought, and with a soul-stealing kiss, he drowned her in passion.

Brea's heart felt as if it were going to burst from her chest.

"Make love to me, Sawyer," she gasped after tearing from his mouth.

"I thought you'd never ask."

The glow of some new and liberating light shined from inside her. Sawyer had given that to her, made her shine. And for the first time in her life, Brea felt extraordinarily free!

Shoving him back, she sat up and shot him a playful smile. "I've ridden a few shoddy donkeys before, but never a stud as sexy as you. How about we saddle up and stampede into the sunset?"

"With or without my spurs on, baby?"

"Surprise me." She laughed. "What am I saying? You already have."

A wicked flame danced in his eyes. "And I plan to keep on doing it, too."

Sawyer plucked her off the bed. Brea let out a squeal. "Where are you taking me?"

"You like surprises. Remember?" Sawyer laughed as he carried her into the bathroom.

"So, we're going to clean us up just so we can get dirty again?"

"Oh, yeah. I plan to get you utterly filthy, darlin'."

She swallowed tightly as the images from her wet dreams came to life in her head. Brea wrapped her arms around his neck and pulled him in for a kiss. "Good, 'cause I'm going to get you smutty dirty, *Neville*."

He narrowed his eyes and growled. Lifting his hand off her left butt cheek, Sawyer brought it down with a loud, stinging slap. Brea let out a yelp.

"I'll turn you over my knee, woman," Sawyer warned.

"Only if I'm bad, right?"

"Are you ready to show me how wicked you can get?"

"Wait. What if I'm good?"

"Trust me, darlin'. You can't get much better. You're nearly perfect already."

"Watch me," she challenged in a sultry whisper.

Bold and sure—feelings Sawyer had evoked inside her—she mentally spread her wings and basked in her newfound confidence. Brea wrapped her hand around his neck and drew him in for a kiss. Forcing his lips apart with her tongue, she grinned at the feral growl rolling from his chest. Sawyer skimmed his wide, calloused hands down her back, gripped her ass cheeks, then pulled her naked body to his. That glorious cock throbbed against her stomach and she purred.

He dipped his fingers in the crack of her ass and toyed with her puckered rim. Tiny sparks of pleasure spread outward and exploded like firecrackers. Brea whimpered and pushed her hips back toward his hand, silently giving him the green light to a little ass play.

Sawyer reached lower, coating his fingers with her pussy juices before smearing the slickness on her gathered ring. Slowly, he worked his finger through the sensitive opening, sending bursts of pleasure to ripple through her.

The heat generating between them turned the bathroom into a sweltering sauna. As they feasted on each other's tongues and lips, Brea slid her hand between their grinding bodies and wrapped her fingers around his cock. She dragged her hand up and down his massive muscle with feathery-light strokes, basking in the thick veins that throbbed against her flesh.

She wanted him inside her…anywhere…everywhere!

When she pulled back, Brea's pulse sped up as she stared into his seductive gaze. She'd never grow tired of looking at him, laughing with him, or giving herself to him.

"Fuck the shower," Sawyer growled. "I'm taking you right here…right now!"

"Where's your condom, tiger?"

"Shit! They're in the nightstand by the bed." Frustration laced his words.

Brea sent him a wicked grin. With her hand still gripped to his shaft, she led him by his cock back into the bedroom.

"This gives a whole new meaning to being led around by your dick," he chuckled.

"You're not complaining, are you?"

"No, ma'am. Not one bit in the world."

He pulled out a string of condoms and tore one off. Brea arched her brow at the several he left sitting on the nightstand. "You planning to use all those tonight?"

"Them and more," he snarled before tearing the package open with his teeth.

Brea reached up and plucked the condom from the wrapper. "I should have eaten my Wheaties this morning. Here, let me do the honors."

"Be my guest." Sawyer placed his fists on his hips and thrust his dick toward her.

"It seems a shame to have to wrap up such a pretty cock."

Sawyer arched his brow. "You on the pill?"

"Yes."

"I'm clean…" His voice broke off and she knew he was waiting for her reply.

"Weed stopped touching me months ago. I went…" Brea shook her head. She refused to spoil the moment talking about that asshat. "I-I'm clean too."

A brutish grin crawled across his lips before he stole the condom from between her fingers and tossed it over his shoulders. "I can't wait to feel you around me."

Pressing his lips to hers, Brea smiled. "Then stop talking."

"I'm not," he murmured. The low vibration of his words tickled her mouth. "You are.

"I guess you'll have to find a way to shut me up, then."

Sawyer broke the kiss and started laughing. "Oh, how I love a challenge."

He removed her hand from his cock and then gripped her hips before capturing her mouth with a hungry kiss. As he advanced on her, the backs of her legs hit the mattress, and with his lips still fused to hers, Sawyer eased her onto the bed. He hovered over her and dragged his tongue down her body.

Brea closed her eyes and sighed as his hands, fingers, lips, and teeth roamed gently over every inch of her naked flesh. Stopping to lick and suckle her breasts, he didn't linger but ebbed toward the juncture of her thighs.

Brea opened her eyes and lifted her head from the pillow. She watched as he gripped her flesh with his capable hands and spread her legs. He brushed his lips and tongue up her thighs. His bristly whiskers tickled. She almost giggled until he nipped his teeth at her tender flesh, only to lave his tongue over each freshly bitten spot. Pulses of pain mixed with pleasure skittered through her while ribbons of lava fluttered in her core.

As he knelt on the edge of the bed, Brea bent her knees, welcoming him inside her. But Sawyer paused and stared at her with a look of pure adoration. Brea's heart soared. He cinched his hands at her waist and hoisted her into the middle of the bed, then braced himself on his palms. Keeping his gaze locked with hers, Sawyer lowered his hips until the crest of his cock aligned with her weeping channel.

"From here on out, it's only me... I'm the only man you'll ever give yourself to."

Her heart fluttered wildly and her eyes grew wide. Surprise, like a flooded creek, swelled inside. Brea swallowed tightly though her mouth had gone dry.

Sawyer cocked his head. "Did you actually think I'd ever let you get away? Not happening. I'm done sleeping alone in my bed, dreaming about you, night after night. I've found the missing pieces of my heart, darlin'…and they're you. Tell me I'm the only one you'll ever want…ever need."

His words singed her soul like a branding iron. His stare grew even hotter, intense and unwavering. He was a rogue, but a damn sexy one.

Karma had indeed come back, but not to bite her in the ass…to save her. Still, this was a complete reversal of every relationship she'd ever known. Part of her felt as if she were learning to walk with two left shoes…foreign…awkward. She prayed she didn't misstep and fall flat on her ass.

If you do, he'll be right there to catch you. Let go. Let him love you…let yourself love him.

Hall-e-fuckin'-lujah! Her heart and head had aligned on the same damn page for once. Though she had no clue if she and Sawyer would last till the end of time. Hell, it could all end tomorrow. But she was willing to see where this crazy, sometimes infuriating man with a huge heart and strong arms would take her.

If she ended up having to wrap another damn tourniquet around her heart one day…so be it. Giving up men and cordoning off her heart wasn't the answer. Life was taking risks, winning, losing, and never giving up on finding the one to share a happy ever after with.

"Say it, Brea," he whispered so low she almost didn't hear him.

"You're the only man I'll ever want or need, Neville Sawyer Grayson." A great big smile speared his face. Brea giggled. "Now make love to me like you mean it."

"There's no other way when it comes to you. Hold on tight, darlin', this ride's about to get wild."

He captured her mouth, swallowing down her whimpers and moans as he slowly inched his thick cock inside her. Brea rolled her hips and wiggled, trying to will her swollen muscles to relax and let him in. When she felt his pubic bone meshed against hers, Sawyer raised his head and smiled.

"You doing all right, darlin'?"

She answered in a dreamy moan. All right wasn't even close.

She was in heaven.

Stuffed full of his incredible cock, suffused in the heat of his body, and held prisoner to his carnal stare—this was better than chocolate or wine or French fries.

He dragged in and out of her throbbing core in a slow, spine-bending rhythm. Lost in the sensation, she squeezed around him as their tongues swirled in tandem. He was savage, gentle, demanding, tender…and the dichotomy of sensations he bestowed overwhelmed. Brea abandoned trying to decipher them all and simply felt…felt it all, with every electrified cell in her body, mind, heart, and soul.

CHAPTER ELEVEN

ENGULFED IN HER heated, wet splendor, Sawyer was going up in flames. Brea was tight...tighter than he'd ever imagined...and slick...so fucking unbelievable he wanted to throw his head back and yell the goddamn roof down. The flames licking at his spine paled to the uninhibited passion pouring from her and flowing into him.

Everything about her was un-fucking-believable.

With his hand wedged between their slapping bodies, he toyed with her clit, watching rapture roll across her face, listening to her whimpers and kitten-like mewls. He'd felt that magical little nub swell on his tongue...knew just how to manipulate his fingers in a way to drive her over the edge. But he wasn't ready to let her fly. Not yet. Sawyer wanted to savor every second of her beautiful suffering.

Unfortunately, he was suffering right along with her. He'd tried to think about Betty White naked, but Brea's cries and the beguiling feel of her body stole his attention back to her.

As he worked her clit with the pad of his thumb, the mounting friction of her clutching heat was shoving him fast toward nirvana. Brea's breathless whimpers grew to keening cries, and he knew she was close.

As close as you are, fucker.

Clenching his jaw, Sawyer struggled to hold on as lightning, white and hot, slashed down his spine and rolled through his balls. Brea wrapped her legs around him and threw back her head. The air grew electric, sizzling with a need so blistering he feared he'd pass the fuck out.

But when Brea screamed his name and clamped down on his driving shaft, he gripped her hips and hammered through her narrowing slit. His nerve endings ignited. The pleasure centers in his brain caught fire, and as she came apart beneath him, he let go.

Squeezing the lush flair of her hips, Sawyer yelled her name. Wave after wave erupted from his cock, showering contracting walls. They rode the surge in a peak of grunts, gasps, and moans until his wrists gave out and he fell to his elbows.

With his face buried in the crook of her neck, Sawyer inhaled the scent of wildflowers and jasmine while Brea lay boneless and quivering beneath him. She was mumbling incoherently now and again, and he couldn't help but smile.

While their breathing slowly began to level out, lingering aftershocks coaxed a couple of grunts and whimpers. Brea lay beneath him, skimming her hands up and down his back in a lazy sweeping motion. Sawyer stroked the curve of her shoulder, and after several long, lethargic minutes, he raised his head.

A slow smile tugged his mouth as he looked at her—eyes closed, lips parted, and a pink glow of completeness painted her cheeks.

Now that's what you call a well-satisfied woman.

Sawyer couldn't agree more with the semi-arrogant voice in the back of his head. Tucking his hand at the small or her back, he lifted Brea's limp body in his arm and then tumbled onto his back. Lying atop him, she nuzzled his chest and exhaled a soft, contented smile.

"I'm glad as hell I vowed no other men but you," she mumbled as the words were getting tangled on her tongue. "I knew the minute I saw you that if we ever…what is it you called it? Oh, yeah…*bumped bellies*, you'd ruin me for any other guy."

Sawyer chuckled. "You knew that the first night in Toot's, did you?"

"Uh-huh."

"You've always been a perceptive little thing." He raised his hands and dusted off his palms. "Now that I've completed that mission…I've got a couple million others I want to fulfill with you."

Brea moaned. The vibration of her lips so close to his nipple made his still-erect cock leap.

"Have you ever played army before?"

"Army?" she asked, clearly confused.

"Uh-huh. I've got a missile that's ready to launch."

She lifted her head and glanced at his cock. Peering at him once more, she licked her lips and sent him a coy smile. "Where do I enlist, Sarge?"

Sawyer's chest shook in silent laughter. Her playful spirit was new, invigorating, and made it too damn easy to love her.

Reaching down, he fisted his cock. "Right here, darlin'."

They spent the entire night, and twenty-four hours after that, jettisoning to the stars and tumbling back to earth. Touching, kissing, licking, and sucking, they discovered all the ways to drain pleasure from one another. He could still hear her cries begging him to stop stimulating her clit after she'd shattered, but he'd worked her through those convulsive minutes until she begged him to soar her higher. There weren't a lot of words spoken, at least not when they were joined as one. That's when they spoke a language all their own…the language of love.

However, in between those straining, blissful orgasms, they showered and snuggled, laughed and talked, ordered pizza and raided Sawyer's refrigerator. Confessions flowed freely, both hers and his. Sawyer quickly discovered he'd never met a woman who'd altered his life quite like Brea.

In the beginning his interest had been purely sexual, even when he thought her the most complicated woman on the planet. Somewhere along the way, his opinion of her had fallen apart, like a defective rebuilt carburetor.

Maybe it was the night she'd gotten locked out, and he'd seen the sassy, determined side of her. Or maybe it was the hot tub fiasco, when he'd glimpsed the scars left by other men. Even then,

Sawyer wanted to move heaven and earth to erase them from her heart. Or maybe it was something as simple as knowing they'd both been wounded but had chosen to survive that made Brea so damn special in his eyes.

While Sawyer might not know precisely why he loved her, he did. Being with Brea made life and everything inside him whole. He wanted to live out his fantasies with her, watch her belly swell and give life to their children, and grow old by her side.

Watching her sleep, his cock soft, spent, and sated, he listened to her even breaths as they floated over his flesh.

The tightening in his chest told Sawyer that he'd found his soul mate.

The corners of his mouth lifted with a hint of a smile, and he closed his eyes and drifted off to sleep.

He woke sometime later with sunshine streaming in through the window. Brea's succulent backside was pressed against his crotch. Her silky hair lay draped over his shoulder as she softly snored. He couldn't wait to tease her about the cute noises she made in her sleep over breakfast.

Breakfast. Shit! Was it Sunday? No, it was Monday. Fuck! A blast of panic blew through his veins. New guests were due to arrive at the ranch…if they weren't already there. Sawyer didn't want to wake his sleeping beauty, but he needed his cell phone to see what time it was. Easing from her sleeping body, he rolled off the bed and searched for his jeans.

They're still piled in the corner, dumb ass.

He grabbed the device from his pants and turned it on.

"Whew, only seven twenty. Plenty of time to wake up Brea proper."

He strolled to the bathroom, and when he returned, Brea was on her back, with her arms open and legs slightly parted. If that wasn't an invitation to violate her in ways to make the devil blush, he didn't know what was. Laying his phone on the nightstand, Sawyer crawled onto the bed. Starting at her ankles, he kissed his way up her body. Mid-calf, Brea moaned, then giggled when he reached her knee.

"Stop. I'm ticklish."

"You probably shouldn't have told me that."

"Don't you dare," she warned.

Quickly drawing up her knees, she caught him square in the jaw. Sawyer let out a growl of pain and cupped the side of his face as lightning exploded through his skull. Brea's eyes grew wide. A look of mortification lined her face.

"Oh, my god. Are you all right? I'm sorry. I didn't mean to—"

"I'm fine, but this wasn't how I'd planned to wake you up."

"Let me get you an ice pack."

Brea started to leap out of bed, but he grabbed her arm.

"No. Really. I'm okay. It just needs a kiss or two." He gave her the saddest puppy-dog eyes he could muster and pointed to his still-throbbing jaw. Brea rolled her eyes and smirked before rising to her knees and dotting a row of tender kisses against his skin.

"Is that the only place that hurts?" she asked coyly.

"Not by a long shot." He thrust his erection against her stomach. "Maybe you can kiss it in the shower."

She laughed and slung her arms around his neck, pulling his mouth to hers. "What makes you think we're going to make it out of bed?"

With a growl, he kissed her and pressed her back to the mattress just as his cell phone started to ring. He inwardly cursed the interruption, but at least it was only a phone and not a shotgun this time.

"Hold that thought," he instructed before plucking his phone off the floor.

Brea flashed him a devilish grin, then spread her legs and began toying with her clit. "Make it fast, cowboy."

"Jesus, woman. How am I supposed to talk to anyone now?" he murmured before scowling at the ringing device in his hand.

"I'm just keeping it warm for you, sugar," she giggled.

"Fuck!"

Though the show on the bed was beyond captivating, a hint of fear slid through him. Noble was calling. The fear that something had happened to one of the family crawled through him.

"Hello?"

"Whatcha doin'?" Noble asked in a taunting, childish lilt. "Something fun, I bet."

"None of your damn business. What do you want?"

"Wow. Someone woke up on the wrong side of the bed. What's the matter…didn't you get any last night?"

"What the fuck do you want?"

"I just called to make sure you remembered that we've got new campers coming in soon, and wanted to see if you needed a ride to work."

"I know. Why the fuck would I need a ride to work?"

"Well, they say jacking off too much will make you go blind. I wasn't sure if you could still see."

"What are you…twelve?" Sawyer spat. "I'll *see* you and your service dog at the ranch later, you blind-assed motherfucker."

"Wait! Wait!" Noble yelled.

"What?"

"Just tell me one thing…was Brea every bit as incredible as I imagine?"

"Fuck off. And stop fantasizing about my woman before I rip your eyes out and you really will need a service dog."

As his idiotic brother howled with laughter, Sawyer hung up. Placing his phone on the nightstand again, he sent Brea—who'd abandoned her masturbation performance and was now sitting up in bed—a look of apology. "Sorry. I thought the call might be important. It wasn't."

She grinned. "Let me guess, one of your brothers calling to give you shit about leaving with me the other night, right?"

He nodded in annoyance. "Noble, the prick."

"I still feel bad that we just dumped Ozzie on your family."

"Don't. I called Mom yesterday while you were taking a nap.

He's doing fine."

"Good. What time do we need to be at the ranch?"

"Couple hours."

Brea stood and walked toward him. Reaching down, she tickled the tips of her fingers up and down his hardened cock. "Why don't we have a little quickie in the shower, get dressed, and then grab some breakfast before we head to work?"

She could have suggested he put on a frilly pink tutu and dance *Swan Lake* in the middle of Main Street, and Sawyer wouldn't have refused.

"I'll start the water," he offered, but didn't move. He couldn't. Her feathery-light caresses had stolen the muscle control from his legs. Instead, he delved into her silky mouth. Tangling his tongue with hers, Sawyer dropped a hand between her legs and teased her already wet and swollen nub.

Somehow they made it to the bathroom and into the shower. But instead of soaping her up and washing her hair, as he'd enjoyed the past two days, Sawyer pressed her up against the tile and aligned his crest to her opening.

"Oh, god," she groaned and wiggled her ass, taking a few more inches of him inside her steamy slit.

"Sorry, but you said a quickie. I'm simply trying to accommodate your wishes."

"Oh, you are. But I think I'm the one trying to accommodate you at the moment. Where did you get such a huge, fat dick?"

"I didn't order it off the computer. I was born this way." He chuckled against her ear before nibbling at the lobe. "Relax, darlin', let me inside your snug, sweet pussy."

Twisting the massaging showerhead free, Sawyer aimed the pulsating spray at her clit. Brea yelped, then gripped his hand and tilted the angle a bit higher. She clutched around him with a pitiful moan as he sank balls deep inside her steamy tunnel. The sounds of wet slapping skin melded with grunts and cries of bliss. And when they shattered together, the reverberation of Brea's screams echoed in his ears for several long, glorious seconds.

When they stepped out of the shower, Sawyer wrapped her in a big, fluffy towel and pulled her against him. As he dropped kisses through the beaded-up water on her shoulders, she rested her head against his chest.

"You'd better watch out. I could grow accustomed to this style of pampering."

"Good, 'cause I'm going to pamper the pants off you," Sawyer growled.

"Too late. You already have…numerous times, but feel free to pamper me as long as you want."

"Even if it's forever?"

Sawyer felt her tense. No doubt she was frightened by his offer. But when she relaxed once more, and simply sent him an anxious nod, he wanted to throw his fist in the air and cheer. Her silent kiss sealed the deal, at least as far as he was concerned. Time would tell if she could grow accustomed to his love and open her heart to him.

BREA'S SKIN TINGLED from both the amazing sex in the shower and the towel Sawyer had used to dry her with. Standing naked in his bedroom, she looked at the clothes she'd worn two days ago, piled in the corner. When she wasn't running around his house naked, she'd covered up in one of his flannel shirts. With a shrug, she dressed in her own dirty clothes, but she wanted to wear something clean.

"I'm going to run next door and change clothes," she called to Sawyer, who was still in the bathroom. "Can I use Barbara's extra key you've got?"

Sawyer stepped into the bedroom with a towel wrapped around his waist and a toothbrush stuck in his mouth. Visions of living with a litany of men over the years doused her skin in an oily film of déjà vu. Brea swallowed tightly as she watched him fish his keys from his jean pocket. As he handed them to her, he plucked the toothbrush from his mouth.

"I'll go over and water the gardens while you change."

"Okay. I'll meet you back at the truck."

Sawyer nodded, then flashed her a foamy grin before puckering his lips to kiss her. Brea laughed and backed away. "Oh, no, you don't. Go spit that out, then you can kiss me."

"Uh-uh."

He shook his head and started chasing her around the room, nearly choking on toothpaste once or twice. She giggled and screamed for him to stay back as he wiggled his Crest-covered tongue at her. Brea raced into the hallway and down the stairs as his deep, rich laughter followed her out the door. She felt like a dolt for even thinking about the dreadful pricks from her past. Sawyer was nothing, absolutely nothing like them. Thank god.

She couldn't wipe the smile off her face as she donned clean clothes in the guest room of Barbara's house. Never in her wildest dreams had Brea thought a man with Sawyer's playful spirit existed. He was buckets full of crazy, in a good way, and every minute she spent with him was new and exciting. And the sex? Holy fuck! It was the best dirty sex she'd ever had. She heard angels sing with every orgasm Sawyer dragged from her. She'd never known she could be this happy, or that life could be so grand.

As she zipped up her jeans, she thought what being with him forever would be like. It would be so much easier if she had a crystal ball, but she didn't. She'd have to take one day at a time. Though she'd spent two nights with him, her things were still at Barbara's and the ranch. Brea hadn't moved in with the man, so that was progress, right?

"A slightly altered version of it." She snorted at her own absurdity. "He even made the earth and stars collide and you didn't profess your undying love for him. Now *that's* progress right there. Huge progress."

No, she hadn't told Sawyer that she loved him, but she did. Still, Brea wasn't ready to say the words. In her warped mind, she figured if she didn't spill the beans, she could still control her emotions...namely protect her heart.

News flash...you've already lost your heart.

She frowned. "Okay, so I obviously still need a little work on that blowing smoke up my own ass thing...but I'm working on it, dammit!" She tugged on her T-shirt and sighed. "Rome wasn't built in a day, you know!"

She heard water running toward the back of the house and guessed that Sawyer was taking care of the plants. Brea took a few extra minutes to blow-dry her hair. She didn't bother with makeup. Ten minutes at the ranch and it would be melting off her face. She didn't want to scare the poor kids looking like a scary raccoon.

As she brushed her teeth, her stomach growled. But it was her need for caffeine that had her body's cravings at DEFCON one.

When she hurried downstairs, she didn't hear the water running anymore but peered out the kitchen window anyway. With no sign of Sawyer, she grabbed his keys off the coffee table and rushed out the front door. Just as she was about to leap off the stairs, she spotted him...arms wrapped around a tall, willowy redhead standing next to a gleaming silver Mercedes sports car. Skidding to a halt on the wooden slats of Barbara's porch, Brea pressed a palm to her heart and stared.

She couldn't hear what the couple was saying...she wasn't sure she really wanted to. Unable to move, she watched as Sawyer gripped the redhead by the shoulders and stared into her eyes. Brea's heart sputtered and threatened to stop. The woman was drop-dead gorgeous, from the top of her perfectly coiffed hair to her designer clothes and shoes. She made the three bitches in Sawyer's hot tub look like mud-crawling skanks. Brea could barely breathe, especially when Sawyer sent the redhead a smile—the same one he'd used to draw Brea into his web of lies so he could crush her moronic and pitifully stupid fantasies. Tears slid down Brea's cheeks.

When the woman reached up and cupped his face, Sawyer

leaned in and kissed her. Kissed her right on her collagen-filled lips.

As if smacked upside the head with a bag of dicks, Brea erupted in a white-hot rage.

After bolting off the porch, biting back her sobs, she ran across the lawn as if the hounds of hell were nipping her heels. With Sawyer's keys cupped in her hand, Brea raised her arm over her head. "Here's your keys, you fucking asshole. I hope you rot in hell!"

Sawyer turned. His eyes were wide like saucers as she launched the heavy ring at him. They nailed him right between the legs. He let out a strangled cry and doubled over before folding to his knees. She didn't wait to see if he recovered...eventually he would. Besides, Miss Rich America was already crouching down beside him, rubbing his back and shooting daggers Brea's way.

She turned and raced back to her temporary house, refusing to let him see her cry like a four-year-old who'd just dropped her ice cream. The minute she stepped onto the porch, she realized her mistake in throwing the keys. She was locked out...again!

Anger overrode pain and humiliation. She kicked the door with her tennis shoe as tears spilled down her cheeks. Brea wanted to curl up into a little ball and disappear.

"Goddamn son of a bitch motherfucking, men!" she screamed. "When the hell am I ever going to learn?"

Refusing to put on any more of a show for Sawyer and his newly acquired *fuck toy*, Brea raced off the front porch, making a beeline to the backyard. She might not be able to get inside, but she could hide...hide and throw her temper tantrum in private without Sawyer having a front row seat and watching her fall the fuck apart.

She found an alcove between the vegetable and flowerbeds. Pushing the tall stalks aside, she sat down in the wet grass. She had no idea how everything had gone to hell in the span of fifteen damn minutes. She and Sawyer had been laughing, loving and...

"Oh, god, I'm such a fucking idiot," she wailed. Drawing her knees to her chest, Brea lowered her head and cried.

Cried for being foolish enough to think she could have a normal relationship with someone as wonderful as Sawyer.

Cried for letting her hopes and dreams overrule common sense.

Cried for the little girl inside who never wanted anything but to be loved.

"Brea!" Sawyer called in a snarl. "I know you're back here. Brea, goddamn it, where are you?"

She covered her mouth to muffle her sobs and tucked herself into a ball. Hopefully, if he didn't find her hiding place, he'd give up and go away. She wasn't ready to face him yet. She needed time to lick her wounds and construct a bitch barrier so thick and strong he couldn't penetrate it with that dazzling smile, loving caress, or toe-curling kisses. But Sawyer was as bullheaded as she was. Brea wasn't going to hold her breath that he'd just give up.

"I have no idea what you think... No, I know *exactly* what you think you saw, or I wouldn't have the Ford logo imprinted on my *dick*!"

She clenched her jaw. It might do him some good to walk around with the logo branded on his big, beautiful cock. She hoped gangrene set in, and his ungodly talented dick would fall right off. It'd serve him right.

Asshole!

"Come out, Brea. I'm not leaving until we talk this misunderstanding through."

Misunderstanding, my fat ass! Did he think she was so naïve not to put the pieces together? He practically shoved that snotty bitch down Brea's throat. No, he wasn't going to *talk* his way out of this!

She remained hidden among the burgeoning brush like an oversized garden gnome. Brea would never find a decent man. Even when she was old and gray and scouting the old folks' home with a purse of Viagra, she'd probably still be striking out.

No, she was going to keep her sorry ass right here. The only way she'd come out was if Sawyer took a Weedwacker and tore the whole backyard down. She knew he'd never do that; Barbara would kill him.

"Fine. Have it your way, darlin'."

Thank god! He was actually going to leave her in peace. Let her hold on to her tattered pride. Let him take off with pretty Miss Rich Bitch—her three-hundred-thousand-dollar sports car, two-thousand-dollar Gucci outfit, forty-four triple Z tits, and twenty-inch waist—Brea didn't need or want him! She hoped Sawyer choked on every inch of her plastic, artificially enhanced body.

Asshole!

A blast of ice-cold water doused her internal fuming. Brea screamed and bolted upright as if her ass had been spring-loaded. Sputtering, she raised her hands as the stream of water continued to pummel her face.

"There you are, darlin'. I knew I'd find you." There was a hint of laughter in his angry tone while Sawyer continued his assault by water hose. "Have you cooled off enough to have a rational conversation yet?"

Turning the water off, he arched his brows. A mixture of irritation and humor danced in his golden-green eyes. Brea was all but certain flames of rage were leaping from hers. Though the morning sun was shining brightly, she was soaked to the skin and shivering like mad. But it wasn't going to stop her from giving the prick with the hose a piece of her mind.

"Rational conversation?" she squawked. "You drown me in icy water and expect a rational conversation? Fuck you…you…asshole!"

"I've already fucked your asshole, darlin'…numerous times. It was fantastic." An arrogant smirk tugged at the edges of his mouth. "If you'd like to sit down and have a chat, I'm sure we can arrange to do it several times more."

"In your dreams," Brea hissed. "The only reason you're not

fucking the collagen out of Miss Mercedes Tits is because you haven't had time to *change the goddamn sheets*!"

Sawyer sent her a sympathetic smile, which only made her all the more livid.

He slowly shook his head. "Brea, I wouldn't take her to bed if she were the last woman on the planet."

"Oh, spare me!" She threw her hands into the air. "I might have been naïve and stupid enough to play into your manipulative hands, but I'm not a complete moron. You'd fuck her all night long and we both know it."

"No. I. Wouldn't." He dropped the hose and ate up the distance between them in three long strides. "The woman you saw me with is Sara…my ex-wife."

Brea's mouth gaped open. Though he could have knocked her over with a feather, she felt as if Sawyer had just landed a right hook to the jaw.

The pageant queens in the hot tub… It all made sense now. Sawyer was bedding women who looked like his ex. So why in the hell had he picked her? She looked nothing like Sara or the hot tub whores.

Brea's stomach pitched and the knife of reality stabbed deep. She'd been nothing but a pity fuck. Big, fat tears welled in her eyes.

"I don't like what you're thinking. I'm about to lose my shit, Brea." Sawyer cupped her chin with a force that almost scared her. And when he pierced her with a probing stare that ripped her soul wide open, she started to tremble. "I don't feel a thing for her anymore."

"Then why were you kissing her?" The pathetic wail that ripped from her throat embarrassed her all the more.

"Come on, we're going inside. You need dry clothes and I need to tell you what happened."

"No. We'll talk out here."

"You're freezing. We need to get you out of these wet clothes."

"*I* need to get my wet clothes off. *You* are going to wait in the kitchen."

"Why? You don't trust me?"

"No. I don't trust myself." The truth rolled off her lips faster than she could stop it.

"Fuck! I thought I'd helped you work past that."

Helped? It kept getting more priceless by the second. Not only had he granted her a pity fuck—well, several, actually—but she'd been nothing but a charity case for him, too? Phe-fucking-nomenal. Could it get any better than this? Oh, wait. It could. She could live under a bridge, dig through garbage, and push her recyclables in a shopping cart all day. That ought to give him plenty of balloons and streamers for the pity party he'd been throwing her.

Following her up the to the back deck, Sawyer unlocked the door and headed toward the kitchen. "Go change. I'll make us some coffee."

Brea didn't respond, simply turned and climbed the stairs. She wanted to lock herself inside the room, but Sawyer would probably kick the damn door down. At the rate things were going, Barbara would be lucky if her adorable gingerbread house was even standing when she came home.

Tearing off her wet clothes. Brea tossed them to the floor of the shower and dressed once again. The rich sent of coffee hit her halfway down the stairs. If Sawyer hadn't been waiting, like an executioner, to *talk*—though as far as Brea was concerned, there was nothing left to say—she would have sprinted to the kitchen for a caffeine infusion.

When she rounded the corner, sitting on the table was a full mug of coffee, waiting for her. Sawyer's sexy ass was resting on the counter, his muscular legs stretched out toward the fridge, with one boot-covered foot crossed over the other. He looked relaxed. And why shouldn't he be? He'd do his best to let her down easy…he probably had that script memorized by now.

Brea wanted to nip this in the bud and send him on his way.

She took a sip of coffee and lifted her chin. "Say whatever you need to, then leave, please."

When that lazy smile stretched across his lips, she wanted to moan. "Oh, I intend to set the record straight, but I won't be going anywhere without you when I'm done."

Dream on, you delusional prick!

Instead of inciting a bigger argument, she kept her smartassed thoughts to herself.

Sawyer pushed off the counter and extended his arm, inviting her to sit at the table. She sent him a scowl but flopped down on a chair. He joined her and cupped his hands around his mug of coffee. A faraway look glazed his eyes as began to tell her about Sara. Brea wasn't interested in the ancient history he was revealing. She simply wanted to know why Sawyer was sucking face with his ex-wife.

"So, when she came to me and told me she was having an affair, I did the only thing I could and filed for divorce."

"So, you never got over her, right?"

"No. I did." He lifted his head and locked eyes on hers. "Like every failed relationship, it leaves scars."

Yes. Brea was an aficionado of those nasty mutilations.

"Sara stopped by this morning to apologize. She discovered yesterday that her husband, the plastic surgeon she left me for, is having an affair…numerous ones, actually."

"Oh, I know how this ends." Brea smiled tightly. "She wants you back."

He wrinkled his brows. "No. She just came to apologize. We'd been friends since second grade, and our marriage ended ugly. We'd been more like friends than husband and wife even when we were married."

"Okay, but that still doesn't explain why you were hugging her, then kissed her."

Jealousy and insecurity oozed from her pores, and Brea hated the way the film of it clung to her skin.

"If any of my female friends came to me with that much guilt and remorse flowing through their system, I'd hold them, kiss them, and forgive them." Sawyer issued a heavy sigh. "After having you in my life, I realized that I'd let Sara's betrayal color my world long enough. Remember when I told you that after my divorce I vowed two things?"

Brea nodded.

"Waking up with a woman in my bed was one. The other was to never lose my heart again and say I do."

Brea wasn't surprised by his confession; after all, she'd sworn to give up men. Of course, she'd failed miserably, while Sawyer had only slipped a little and allowed her to spend the night.

"Makes sense. We do what we have to in order to protect ourselves. I get that, more than you know." She shrugged.

"I'm sure you do. But do you *get* what I'm trying to say to you, Brea?"

"Of course I do. You told me the first time that you kissed me, no regrets. There are none. It's cool. You can go. I'm not going to fall apart or stalk you. Can you do me a favor, though, and bring Ozzie back home with you tonight? Just put him in the backyard. You don't need to come to the door or—"

"No!" Sawyer barked. Clenching his jaw, he stood and rounded the table. Brea could feel the anger rolling off him in potent waves. "You don't hear what I'm saying. Not at all."

She craned her neck and looked up at him. With him towering over her, Brea was clearly at a disadvantage. Rising to her feet, she tried to keep his tormented green eyes from wreaking havoc with her dissolving mask of bravery.

Do not fall apart. Do not cry.

The mantra spooled through her brain as she clenched her hands into fists. She found it ironic that the angrier she grew, the more relaxed Sawyer became. Nothing was making sense. The whole conversation, or rather his kiss-off, had some weird and bizarre vibe to it. Maybe Sawyer wanted to part ways as friends, like with his ex. Though none of Brea's past relationships had ended civilly, she'd give it a shot. Hell, it would be another first, and maybe take some of the sting away.

As if! her subconscious snorted.

Dragging the mantra through her brain once again, Brea was stunned when Sawyer reached up and cupped her cheeks.

"I not only want to wake up with you in my arms every morning, Brea, I want you to be the woman I watch walk down the aisle to me, wearing a frilly white gown and smiling with tears of happiness shimmering in your eyes. Then I want to take your hand and say I do one more time…to you."

The room began to spin. Her knees wobbled, and her heart was lodged so far up into her throat she knew she'd never swallow again. Like a fountain, tears spilled down her cheeks.

"I want to raise a family, five…six little Graysons running around the backyard, and learning how to bring memories to sick kids out at the ranch. I want sit in the hot tub at night, stare at the stars, and make love to you until sunrise. I want to spend my life with you…and grow old together, forever."

She wanted him to repeat the things he'd just said for fear she was having a stroke and that his real words were simply being discombobulated in her brain. But when he bent and pressed his lips to hers, kissing her with a passion so strong her spine turned to jelly, Brea knew she'd heard him just fine.

"That night Emmett blew out the window, you asked me if I loved you and I said no? I lied. When you wanted to know if I'd ask you to move in with me? I lied then, too."

She issued a watery laugh.

"I love you, Brea. You make me feel what love's supposed to be like. Move in with me, darlin'. We'll set a wedding date whenever you're ready. But stay with me. I want…no, I *need* you in my life."

Say yes, or you'll need a lobotomy to make you forget this amazing man…and even that might not work…just sayin'.

"I love you, Sawyer. I think I fell in love with you the first time I saw you. I-I just tried to…"

"Do what you needed to do, to protect your heart," he finished for her. "I won't break it. I swear. You might get pissed off at me from time to time, but I'll never break your heart. I promise."

Brea wrapped her arms around his neck and kissed him…kissed him with all the love, hope, and happiness that was exploding inside her.

EPILOGUE

A TORRENTIAL RAIN was blowing sideways. The white wooden folding chairs were being tossed across the monster-sized deck at Sawyer's family ranch like tumbleweeds. Brea was holed up in the guestroom on the second floor with her mom, Jade, Barbara, and his mother, while Sawyer stood by the sliding glass door, peering up at the black clouds rolling by. He wondered why he and his yet-to-be-seen—because it was supposedly bad luck—beautiful bride-to-be had thought a wedding in April would be perfect. It was perfect, all right—a perfect disaster.

Tugging the tie at his throat, Sawyer flashed a grim expression to his best man, Colton.

"Don't give up. The storm's bound to blow over soon," his friend assured. "Your brothers and I will set things right outside, once it stops. Everything will go off without a hitch."

Sawyer issued a noncommittal grunt.

"They say rain's good luck on your wedding day. It was pouring cats and dogs the day Jade and I tied the knot. Remember?"

"Yeah, but your wedding was inside a church. No risk of your guests needing a raft and oars to make it to the reception." Sawyer glanced over his shoulder at the throng of guests crammed and waiting inside his parents' house. "Look around us, man. Nearly everyone in Haven is here...sweating like a roofer in August. No number of fresh flowers is going to mask the smell of body odor, especially mine, if we can't herd them out of the house soon."

Colton leaned in close. "I hate to tell you this, man, but nobody is sweating, but you. You're not having second thoughts, are—"

"Kiss my ass," Sawyer hissed. "No. I'm worried Megan is going to get too close to the knives in the kitchen and start using Nash for target practice."

Colton chuckled. "Jesus…if looks could kill, your brother would be a dead man. And not just from Megan. Her daddy looks none too happy."

"I know. The last thing I want for Brea's special day is a damn knock-down-drag-out between my brother and a pissed-off old man. There's no stories of blood being spilled on your wedding day and we both know it."

Colton laughed. "True."

Sawyer exhaled a heavy sigh and tried to will the storm away. He was grateful… Aside from Megan and her family, everyone was wearing smiles and taking the delay in stride. Even Brea's dad and his were off in the corner swapping stories and laughing.

"I know it's none of my business, but," Colton whispered. "is Gina the woman you weren't thrilled that Nate was getting mixed up with?"

Sawyer's heart sped up slightly. "Why would you ask that?"

"Oh, just curious. They can't keep their eyes off one another. It's pretty damn obvious."

"Shit," Sawyer murmured. "Just as long as they keep their hands off each other, we'll be fine. I don't want Mom stroking out if they don't. Talk about sucking the joy out of every damn anniversary. Shit!"

"You worry too much," Colton said with a chuckle.

Lightning splintered the sky, followed by a crack of thunder that shook the house.

"Come on, God. Give us a break. If not for me…for Brea," Sawyer groaned.

Ten minutes later, the sun was out and his heart lifted. As promised, Colton and his brothers were righting the chairs and drying them off as the guests mingled on the deck.

Sawyer watched as Brea's father climbed the stairs to fetch his daughter. The reality of what he was about to do landed in his gut like an anvil.

Suddenly, he felt the familiar grip of his father's hand on his shoulder, and Sawyer instantly calmed.

"You have that same look on your face again." Norman grinned.

"What look?"

"The one you had the day we lost Norris at that amusement park in Dallas when he was six." His father sent him a hard stare. "If you're not sure of this, son, you don't have—"

"No, Dad. I'm sure. I'm doubly sure. Just had a wave of…"

"What the fuck am I doing?" Norman laughed.

"Yeah."

"I'd be worried if you didn't. She's a fine girl. Perfect for you. Hell, the first day you brought her to the ranch, your mom told me then that you'd found your soul mate."

"She did… I mean, yes. I did."

"Then let go of your worries. Set your sights on living a long, happy life with Brea, Neville."

"Sawyer."

"Hardheaded little…"

"Hey, I love you, Dad." Sawyer's voice grew thick.

His father's eyes misted. Wrapping him in a manly hug, Norman slapped his back. "I love you, too, son."

His mom came down the stairs wearing a smile from ear to ear. "Brea is gorgeous…just gorgeous. I can't wait to see the look on your face when she walks through the door."

"Well, let's get you seated then, Momma. We don't want to keep our boy waiting now do we?"

"Oh, just a minute," Nola scolded. "I haven't even told Neville—"

"Sawyer," he and his father corrected in unison.

"Our *son* how handsome he is in his tuxedo."

"I'll wait for you by the door, precious." Norman smiled.

Tears filled his mother's eyes as she stared up at Sawyer. She hadn't been this happy the first time he'd gotten married. That fact only served to solidify what he knew in his heart…Brea was his life.

"I know you'll make her happy, sweet boy. And I know in my heart she'll do the same for you. I love you…love you with all my heart."

Sawyer bit back the lump of emotion lodged in his throat. "I love you, too. You're the best mom a kid could ever have."

Nola swiped away her tears, kissed his cheek, and then hugged him tight. "Be happy," she whispered in his ear, then let him go. Wiping her eyes once more, she draped her hand over his father's arm and walked outside.

Sawyer stood on the deck beside Colton. The preacher stood a few feet away, and sitting at his feet was Ozzie wearing a black bow tie. Sucking in a deep breath as Jade, with her visible baby bump, stepped through the door, Sawyer darted a glance at Colton. The goofy, love-struck grin that spread across his friend's mouth made his shoulders shake in silent laughter. Sawyer knew he'd look just as stupid in a couple more seconds, but he didn't care. No fucker on the planet was half as lucky as he was.

Brea's father stepped out next. He moved to the side as he took his daughter's arm. When she cleared the portal and raised her head, Sawyer nearly swallowed his tongue. He drank in Brea's lush, ripe lips and the swells of her breasts that were all but pouring out of the strapless white gown covered in lace and hugging her beguiling curves. But the glow of sheer joy that lit her face and sparkled in her eyes was what took his breath away.

When Brea sent him a quivering smile, Sawyer grinned. Knowing she was nervous only furthered his resolve to give her…everything. To calm her with reassurance when her insecurities threatened to drag her under, like now. To bolster her courage and face the bumps life tossed their way as one. To shower her and the family they'd create with all the love in his heart, till life left his body.

The preacher's words were at first nothing but a buzz in his ears. All Sawyer could focus on was Brea...his beautiful, headstrong, sassy, thrilling, erotic, and sensual Brea.

He took her hand and grinned as that electric current sped up his arm. A little voice in the back of his head told him to get used to it. She'd always charge his system in this same way.

"Do you, Neville Sawyer Grayson, take Brea Rosalind Gates to be your lawfully wedded wife? To have and to hold, from this day forward, for better for worse, for richer or poorer, in sickness and in health, forsaking all others until death do you part?"

Sawyer squeezed Brea's hand and gazed into her twinkling dark eyes. Then swallowed and smiled. With a voice loud enough to be heard in heaven, Sawyer nodded, resolutely and said, "Hell, yes, I do!"

She was a vision
An angel.
His wet dream.
His bride.

ABOUT THE AUTHOR

USA Today Bestselling author **Jenna Jacob** paints a canvas of passion, romance, and humor as her alpha men and the feisty women who love them unravel their souls, heal their scars, and find a happy-ever-after kind of love. Heart-tugging, captivating, and steamy, Jenna's books will surely leave you breathless and craving more.

A mom of four grown children, Jenna and her alpha-hunk husband live in Kansas. She loves reading, getting away from the city on the back of a Harley, music, camping, and cooking.

Meet her wild and wicked fictional family in Jenna's sultry series: ***The Doms of Genesis.*** Become spellbound by searing triple love connections in her continuing saga: ***The Doms of Her Life*** (co-written with the amazing Shayla Black and Isabella La Pearl). Journey with couples struggling to resolve their pasts and heal their scars to discover unbridled love and devotion in her contemporary series: ***Passionate Hearts.*** Or laugh along as Jenna lets her zany sense of humor and lack of filter run free in the romantic comedy series: ***Hotties of Haven.***

Connect with Jenna Online
Website: www.jennajacob.com
Email: jenna@jennajacob.com
Facebook Fan Page: facebook.com/authorjennajacob
Twitter: @jennajacob3
Instagram: instagram.com/jenna_jacob_author
Amazon Author Page: http://amzn.to/1GvwNnn
Newsletter: www.subscribepage.com/jennajacob

OTHER TITLES BY JENNA JACOB

The Doms of Genesis Series
Embracing My Submission
Masters of My Desire
Master of My Mind
Saving My Submission
Seduced By My Doms
Lured By My Master
Sin City Submission
Bound To Surrender
Resisting My Submission (March 21, 2017)
Craving His Command (May 23, 2017)

The Doms of Her Life – Raine Falling Series
(Co-authored with Shayla Black and Isabella LaPearl)
One Dom To Love
The Young and The Submissive
The Bold and The Dominant
The Edge Of Dominance

The Passionate Hearts Series
Sky Of Dreams
Winds Of Desire (Coming Soon)

Hotties Of Haven Series
Sin On A Stick
Wet Dream

Made in the USA
San Bernardino, CA
12 January 2018